THE NORTHWOODS

By the Author

In Between

The Man Who Was Not

The Northwoods

Visit us at www.boldstrokesbooks.com

THE NORTHWOODS

by

Jane Hoppen

2018

ISBN 13: 978-1-63555-143-3

THIS TRADE PAPERBACK ORIGINAL IS PUBLISHED BY
BOLD STROKES BOOKS, INC.
P.O. BOX 249
VALLEY FALLS, NY 12185

FIRST EDITION: MARCH 2018

CREDITS
EDITOR: CINDY CRESAP
PRODUCTION DESIGN: STACIA SEAMAN
COVER DESIGN BY TAMMY SEIDICK

Acknowledgments

Thank you to my editor, Cindy Cresap.

To Sharon Morrison

CHAPTER ONE

Evelyn Bauer was as ready as she ever would be to transform into a man. She laid out the logging clothes that had belonged to her husband, George, on the bed. As the bitter, brutal Wisconsin winter required, the clothes were mainly made of wool. Evelyn fingered a large checkered coarse shirt, brightly colored with rust, pine green, and brown. The woolen pants that she would pack were cut off at the knees for easier movement. She set aside two wool caps, a pair of mittens and gloves, and a deep red mackinaw, and she put a pair of rawhide shoepacks on the floor near the bed. They would serve as her boots and were made large enough so that several pairs of wool socks could be worn. These were the clothes that Evelyn would don for the good of her family.

Two months earlier, near the end of a very dismal harvest season, Evelyn went to the cornfield on the farm's northern section to fetch George for dinner. He hadn't responded to the dinner bell when she rang it, and she didn't mind the stroll. The evening was just edging into dusk, the sky's burnt orange melting into a soft violet blue. After calling and calling for George and getting no answer, Evelyn finally found him in the far end of the field. He had collapsed in the dirt, surrounded by leftover stubble—bent stalks and discarded husks. She was unable to revive him, and the doctor had said that the cause of death was a heart attack.

The burial was a simple affair, attended only by Evelyn; their three children; Evelyn's sister, Helen; and George's brother, Will. A minister from the small church down the road spoke a few words, and Will and one of his farmhands buried George beneath a birch tree that stood behind the house. During the days that followed, Evelyn mourned the loss of George, the loss of his kinship. They had grown up on neighboring farms and became fast friends in youth; their families often gathered together for summer picnics and visited during the winter to break up the long, monotonous stretches of icy cold. Their marriage had been a given, a matter of necessity dictated by nature. Evelyn's father died when she was only seventeen, and her mother had passed away three years earlier. Her sister was already settled in town as a teacher, and with little discussion, Evelyn and George married soon after her father's death. George joined Evelyn in the running of her parents' farm, and his brother took over the Bauer family farm.

Evelyn fingered the mackinaw that George had once worn. A tear slid down her cheek. *I never thought I'd be without you this soon, George.* He had been such a key in the fabric of their daily living that, even two months later, she would find herself calling out his name. Evelyn had always been grateful for George's kindness and his companionship, though their relationship had not been one of great passion. Evelyn had little understanding of the concept.

George had been a good-natured man, though not a man of many words, and when it came to the sensibilities of affection, he had always been at a loss—reserved and awkward. The marriage was a means of survival, a partnership built to withstand the hardships of the land. To Evelyn, George was more like a brother figure, and with the daily work on the farm being so strenuous, their sexual encounters were always fumbling and rushed affairs. By the time the act was over, George quaking into an orgasm, Evelyn was just beginning to feel some stirring. George would pass out beside her, exhausted, and all she would feel was frustration, lying beside him, awake in the night. Some nights after George had fallen into deep sleep, snoring beside her, Evelyn had let her hand slide past her belly, between her legs, where her fingers provided the release she desired. Any sexual pleasure that Evelyn had had in life, she had given to herself. Evelyn and George did have their three children, though—Peter, Karl, and Louise—and together they had maintained a substantial farm, with the usual ups and downs, the precariousness of farming always close at hand.

That year had been a hard one for the Bauers, and their crops had suffered greatly. Weeks of heavy rain in the spring had caused the Wisconsin River to overflow just after planting, flooding the potato fields on the south end of the farm and rendering the land useless. The income from the few crops that remained, the corn and the wheat, was barely enough to survive on throughout the long winter months. When Evelyn surfaced from the shock of George's sudden death, she realized that with a farm to manage and three children to feed, she had to do what he had done during the winter months after a bad harvest—head north to work in the logging camp. Evelyn lifted the heavy mackinaw and held it before her. She would take George's place—as George.

As Evelyn began to put on the clothes, she wasn't surprised at how well they fit. She was a big woman, of German stock, and she and George had the same tall, sturdy build, though George had lacked her breasts and full curves. The outfit wasn't really that foreign to Evelyn. She found dungarees more suitable to her work on the farm and, unlike her sister, Helen, who lived in town and taught in the one-room schoolhouse, she wore a dress only a few times a year, which wasn't unusual. Many women from her territory were as masculine as the men and were used to toiling as much as any man. Some of the farm wives wore long prairie dresses, but many others, like Evelyn, found them a nuisance. One day, Evelyn had stopped by the mercantile store in town and the owner had shown her a newspaper that touted the latest styles some women on the East Coast were wearing.

Evelyn had grunted at the picture and said, "They must be ladies of leisure. No work would ever get done in a getup such as that."

Evelyn gazed at the clothes she had laid out. Next to them she added a pile of rags and the pocket watch that had belonged to George. She knew she would be the only logger packing those items, but she would also be the only one who was menstruating. She would need the watch so she could be sure to wake before the others when she needed to change and hide the soiled rags that she would pin to her undergarments when necessary. Evelyn pulled on a pair of long johns and the heavy woolen pants. Before she put on the shirt, she removed her stays and grabbed an old bedsheet from a trunk. She tore off one wide long panel and folded it lengthwise. She would have to bind her breasts if she was going to pass as George. Slowly, she wound the cloth over her chest in smooth layers, not so tight as to restrict movement or breathing, but tight enough to adequately flatten her breasts. She adjusted the bandage, striving for maximum comfort, as she knew that the binding would need to remain in place for the duration of her time at the camp. Because of the frigid conditions and the lack of water, none of the loggers bathed—ever. Evelyn shook her head as she tried to imagine the stench that must accumulate in the bunkhouse as the months passed. She fastened the binding with two large pins and put on the shirt.

With the stink of the bunkhouse in mind, she went to the dresser that had belonged to George and opened the top drawer. She removed his pipe and a pouch of tobacco. She fingered the pipe. She wasn't really a smoker, had taken only an occasional puff whenever George had his nighttime smoke, but she thought the pipe might give her an excuse to escape the bunkhouse for a few moments in the evenings. Evelyn put the pipe and tobacco in the canvas pack that would hold all her belongings for the winter months. She also took George's straightedge razor off his dresser. She would need it so she could at least go through the motions of shaving. Just as she was shoving it into the pack, the door to the bedroom creaked open and her sister stepped in. She had been staying with Evelyn since George's death, helping to prepare the farm for winter and to care for the children.

"Are you sure this is necessary?" Helen asked as Evelyn pulled on a pair of thick wool socks.

Evelyn looked at her sister, three years her senior. She was more petite than Evelyn, with dark brunette hair that fell only to her shoulders. In town, Evelyn had heard folks refer to Helen, thirty years old and unmarried, as a spinster. She knew Helen wouldn't care what they called her, and in some ways Evelyn envied her status, so untethered. She lived with another woman, Jess Moore, who helped her run the school. Evelyn had always suspected that their relationship was more than a friendship, that perhaps they had a more intimate connection, something she sensed in the way they sometimes gazed at each other, but she never asked. Such matters were not discussed.

She did walk in on them one day, though. She had traveled to town for supplies and stopped by their home. As was the custom, she had rapped on the front door and entered. She followed the scent of baking bread into the kitchen, and when she stepped into the room, she found Helen and Jess in an embrace that was a bit more than casual. When they realized she was in their presence, they released one another and stood looking at her unabashedly.

"Bread smells wonderful," was all Evelyn had said.

She'd had no idea what else to say. Two women comforting one another, hugging, was not an uncommon scene, but this embrace seemed different. Evelyn hadn't wanted to cause discomfort by asking questions, nor did she want to seem naive. She didn't even know what questions she would ask. Helen had moved over to her side nonchalantly and lightly kissed her on the cheek.

"Hello, sister."

Nothing more was said, and they sat down to indulge in warm slices of bread and cups of hot coffee.

"Don't see any way around it," Evelyn said. "If I don't go, we won't have any way to get the provisions that we need come springtime. I won't have the money to buy seed or hire hands. The farm would be a disaster."

"I worry about the kids," Helen said. "George has been in the ground only two months now."

Evelyn worried about the children, too. Their father had been a good man, a mild man, and the children were fond of him and loved him dearly. She could sense the ache of their loss, the echo of his absence. Peter, the eldest at age ten, had always tried to emulate George, trudging out to the barn and fields with him before the break of dawn and joining him by the lake in the late summer afternoons to try to snag some trout or walleyes.

He had grown sullen since George's passing. The younger boy, Karl, was seven. He had also insisted on being in close proximity to George whenever possible, angling for a place on his lap when they sat outside on the porch in the summer, or inside near the woodstove on dark winter nights. Every morning since George's death, when Karl came down to find his father absent from the breakfast table, he burst into tears. Even little Louise, who was four, had always vied for a place near her father's side. She didn't understand that her father's absence would be permanent and often asked, "Papa? Where's Papa?" The void of George's presence would not be easy to fill.

"I'm doing this because of the children," Evelyn told Helen. "If we'd had a better harvest, I wouldn't even think about it. But all the rain early in the season took its toll. Most of the fields were waterlogged, and the root cellar's only three-quarters full. I can't take a chance."

"I worry about your safety," Helen said. "The work at those camps can be deadly, and what do you think will happen if the other loggers figure out that you're not George?"

Evelyn shrugged.

"Guess they'll send me home. Guess it's up to me to make sure that doesn't happen. Let me finish dressing and you can tell me what you think."

"All right," Helen said. "I'll go down and tend to the stew."

Evelyn glanced out the window.

"If you don't see the children heading back from the barn yet, ring the dinner bell," she said. "It'll be getting dark soon."

"Will do," Helen said as she left the room.

As Evelyn finished dressing, she wondered how George had fared at the logging camp. He wasn't much of a complainer, and when he returned home in the spring, the logs having been delivered downriver, he wanted to hear more about her winter with the children, the happenings on the farm and about town, than he wanted to recount the long, laborious days and nights at the camp. Whenever Evelyn had asked George about the camp, his reply was always simple.

"There's not much to tell," he'd say. "Every day was the same day, and every day was a long one."

She knew he had disliked going to the camp, but he took it all in stride, just as she would. She, however, would have the constant worry of being discovered. George did mention to Evelyn once that some of the men called him Quiet George because he never participated in the nightly singing and storytelling. George stayed mostly to himself when at the logging camp, and for that Evelyn was grateful. That would make her taking his place that much easier. George wasn't a regular at the camp either, like many of the other men. He'd gone to work there only twice since Peter was born. No one would be able to remember George Bauer well enough to call her into question.

Just as Evelyn finished putting on the clothes, she heard the children entering the house, and the scent of the stew she had prepared earlier in the day wafted up through the wooden rafters. She stood before the dusty, dim mirror in her new clothes. They were bulky, awkward. She put on a cap; wrapped a sheath of her long, wavy hair around one hand; and tucked it under the cap. She would ask Helen to cut her hair for her that night after dinner. She stepped away from the mirror and spoke, pushing her voice down as low as possible.

"George Bauer," she said. "I'm George Bauer from Maple Grove."

Her voice cracked, and she cleared her throat and tried again.

"Well, this winter I will be a woman of few words," she finally said after a few attempts, displeased with her performance. "Quiet George it is."

The chattering of the children below rose to the bedroom, and Evelyn took one last glimpse of herself and went downstairs to join them. When she reached the bottom of the stairs, the children turned their attention to her. Evelyn settled her eyes on them. Peter was tall and lanky, growing into himself, with a mop of reddish-brown hair and a band of freckles across his nose. Being the eldest, he took things seriously and had a somewhat stern personality. Karl was about a foot shorter, with a stocky build, blond hair, and light blue eyes. He was more easygoing and lighthearted than his brother. Louise was a pudgy little girl, with wavy brown hair and hazel eyes, and she was generally joyous. Peter was the first to stammer any words.

"Ma, why are you wearing Pa's clothes?"

"I've got to go north for the winter," Evelyn told the children. "I'm taking your father's place at the logging camp. Aunt Helen is going to stay here with you, and I'll be back as soon as I make enough money to keep the farm going and food in our bellies."

Karl ran over to her from the other side of the room and clung to one of her legs as she ran a hand through his hair. Little Louise turned her face into the folds of Helen's dress. Peter's eyes filled with tears.

"I want to go with you," he said, his voice pleading.

"The camp's no place for a child," Evelyn said. "And I need you here, to help your aunt with your brother and sister, and the farm. You know how this farm runs better than anyone. You know how to tend to the animals, keep the barn clean. Your father taught you well."

"But, Ma…"

"This is how it has to be, Peter," Evelyn said. "We need to make your father proud. Now, get out the bowls and spoons while I bring the food to the table."

"All right," Peter mumbled, as tears began to stream down his cheeks.

Evelyn went to his side and wrapped her arms around him.

"It'll be okay," she assured him. "It's only for the winter, this one winter. You know I wouldn't go if I didn't need to. Your uncle will help you with the farm. Just listen to him and your aunt and you'll be fine."

Peter sighed and shuddered against her. Evelyn released him and went to gather the food for their meal. Peter slumped away to prepare the table. Evelyn took a loaf of bread she had baked the day before and carved thick slices. She moved the pot of stew to the table and began to ladle it into bowls. The silence in the room was palpable, and as everyone gathered around the table, a mood of dark grimness seemed to join them. Peter's lips trembled.

"When do you leave?" he finally asked.

"I'm not sure," Evelyn said. "Your uncle's stopping by tonight so we can decide. He'll be taking me up to the camp in his wagon. We'll have to leave before the first snow."

Karl pushed his bowl away, only a few small nibbles gone, and started to cry. Helen gently rested a hand on his shoulder and tried to lighten the mood.

"Your mother will have some grand tales to tell you when she returns home," she said. "Paul Bunyan and his blue ox Babe—they're always up to something."

Only Louise, who didn't grasp the gravity of the situation in any way, giggled and merrily swung her legs back and forth beneath the table.

Just as they finished their dinner, silent except for occasional sniffles from Peter and Karl, there was a knock on the door and Will entered. He resembled George in many ways, with his thick mop of brown hair and matching brown eyes, but he didn't have George's girth. Will was tall and lean, his arms dangling by his sides. As he stepped into the house, his eyes landed on Evelyn, and he turned pale. Evelyn had sent word of her plan to him by way of Helen. He shook his head.

"You're almost the spitting image of him with all that gear on," he said. "If I didn't know better…"

"Think I'll pass?" Evelyn asked.

"As long as you can keep up with the work," Will said. "I think so."

"George was a sawyer, and you know I'm no stranger to the ax. I reckon I can take down a tree as well as any man."

The boys sat silently while Louise played with a doll in a corner near the stove. Helen cleared the table and put things back in place.

"When do we go?" Evelyn asked.

"Weather's taking a change," Will said. "Cold's setting in, and it's already mid-November. First freeze was two nights ago, so the first snow's not far behind. Can you be ready in three days' time?"

Evelyn looked at Helen, who nodded. She then looked at the children. Peter and Karl gazed at her with dread. She knew that leaving sooner would give her children less time to fret over what was to be.

"I'll be ready," she said.

"I'll be by at the break of dawn," Will said. "It'll be a full day's travel."

"Coffee, Will?" Helen offered. "Still have some warm on the stove."

"Sounds good."

He pulled a chair up near the stove, and the children gathered around him. He turned to Peter.

"You going to help me keep this farm in good shape, son?" he asked.

"Yes, sir," Peter said glumly.

Will placed a hand on Peter's shoulder. He had the same kindness that George had harbored.

"We'll just make sure we keep things running smoothly so your mother doesn't come home to any surprises," he said.

Helen handed him a cup of steaming coffee, and Will settled in his chair.

"Who's up for a story?" he asked the children.

Louise and Karl clapped their hands in excitement, and even Peter smiled slightly. Evelyn sighed with relief, seeing him relax for the first time since she told him she would be leaving.

"Did I tell you the one about the night I was driving the horse and wagon down a dark road and came upon a barn dance?"

"No," the children said in unison.

"Well, one cold rainy night I was traveling down a road that didn't seem to end," Will said. "I drove and drove, and then suddenly, I saw a dimly lit barn off the side of the road, not too far away, in a field. I headed toward the barn and heard music. Ah, I said to myself, they must be having a dance. When I reached the barn and went inside, I came upon the strangest barn dance I've ever seen."

Evelyn sat beside Helen at the table and listened as Will's voice blanketed the room, the wind outside rising to a shrill whistle. She looked about the home that she had lived in all her life—as a child, and now as a mother. The house was simple—two stories, with two bedrooms and a small fireplace in the upper loft. The kitchen, which housed the woodstove, a small baker, and a dining table, was downstairs, as was the sitting area, the rooms separated by a large brick fireplace. In the sitting area were a wide bench and two wooden chairs. A small hallway off the kitchen led first to the pantry and then out to the backyard and the outhouse. The root cellar was under the kitchen floor, accessible by a trapdoor, which opened to steep, slanting steps.

Like most farm homes of the time, the structure was modest, but it had all the basic comforts and necessities, and Evelyn's stomach churned when she thought about the conditions she would be living in that winter at the logging camp. She stood and went to look out the window near the woodstove. The trees had been stripped down to gaunt figures, bent and gnarled, and fallen leaves drifted back and forth in the winds, like the tide, ebbing and flowing. She felt the coldness of the wind on the other side of the window. The winter would be a frigid one.

After Will left and Evelyn settled the children into their beds, she went to her bedroom to get a pair of scissors. She examined herself in the mirror again. The next time she did so the hair that reached midway down her back would be gone. That was the last element of herself that she could change, physically. Mentally, she had no idea how to prepare for her venture. She was entering a grisly world, and the one thing she knew was that she could show no weaknesses, harbor no vulnerabilities. She turned from the mirror and went downstairs. Helen glanced at her and Evelyn handed her the scissors.

"I need you to cut my hair," she said.

"Ah, the final step of your transformation," Helen said.

"Make it as short as you can," Evelyn told her.

They laid an old sheet on the floor, and Evelyn set a chair on it and sat. She released a jagged sigh as Helen gathered the thick tresses of hair in one hand and slowly began to cut. Chunks of hair fell to the floor. Neither of them spoke, almost as if that act signified a time of great change for both of them. Helen finally cleared her throat and broke the silence.

"Have you thought about how different your life will be now, without George?" she asked.

Evelyn glanced down at the hair gathering on the sheet below.

"Beyond this?" she said. "Not really. Despite the obvious. All the responsibility is mine now—the children, the farm."

"Perhaps you'll marry again at some point in the future," Helen said.

"Can't imagine being with any man but George," Evelyn said. "Even that marriage, as you know, was born more of circumstance. Until now I never wondered what I might have done if George hadn't been waiting for me on the sidelines after Mother and Father passed away."

"Maybe you would have tried to manage the farm on your own," Helen said. "Or you could have met another man."

"That doesn't seem likely," Evelyn said. "What about you? Have you never met a man who...?"

She fell silent. She knew better.

"I'm perfectly content with my life," Helen said.

"With Jess?" Evelyn asked.

She had never broached the subject before.

"Well, yes," Helen said. "She is my best friend, my confidante."

"But what about...?"

"Intimacy?" Helen asked. "Love?"

Evelyn felt herself blushing. She nodded.

"We share the same bed," Helen said. "I'm sure you've figured that out by now. We share everything. I would be devastated without her."

"I have often wondered about the breadth of your relationship," Evelyn said. "Even after I walked in on you two that one day...I wasn't sure. I didn't know what to think. Why didn't you ever tell me before?"

"That day you saw me and Jess I thought you were embarrassed, uncomfortable," Helen said. "I thought you might be against it."

"I was just caught a bit off guard," Evelyn said. "I would never judge you. I just didn't know what to say. We have taken such different paths. You never did consider staying on the farm, did you?"

Having been born into a farm family with only daughters, Evelyn and Helen had helped their father with the bulk of the farm work. Helen did so begrudgingly, but Evelyn embraced it wholeheartedly. She loved the connection to the land—putting her hands in the soil, tending to the crops, reaping the fruits of the harvest. The rhythms of the different seasons drew her in and drove her.

"Not really," Helen said. "I didn't dislike the farm, but you know I always took more of a liking to town, and to books. I wanted something different, and I realized in my teen years that my attraction was toward women. Do you remember Emma May?"

"Of course," Evelyn said. "Her folks had the apple orchard we always went to."

"She was my first crush," Helen said. "We had a few occasions of exploration in the barn on the days when we would visit, but we never did see each other enough to pursue it."

"I never knew," said Evelyn.

"You know, you don't have to be with a man again, marry," Helen said. "This time the choice is yours. You can raise the children and run the farm on your own. Jess and I will always be here to help you."

That thought had never before entered Evelyn's mind. No other words were said, but she found herself harboring an ache, deep down, as she wondered if she could ever have what Helen had—a relationship that was anchored by more than survival and necessity.

When Helen finished cutting Evelyn's hair, she held a hand mirror up before Evelyn so she could see. Evelyn studied her new self.

Evelyn had been trying to put up a strong front since her decision to go to the camp, but alone with Helen, she spoke frankly.

"I'm afraid of what I might encounter up in those woods," she said. "My only reference to men, really, is George and our father."

"Both well-mannered men," Helen said. "Father had such a good sense of humor."

"He did. I know the men I am about to be surrounded by will be nothing like him. I'm guessing they will be a rather brutal lot."

"I wish you didn't have to go," Helen said.

"So do I," Evelyn admitted. "I don't know of any other way, though. I have to save this. This is all I have—my children, the farm."

"I know," Helen said. "I know."

Evelyn gathered up the sheet from the floor and took it outside to release the hair to the winds. She returned inside to sweep up any leftover remnants. She looked at Helen.

"I wish George had told me more about the camp, but I realize now he was probably sparing me his misery, which makes me worry even more. I have no idea what to expect."

"Then expect the unexpected," Helen told her.

"I will," Evelyn said before turning away and heading up the stairs.

"Good night, sister," Helen said.

"Sleep tight," Evelyn replied.

In her room, Evelyn stood before the mirror once again. If she didn't know better, she could see herself as a man. She didn't mind what she saw in the mirror, as she had never been one to home in on her femininity. She looked at herself and pondered her life. A husband and children had always seemed to be a given, only because there were no other apparent options. Unlike Helen, Evelyn had seen no path other than marriage. But now… Besides her trepidation, she felt a small burst of excitement travel through her. A part of her was thrilled to embark on the first real solo journey of her life, though she was also intrigued and overwhelmed by the thought that she would be making that journey disguised as a man. Either way, she was ready to take George's place.

❖

Evelyn's last meal with her children and sister the night before she left for the logging camp was a somber one. Few words were spoken and the winds outside howled, reminding everyone of the long winter that was about to descend upon them. Evelyn sat with Louise in her lap and tried to console Karl and Peter. Helen sat silently with a solemn look on her face, and Evelyn knew she was worried.

"You boys know I'll return as soon as I make enough money to help us out here," Evelyn said.

"Before spring?" Peter asked.

"I hope so," Evelyn said. "I'll definitely be back for planting time. You just stick to your chores and take care of your brother and sister, and winter will be over before you know it."

"I guess," Peter said.

"I'll help," Karl chimed in, slinging an arm around Peter.

"I want you boys to go out to the shed now and get me your father's ax," Evelyn said as Louise shifted in her lap.

Evelyn watched them as they pulled on coats and hats and headed outside. Helen rose to clean off the table, and Evelyn hummed to Louise as she rocked her back and forth. Louise's eyelids slowly fluttered and closed. With Louise finally sleeping calmly in her lap, Evelyn bent over and lightly kissed her forehead as her own eyes filled with tears. The children didn't know that she dreaded her journey as much as they did. Never before had she spent even a day away from them, and her heart sank as she thought of them being absent from her life for so long.

She heard stomping outside the door, the boys cleaning off their boots before entering. When they walked in, Evelyn gestured for them to be quiet as she stood with Louise in her arms and took her upstairs to put her to bed. When she returned downstairs and joined the boys, Peter handed her the ax. Evelyn examined it. George had always taken meticulous care of his tools, and the ax was no exception. The bit was sharpened and the head was oiled and securely fastened to the handle. She checked the handle for any cracks or splits and smiled when she saw the initials that George had carved into the bottom of the handle—GB. She set the ax down. She pulled the boys close to her and hugged them tightly.

"Don't know how I'm going to make it without seeing you boys every day," she said.

Peter looked up as tears traced down her cheeks, and he tightly wrapped his arms around her waist.

"It'll be all right, Ma," he said. "Me and Karl will do whatever Uncle Will and Aunt Helen say, and we'll take good care of Louise."

"Yep," Karl said.

"I know that," Evelyn said. "Your pa and I couldn't have raised better boys. But I'm going to miss you every day. You head upstairs now and I'll come tuck you in."

The boys hugged Helen good night and went upstairs. When Evelyn stood to join them, Helen handed her a tiny booklet tied together with string and a stub of a pencil.

"I made you this so you can track the time," she said.

Evelyn fingered the hand-fashioned calendar and flipped through the pages.

"You went all the way to May," she said.

"Well, we've had many an Easter snow," Helen said.

Evelyn grunted.

"Let's hope that's not the case this season."

"I'll keep my fingers crossed," Helen said. "Either way, when you return it will be a new year."

"I reckon just returning home will make 1853 one of my best years ever," Evelyn said.

They looked at each other steadily and then silently embraced.

❖

That night as Evelyn lay in bed listening to the wailing of the winds outside, she ran a hand over the empty space in the bed beside her and thought of George. She knew he would think she was doing the right thing. She missed the sense of him, his partnership, the comfort of his presence, even his arms, sturdy around her. The prairie was a difficult place to stand alone. She felt an ache in the pit of her belly, a gnawing loneliness, and she thought that, if nothing else, she would be too busy at the camp, too exhausted, to dwell on her loss and the newness of her life.

Before turning off the kerosene lamp that dimly lit her room, Evelyn fingered the book lying on her nightstand—Charlotte Brontë's *Jane Eyre*. Evelyn had borrowed the book from Helen, the source of all her reading materials. She had already read the book three times, marveling each time at the passion and turmoil between Jane and Mr. Rochester. She had had plenty of turmoil and hardship in her life, but she didn't even know if she would be able to identify passion, which made her even more curious. She thought about her conversation with Helen. She had always known that relationships between two women or two men existed, and she had always assumed they entailed all the same facets as a relationship between a woman and a man, but she sensed that Helen and Jess's relationship was more rooted in passion. Evelyn couldn't even imagine a circumstance where that might occur for her. As soon as she returned home from the camp, she would be back to running the farm, and that would be a solitary existence, except for the children. She ran her hand over the cover of *Jane Eyre*, feeling as if she would probably never experience the romance within those pages.

CHAPTER TWO

As the horse-drawn wagon traveled slowly over the dirt road, Sarah Bell sat solemnly beside Sam Hardy, the older brother of Abigail Hardy, Sarah's lover for six years, the woman they had buried that day. Abigail had died of pneumonia at the early age of thirty. Sarah was numb and stunned, and she rode with Sam in a daze.

Sarah had been orphaned at the age of eight, when her parents died of typhoid fever. She was raised in the orphanage outside a little town called Pine Creek, and at the age of seventeen, she was taken in by the local seamstress, Abigail Hardy, to help her with her business. Abigail, seven years her senior, gave Sarah a room to stay in and full rein of the house, and they soon became close friends, spending nearly all their waking hours together.

Six months after settling into the Hardy house, Sarah realized that she was not only fond of Abigail, but she was also attracted to her. Abigail was a slender, pale woman with long blond hair and freckles that spread across the bridge of her nose and cheeks, and one could easily get caught in the sea of her moss green eyes. Neither her feelings for Abigail nor her attraction to her were foreign to Sarah, as she had harbored a secret crush on another girl at the orphanage, Molly, ever since she was thirteen. When they were caught kissing in the bathroom by a member of the staff, they were quickly separated, and their budding romance was squelched.

As Sarah and Abigail spent more time together, Sarah would

steal glimpses of Abigail whenever she wasn't looking, tracing the lines of her body with her eyes. She waited for those moments when their fingers would brush against each other or when their bodies briefly touched. She never suspected that Abigail might feel the same way that she did.

When the house that Abigail and Sarah had shared came into view, Sarah remembered the first time that she and Abigail had made love. Abigail was tailoring a pair of trousers for a young, small-built man who lived in town. He couldn't make it by the shop for a fitting, and since they were approximately the same size, Abigail had Sarah step in for him. Abigail first fitted the waist and then moved on to the inseam of the pants. She ran her hand along the inside of one of Sarah's legs, and as she moved her hand toward the crotch area, Sarah trembled and caught her breath. She felt herself moistening between her legs. Her knees nearly buckled as Abigail spoke.

"Is something wrong?" she asked.

"No," Sarah said. "I simply…"

As Abigail continued to adjust the pants, Sarah shuddered and spoke again.

"Please," she said.

Before Sarah knew what she was doing, she found herself pressing against Abigail, seeking out her lips with her own. They kissed, long and hard, tongues twisting. Abigail led Sarah to her bedroom and closed the door behind them.

❖

The wagon finally lurched to a stop in front of a small, quaint house, the only home Sarah had known since she left the orphanage. Sam climbed out of the wagon, walked over to Sarah's side, and helped her down. For a moment, they both stood in silence, staring at the house.

"I want you to know that you can keep the house," Sam said. "As you know, it belonged to our parents, and I have the farm and my own home to look after. I've got no need for another house, and Abigail would want it this way. From the day you arrived, she wanted this to be your home as much as hers."

"Thank you," Sarah said. "You have no idea how much your kindness means to me."

She was, indeed, relieved. She had spent the three days since Abigail's death in a state of both mourning and fear, sometimes edging on hysteria. *Where will I go? What will I do? How will I handle life on my own?*

Without saying anything else, Sam left her side and climbed back up into the wagon.

"I'll check in on you in a week or so to see how you're doing," he said. "I have no idea what my sister's and your financial situation is, but you might need some additional income now that Abigail is gone. You can let me know."

"I will," Sarah said.

She stood in front of the house and watched him turn the wagon around and head back down the dirt road. When the wagon became a distant dot, Sarah finally entered the house, closed the door behind her, and began to aimlessly wander from room to room. When she reached the bedroom, she sat in a rocking chair near a window and gazed out at the pale gray clouds and the barren trees. At twenty-three, she was again alone in life, with no anchor, nothing to hold on to, except for the house that Abigail had shared with her—home. She gulped in a deep breath and started to sob. She lay down, pulled a blanket over her, and closed her eyes to darkness.

The next morning, Sarah woke early; the sun was slanting through the bedroom curtains. She rose, somberly prepared herself for the day, and went to the kitchen to make a pot of coffee. When it was done, she poured herself a cup and went into the parlor, where she sat at Abigail's desk. She ran her hands over the smooth, polished wood. She then methodically began to go through the drawers, trying to find the bank records and ledgers that Abigail had kept. She spread them out on the desk and began the process of laboriously going through them. Abigail had always managed their finances, and Sarah had never thought to inquire into their situation. She had taken so much for granted.

As Sarah paged through the ledgers, gazing at Abigail's handwriting, she remembered watching Abigail, perched at the desk, penciling in numbers in the various books. Abigail was a meticulous record keeper, maintaining one ledger for the tailoring business and another for the household. The business ledger revealed that the income from the tailoring was barely sufficient after monies were deducted for sewing supplies and the household expenses. Sarah knew her situation could be worse, much worse, but she realized how frugal Abigail had been while providing a most comfortable life. Now Sarah would have to do the same, but she would be making money from her work only. She perused the bank records, which showed a small amount of savings.

By the time Sarah took a break to make some lunch, she realized that her financial outlook was rather grim. With Abigail gone, she would definitely need another way to make money. She would never draw in as much income as they had together. She pushed the chair away from the desk and began to pace around the house, wringing her hands. She had no idea how she would manage in the future, standing on her own. Her and Abigail's few friends were as strapped as she was, if not more, each struggling in her own way. She and Abigail had felt fortunate. Now she knew she would need to speak to Sam, though she had no idea what he might be able to do to help her.

Nine days after Abigail's burial, Sarah was outside preparing the yard for winter, the cold November wind creeping up her dress, when she heard the clatter of a wagon and turned to see Sam drawing near. He pulled up in front of the house.

"Sarah," he said as he climbed out of the wagon.

"Good morning, Sam," Sarah said.

She was relieved to see him, as each day she was growing more worried and anxious about her situation. She'd had no customers since Abigail passed away, and though she thought some folks might be allowing her time for grieving, she didn't know what to expect in the future.

"How are you faring?" Sam asked.

"The days are difficult," Sarah said. "Perhaps things will improve over time."

An awkward silence settled between them. Sarah didn't really know Sam that well. He had never been a frequent visitor, with his farm to tend to, and he was away during the winter months.

"Is there anything you need?" Sam finally asked.

Sarah hesitated for a moment and then spoke.

"I've gone through all the financial records, as you suggested," she said. "I'm unsure of how prosperous the tailoring will be in the future, with Abigail gone. I'll most likely need to supplement my income somehow."

She watched Sam as he shifted from foot to foot. He scratched his head and cleared his throat.

"I wish I had the means to help you, but I'm a bit strapped myself," he said. "You could come to the logging camp with me this winter and work in the cook shanty until you figure things out. I lost one of my flunkies last year, so I'm a few arms short. The money will be enough to sustain you here for the next year."

Sarah gulped hard, feeling as if her breath was stuck in her throat, anxiety coursing through her. She had heard tales about the logging camps—long hours of endless work, cramped quarters, freezing conditions, lice, months without bathing. The logging camps were all grit and no glamour. Sam had been the head cook at the Hodag Camp for years.

"What would I be doing?" she asked.

"Cooking, cleaning up the shanty," Sam said. "I won't try to deceive you. The days are long and hard."

"How long would I be there?" Sarah asked.

"At least until April, maybe longer. Everything depends on the weather, what kind of winter we have."

A part of Sarah thought that going away for a while might help her overcome her grief and loneliness.

"When would we leave?" she asked.

"Two weeks," Sam said.

Sarah looked at the huge, strapping man, his arms as thick as logs, and his hair a curly, brownish-blond mane. His face was pocked, and he had a beard that fell to the middle of his chest. Sarah knew that at the camp they called him Mighty Man Sam. He was a man of few words, and he and Abigail hadn't been that close, with a number of years between them. Abigail had told Sarah that Sam had rather drifted off, become more isolated, after their parents had passed away.

"I guess my predicament leaves me little choice," she said as knots tightened in her stomach.

She felt as if she might be sick.

"Pack your warmest clothes," Sam said. "Other than that, bring only what you absolutely need. There will be a younger girl at the camp this year, my helper's daughter. They'll stay with me in the cook shanty. You can stay in a small shack near the shanty. There's a cot in there and a small stove. I'm thinking you'll need some privacy."

Sarah felt only slightly relieved.

"Thank you," she said quietly.

"I'll check on you in a week to make sure everything's in order," Sam said.

"I'll start to get ready, then," Sarah said begrudgingly.

"Good enough," Sam said.

He returned to the wagon, climbed in, and grabbed hold of the reins.

"See you next week," he said as he pulled away.

"Bye, Sam," Sarah said.

Nausea nudged its way into her belly. She couldn't move. *My God, a winter in a logging camp. I'll be surrounded by men.* She knew some of them would be decent, like Sam, but the others...She didn't dislike men, but she felt no attraction to them or their ways, wanted no dependency upon them. During her years living with

Abigail, Sarah had been approached by a few of the town's men, asking for courtship. Sarah always felt that those men, even those with more timid and mild personalities, saw her only as a vessel for sex and motherhood. Even if she did desire to be with one, no man would ever see her as an equal partner.

When she finally went back into the house, she wandered to the kitchen. With trembling hands, she picked up an empty cup, and in a surge of both defeat and rage, she hurled the cup against a wall and it shattered into splinters.

"Why did you leave me, Abigail?" she wailed. "This isn't how life was meant to be."

She sank into a chair and sobbed.

Sarah spent the days that followed Sam's visit sorting through her clothing, selecting only the heaviest garments, anything that might protect her from the harshness of the Northwoods in wintertime. She grimaced at the thought of being surrounded by the burliest and rowdiest of men for the long, drawn-out winter—from November until the end of March or April. The only other female in the camp would be the other flunky. She, at least, would have the companionship of her father. But Sarah…She would be on her own. She tried to push that thought away. If she thought about it too much, Abigail's absence became too agonizing, and she could feel herself plunging into darkness.

❖

Two weeks after Abigail's funeral, Sarah and Sam headed to the logging camp. They needed to arrive ahead of the others so they could prepare the cook shanty before the throngs of hungry loggers were upon them. Everyone knew that a camp was only as successful as the cook shanty was good. If the men weren't fed decent food, in rather copious amounts, they wouldn't survive the rigors of the forest or logging.

Sam and Sarah spoke little on their day-long trek to the camp. The wind bitterly blew around them the entire trip, and Sarah kept herself covered beneath a big wool blanket, exposing only her eyes. As they entered the Northwoods, the land so different from that surrounding Pine Creek, Sarah was both mesmerized and frightened. The dark pine trees towered above them, scenting the air in evergreen, and the winds traveling through them sounded like muted voices and muffled screams.

When they finally reached the camp, Sarah panicked at the sight of the primitive, drab scene—her home for the coming winter months. She and Sam climbed out of the wagon, and as Sam unharnessed the horses, he explained the layout to Sarah.

"The longest building you see there is the bunkhouse, where the loggers stay. They don't spend much time in there, only nights and Sundays."

Sarah gazed at the building, long and low, constructed of logs laid lengthwise. The bark was still on the logs and the chinks were filled with moss. She saw only two tiny windows, and she couldn't imagine how fifty or more jacks could squeeze into those quarters.

"The smaller building right on the left side of the bunkhouse is the cook shanty. That's where we'll be spending our time, us and the other two. My helper's name is Mack, and his daughter's name is Annie. You'll be staying in that tiny shed over there."

He led the way to the shed and Sarah followed, carrying the satchel with her belongings. When they reached it, he pushed the door open. The shed had one tiny square of a window, a cot, a little table and chair, a kerosene lamp that hung from the ceiling, and a small woodstove. Sarah swallowed hard. The air in the shed was stagnant, and she felt as if she might suffocate. She had no idea how she would be able to sleep there, though she knew it would be better than bunking in the cook shanty with Sam and the others. She set her satchel on the cot. *I'm never going to survive this. What was I thinking?* She and Sam went back outside, and Sam continued describing the logging camp.

"The building to the right of the bunkhouse is the stable for the horses. The shed next to that is used for shoeing the horses. That's where the teamsters and the foreman sleep. The outhouses are in the back, between the bunkhouse and the cook shanty. There's a stream a short walk beyond them. That's where we'll be getting our water."

"This is it?" Sarah asked. "This is the entire camp?"

"That's right. Our supplies start coming in tomorrow. Tonight we can settle in, and tomorrow we'll start to prepare the shanty. We need to scrub it down good with boiling water, try to get rid of the lice, though they're bound to come back."

Lice. Sarah nearly gagged at the thought. She followed Sam as he took the horses to the stable and put out some feed for them. He then guided her toward the bunkhouse, opened the door, and gestured for her to step in. Even though it hadn't been used since the previous winter, the wall of odor that hit her as she entered was rancid—a vile mix of tobacco, dirty socks, and stale sweat. Sarah nearly choked on the smell.

"You'll probably never need to come in here, but you might as well take a look at where the loggers will be living," Sam said.

Kerosene lamps hung from ropes that ran across the room from the ceiling's rafters. Sam struck a match to one and it dimly lit the room. Sarah scanned the quarters. The bunks were built along the two longer sides of the room in two-deck style, and each bunk had a bale of hay and a blanket on it. There weren't any chairs. Instead, a bench made of a wide board that projected from the lower tier of bunks provided sitting room.

"Besides the bunks, that's the only place the jacks have to sit," Sam said. "We call it the deacon's seat. The jacks gather there for cards, music, and storytelling. That's about the only entertainment we've got up here. No drinking or gambling. Over there's where the jacks wash up and sharpen their axes and tools, repair their equipment."

He pointed to a corner where a washbasin, water pail, and grindstone were in place. Sarah's eyes traveled from the corner to the center of the room, where a huge potbellied cast iron stove stood.

"That stove provides the only heat," Sam said. "At night, the jacks hang their wet socks and mittens on the stringers above and beside it so they can dry by morning time. That's a smell that'll nearly knock you out."

He chuckled to himself. Sarah almost became ill with the sight and scent of the quarters. What kind of men could live in these conditions, she wondered, knowing that she was soon to find out. Sam put an arm over her shoulders, a bit too comfortably, and pulled her close to him.

"You let me know if any of the jacks give you a hard time," he said. "I'll put an end to that." Without removing his arm, he led her to the door. "We should move on to the cook shanty now."

Sarah was uncomfortable with Sam's closeness, but she didn't want to say anything. She would need him in the upcoming months. She just hoped that she would find him trustworthy, and she then remembered an incident that had happened so long ago that she had almost forgotten.

About six months after Abigail and Sarah became intimately involved, Abigail had noted a change in Sam.

"My brother seems to be intruding on my territory a bit lately," she said. "He's been coming around more than usual. I think he might sense that there is something more between us now."

"Wouldn't he say something?" Sarah asked. "Do you think he would care?"

"Only if he's taken a liking to you," Abigail said. She wrapped her arms around Sarah, nibbled on her ear, and whispered, "Which wouldn't be hard to understand."

"Should we be worried?" Sarah asked.

"I don't think so, though I will be keeping an eye on him in the future," Abigail said. "I don't particularly like him lurking around, and I do believe I've seen him taking rather longing glimpses of you."

"Maybe you should tell him about us," Sarah said.

"Our business is our own," Abigail said. "Besides, as you know, Sam and I aren't that close. We have ten years between us, and he was always working in the fields with Father when we were young. My mother kept me close to her side, teaching me how to cook and sew. Sam never was very talkative. He's always been rather ornery, gruff in his own way, but he is my brother."

"Has he ever courted any of the women in town?" Sarah asked.

"A few, though that has never seemed to last long," Abigail said. "I think he might be a bit of a brute with the ladies. He started to drink heavily after our mother and father were both gone, and whiskey can make even the kindest man turn wicked."

Two months after that conversation, on a warm summer morning, Sarah had been in the garden tending to the flowers, watering and weeding, when she heard a wagon approach and turned to see Sam. He pulled up beside the house and tied the horse to a post. She expected him to go directly to the house and was surprised when he headed her way.

"Good morning, Sam," she said.

"Za-rah," he said, his voice sounding sluggish and slurred.

Sarah then noticed an awkward staggering in his step. When he finally was in front of her, she could smell the stench of whiskey.

"Came by to ask you to the Harmons' barn dance tonight," he said.

Sarah felt herself reddening as she stood before him, speechless. She didn't know what to say. She couldn't say yes. No part of her wanted to say yes, but she also didn't want to offend him, for he was Abigail's brother.

"Cat got your tongue, there?" Sam asked, as he nearly stumbled into her. He reached out and rested a heavy hand on her shoulder. "I think we'd make a fine pair on the dance floor."

Sarah had tried to back away, but Sam had a firm grip on her. Just then, she heard the front door creak open and slam shut.

"What's on your mind, Sam?" Abigail asked as she approached him and Sarah.

Sam removed his hand from Sarah and swung around, nearly losing his balance.

"Thought I'd invite Sarah to a dance," he said. "I bet she's a helluva dancer."

"You've been drinking, Sam," Abigail said. "You already smell like a saloon and it's still morning."

"Just a little hair of the dog," Sam said, a sloppy smile spreading over his face. "Got a little carried away last night."

"I'm sure tonight won't be any different," Abigail said. "And you're too old to be taking Sarah to a dance. You're more than ten years her senior."

The smile vanished from Sam's face, and he turned away from Abigail and twisted about to face Sarah again. She dropped her eyes to the ground. Just as Sam reached out to her, Abigail snagged one of his arms and pulled him back.

"That's enough, Sam," she said sternly. "You need to go home, have some coffee, and sober up. You'll feel better tomorrow."

Sam grunted loudly and Abigail steered him toward his wagon. Sarah watched, relieved. Abigail waited until Sam's wagon was well down the road before returning to her side. She looped an arm around Sarah's waist.

"I'm sorry about that," she said. "Has he ever approached you before?"

"Never," Sarah said. "I was so startled I didn't know what to say. You came out just in time."

"I saw him through the kitchen window," Abigail said. "I guess I was right. He's probably had you on his mind for some time."

She had kissed Sarah on the cheek, and they went to the garden together to finish their tasks. Sam never did approach Sarah again, and she had simply regarded the incident as a one-time occurrence, fueled by the liquor. Now that she was sequestered with him at the logging camp, she hoped she was right.

When they reached the wagon, Sam finally released her and started to unload his bag and a few other supplies he had brought with him. They then went to the cook shanty and Sam pushed the door open.

"After you."

Sarah stepped into the small building that was just as crude as the bunkhouse. Two long tables made of rough pine boards flanked with benches were on each side of the shanty and ran nearly the length of the building. In the back were a large woodstove and a small fireplace. Above them, stringers ran crosswise over the cook's and flunkies' stations, from which hung kettles, frying pans, baking dishes, cleavers, meat saws, ladles, and big spoons. Next to the stove was a large baker where the pies and biscuits were prepared. To the right of that was a table where the food was prepped, and to the left of the table was an area with a large basin that was used to wash the dishes, utensils, cups, pots, and pans.

"There's no talking during meals," Sam said. "The men need to eat quickly, and if they were all in here talking, the sound would be deafening. As it is, you can hardly hear yourself think. If they want more food or a refill, they'll gesture to you."

"What are my duties?" Sarah asked as she tried to imagine maneuvering around that small structure filled with men.

"You and Annie will wake an hour before me and Mack to carry in the wood; build the fires in the fireplace, the woodstove, and baker; fetch the water we'll need for the first half of the day; put on the coffee; and begin peeling potatoes." Sam pointed to a door in the rear of the shanty before continuing. "That door goes out back, where you'll find the ice house, root cellar, and woodpile."

Sarah looked around the shanty.

"Where do we keep the water?" she asked.

"In that barrel there," Sam said. "It should always be at least half full."

"Okay," Sarah said.

"When you're done with those duties, you'll wake the teamsters before everyone else. Just pound on their door. They need to feed, water, and harness the horses before chow so they're ready to go as soon as the jacks finish eating. You ring the triangle that's hanging outside the door at four thirty to wake the rest of the jacks, and again fifteen minutes later to let them know breakfast is on."

"Is that it?" Sarah asked naively.

Sam let out a loud laugh.

"That's just the beginning. You and Annie will wait on the tables during breakfast and dinnertime. Just keep the plates filled with food and the mugs topped off with coffee. As soon as breakfast ends, you'll clean off the tables and wash the dishes, pots, and pans. You'll spend the mornings preparing food for the next day's lunch buckets, slicing bread, making sandwiches, and wrapping pie, cake, and fruit. Mack and Annie will deliver the buckets to the loggers in the woods each day. While they're doing that, you'll prepare for dinnertime in the afternoon, whatever needs to be done."

Sarah looked around at the bare bones of the shanty.

"What do the loggers eat?" she asked.

"Your basic fare," Sam said. "Only what can keep in these conditions—salt pork fried with potatoes, beans, biscuits, dried fruits, shoepack pie. The pie is nothing but sugar, vinegar, water, and cornstarch. I've got a good recipe for bean hole baked beans that I'll be showing you. They're easy enough to fix, and they stick to the ribs. They're usually made outside in a hole dug into the ground and filled with embers, but up here the ground's too frozen for digging, so we use the fireplace instead. You just put your beans and molasses in a heavy pot or earthen jar, bury it in the fireplace, and bank it with coals before you go to bed. They'll be ready by morning."

He pointed to two bunks against the opposite wall.

"That's where Mack and I will be sleeping," he said.

He walked over to a door on one side of the room and opened it.

"Mack's daughter can bed down in here."

Sarah took a deep breath and stepped into the room, barely big enough for the crude cot, wooden chair, and tiny table that it held.

"That's it," Sam said. "This is the camp. You might as well settle into the shed for the night. It's been a long day, and the days to follow will only get longer. You can wash up in the basin by the dishwashing station if you want. Tomorrow, I'll give you a few more things for the shed to make it more convenient for you. This has enough grub in it to hold you for the night."

He handed her a brown paper parcel.

"Thank you," Sarah said. "For everything."

"With all these men rolling in, you'll be a sight for sore eyes," Sam said.

His eyes settled on Sarah long enough to make her feel uneasy.

"Good night, Sam," she said as she exited the shanty.

❖

Her first night at the logging camp, in the tiny shed, Sarah felt a sudden surge of fear when she ventured out in the dark to use the outhouse and realized how vulnerable she was in that arena. She didn't really fear the animals that roamed the woods at night—the bears were already hibernating—but any one of the men who would be in that camp could easily take her down. She had no protection. She had never felt so alone and isolated. The first thing she did when she returned to the shed, before lying down that night, was wedge the chair beneath the shed's doorknob. That was her only way of deterring a stray jack from entering. She knew it wouldn't keep him out, but it would give her warning. She would secure one of the pots from the shanty the next day to keep in the shed so she could avoid going out into the night to use the outhouse. Soon she would be surrounded by a sea of unruly men, and she could think of no other way to protect herself.

After she built a fire in the woodstove, she yawned and finally removed her boots and outer layer of clothing and stretched out on the cot. She pulled the thick wool blanket tightly over her. As tired as she was from the day of travel, she couldn't sleep. The winds whipped and whistled, while tree branches snapped. Every sound outside seemed to be amplified, the creaking of the trees and the occasional calls from night birds. The cot was uncomfortable, hard and unyielding, and though she welcomed the glow from the small woodstove, it barely kept the shed warm enough. She knew that as the temperatures dropped, it would be almost unbearable. She closed her eyes and thought of Abigail, wishing her life could be as it once had been, with Abigail's body warm against hers, soft arms around her, holding her close. Tears traced down her cheeks.

The first week that Sarah and Sam were at the camp, they spent the time from sunup to sundown unpacking and storing the supplies that were delivered on the second day and thoroughly cleaning the shanty, scrubbing down the floors, tables, and benches with boiling water to try to eradicate the lice that had nestled in during the warmer months and to wash away the dust that had settled over everything. Sarah cringed the entire time.

Sam began to stockpile firewood, and Sarah scrubbed the pots and pans, plates and cups, and utensils. The work was so constant that there was little idle time, which relieved Sarah. She didn't need to worry about conversation and everyday courtesies, and she was even more relieved when the cook's helper and his daughter arrived the first day of the second week. Sarah had just returned from getting a bucket of water when their wagon pulled up. She watched as they got out of the wagon and gathered their belongings. The man, Mack, was a compact, rather stout man, with a shock of red hair and a short bush of a beard. His daughter, Annie, was a small, mousy-looking girl with shoulder-length, curly strawberry-blond hair. With Sam nowhere in sight, Sarah greeted them.

"Hello," she said. "I'm Sarah, the other flunky."

"Mack," the man said. He thrust out his hand and firmly shook Sarah's. "Mack McGee, and this is my daughter, Annie."

Sarah smiled at the girl.

"We'll be spending a lot of time together the next few months," Sarah said. "I'm so glad you're here."

She felt relief to no longer be the only person in the camp with Sam.

"Where's Sam?" Mack asked as he surveyed the camp.

"He's out beyond the river chopping some firewood," Sarah said. "He told me you two would be bunking in the cook shanty with him. He cleared out the small room in the back for your daughter. I'll be staying in that little shed there."

She pointed to the structure.

"Well, then, let's put our gear in the shanty and get cracking," Mack said to Annie.

They gathered their belongings and took them into the shanty and immediately came back out.

"I'm going to track down, Sam," Mack said. "Annie can join you in the shanty so you can show her the ropes."

Sarah picked the bucket of water back up and looked at Annie.

"Will do," she said. "Follow me."

Mack took off into the woods, whistling a cheerful tune that filtered through the trees. Sarah headed into the cook shanty with Annie trailing her.

"We spent the last week cleaning the place so it's not half bad," Sarah said as they stepped inside.

"It's so…simple," Annie said.

"It is rather crude," Sarah agreed. "I have to admit that I spent my first two days here in a near state of shock."

"I can see why," Annie said.

The look on her face was grim.

"Sam said the loggers will start to arrive toward the end of the week, so you're here just in time," Sarah said. "I'll show you where the supplies are and go over our duties. Our days will be long ones."

"I'd be lying if I didn't say I'm dreading this," Annie said.

"You seem so young," Sarah said. "Have you been here before?"

Annie sighed.

"This is my first winter," she said. "I'm fourteen now. Father says he needs me here, but my mother doesn't take kindly to him pulling me out of school. I'm hoping that when he's old enough, my brother Jacob will take my place."

"How many brothers and sisters do you have?" Sarah asked.

"Two brothers and one sister," Annie said with a tinge of sadness in her voice. "I'm the oldest. As much as I argue with my brothers, I'll miss them both, and my mother and sister. I'm going to be so lonely up here. Father already forbade me from talking to any of the loggers."

"That's probably wise," Sarah said. "I imagine they're going to be a rather rogue gang of men."

"I guess we'll find out soon enough," Annie said meekly.

"As the only two females here, we'll have to look out for each other," Sarah said.

Even as she spoke those words, Sarah knew that Annie would be far less alone than she would. She, at least, would have her father by her side.

CHAPTER THREE

When Evelyn arrived at the logging camp, the air was bitter cold and the ground was already frozen, rock hard. A thin layer of snow dusted the trees and earth, and the sky was bright and clear, a solid aqua. Monstrous, hundred-year-old trees, many of them pines, seemed to span into forever, like an endless ocean of dark green. The grandeur of the land gave Evelyn comfort, solace, and she took a deep breath of the fresh, chilled air. She climbed out of the wagon, and Will tossed her the canvas pack. Their eyes locked for a moment.

"Watch your back," Will said.

Evelyn nodded.

"Watch my children," she told him.

"They'll be fine," Will said. "We'll all be fine."

Evelyn watched as he turned the wagon around and headed back the way they had come. When the wagon finally vanished from sight, she yearned to run after it, but she stood in place. She gazed at the small army of men that surrounded her, roaming about the camp grounds, their booming voices resounding through the woods, and she felt a sharp twinge of panic burrow into the pit of her stomach. She felt intimidated. She knew many of the men were long-term lumberjacks. Others, like her, were just trying to make a living for their families. Evelyn had never seen so many men gathered in one place, and she realized in that moment how isolated and sheltered she had been in life. She had spent nearly all her time on the farm with George and the children, seeing outsiders only when they had gone to town for supplies or visited a nearby neighbor. No part of her could have envisioned the realm she was entering.

"You check in yet?" asked a man with a jet-black handlebar mustache that curled into two question marks at each end.

"Just got here," Evelyn said, so conscious of her voice that her palms instantly became sweaty. "Name's George Bauer."

"Been here before?"

"Two times. Last time was three years back."

The man riffled through his papers.

"Here you are," he said. "You're a sawyer?"

"Sure am," Evelyn said.

"I'm the foreman, Johnny Jones. You know how things work around here. No gambling, no booze, and we'll get along just fine. Some of the jacks are still arriving, but we've already had a crew in the woods for a week now. You'll be starting tomorrow. Dinner's in about an hour. You can find yourself a bunk to settle in until then."

Johnny pointed to the long, low bunkhouse. Evelyn took it in. No part of her believed the structure could withstand a wicked storm or provide sufficient warmth for the winter. Just as she was about to head to the building, a young boy, he didn't look older than fourteen or fifteen, bare-cheeked except for the peach fuzz that feathered his face, rode into camp on a horse that was definitely nothing to brag about—more like a haggard plow horse. The horse's nostrils emitted puffs of white and its body steamed from exertion in the wintry air. As the boy was about to dismount, Johnny Jones yelled out.

"Whoa, now! You stay right where you're at, boy. What're you doing here?"

"I came for work," the boy said.

"We don't allow jacks to bring their own horses up here, boy. Unless you're a teamster. You a teamster?"

"No, sir," the boy answered.

"Well, we don't need any distractions, and we definitely don't need another mouth to feed," Johnny said.

By then some of the other jacks had gathered around the boy and his horse. One jack, with long, curly brown hair that fell like a drape past his shoulders and a thick beard that resembled snakes coiling down his chest, bellowed loudly, a sound that rose to the treetops.

"Can't believe that old mare actually made it up here," he said. "You might have to carry her halfway back."

The other jacks laughed and the boy reddened.

"Where you from, greenhorn?" Johnny asked.

"From outside Baxter," the boy answered quietly.

"Better head back that way, boy," Johnny said.

"My pa's dead," the boy pleaded. "The horse was my only way up here. I need the work. It's only my ma and my brothers and sisters now."

"What's your name, kid?" Johnny asked.

"Henry," the boy said. "Henry Jankowski."

"A Pole and a greenhorn, huh?" Johnny said.

The boy lowered his head.

"Yes, sir," he said.

Johnny hesitated a moment and then nodded.

"All right," he said. "Don't make me regret this. Greenhorns only get one chance."

The jacks who had gathered around laughed and hooted as the boy got off the horse.

"Horse shed is that way," Johnny said. "Don't take all day."

The other jacks laughed again. As the boy headed to the shed, with the horse plodding behind, Evelyn grabbed her pack and trudged toward the bunkhouse thinking this was a land of little empathy. As a mother, she wanted to protect the boy, defend him, but she moved on. When she reached the bunkhouse, she paused, took a deep breath, and tried to steady herself. For the first time, she felt fear. She pushed the door open, and as soon as she entered the bunkhouse, the stench that rose around her almost made her double over. Men were squeezed into every corner of the small space, and their voices droned on like cicadas, a constant scratching sound.

Evelyn scanned the room and spotted a vacant lower bunk. She walked over to it and put down her pack. This will be my home for the next few months, she thought with trepidation. Before she could think another thought, she turned and quickly headed toward the door. She bolted into the woods, and when she was out of sight, she bent over, her hands on her knees, and vomited, bile pushing past her lips. Evelyn felt tears well up in her eyes, and she straightened herself and gulped in air to settle her nerves.

"You can do this," she said to herself. "You have no choice."

The rush of the winds high in the trees sounded like a plummeting waterfall, almost deafening. She looked up at the trees, swaying side to side, and felt a sense of calmness. She turned from the woods and headed back to the bunkhouse.

❖

Evelyn went to the bunk she had selected, the top one now occupied by a man with his legs dangling over the side. He was a tall, rather skinny, long-limbed logger, who appeared to be nearly seven feet tall. He had a mane of stringy dirty blond hair and his beard, not thick, but wispy, hung over his chest.

"I was wondering who my new bunkmate was," he said as Evelyn sat. "I'm Jack. Folks here call me Whiskey Jack, though the whiskey part doesn't account for much in these parts. Not a drop in sight."

Evelyn reached out and firmly shook his hand.

"Keep an eye on that one," the man in the bunk to the left of Evelyn's said. "Word is that if you get in a fight with Whiskey Jack, he'll wrap himself around you like a boa constrictor and squeeze the life right out of you."

Whiskey Jack reached down with one long arm and smacked the man on the back of the head.

"Hey," the man growled.

"Don't pay him any mind," Whiskey Jack said. "We call him Gabbie. He'll talk your head off if you let him, but he does tell a damn good story."

Gabbie was a stocky man with wavy dark brown hair, a scrubby bush of a beard that was trimmed to just below his chin, and a slanted grin. Evelyn glanced from one man to the other, trying to discern how serious they were. She had heard stories about the fights at the camps.

"I'm George Bauer," she said.

She focused on keeping her voice low and steady.

"Where do you hale from, George?" Whiskey Jack asked.

"Farm outside Maple Grove."

"Maple Grove, eh? It's nice in those parts. I'm from Munson, but I spend most of my time up this way. You snore much, George?"

"Only when I sleep," Evelyn answered.

Whiskey Jack laughed and fell back into his bunk. He sat up again only when the clanging of the triangle signaled dinner time and the loggers rushed to the door and out of the bunkhouse in a stream, like a line of ants heading toward their hill.

Once inside the cook shanty, with the scent of food rising from the stove and tables, Evelyn realized how hungry she was and took the first available seat that she saw. The men surrounding her nodded at her in greeting, and she nodded back. She quickly glanced around the room. The men were crammed around the tables, elbow to elbow, and the tables could barely be seen, every inch of them covered with bowls, platters, plates, and cups. The sea of loggers was a menagerie of burly look-alikes, all wool and suspenders. Most of the men had short hair accompanied by mustaches or beards, and distinguishing one logger from another was not an easy task. Some of the men obviously knew each other. Others, like Evelyn, sat surrounded by strangers.

Despite the no talking during meals rule, the sound was deafening—an endless drone. As emptied bowls and platters were replaced with full ones, the shanty was an avalanche of noise, with flatware clanking and cups clapping down on tables. Even with three children and George, Evelyn's home in Maple Grove had always been moderately quiet. But with this assembly of men, she didn't think silence ever took root. The smell of the food made Evelyn's stomach growl, and like the others, she began to fill her plate—baked beans, biscuits, salt pork, dried apples and prunes, and pies. She appreciated the simplicity of the food—solid, stick-to-your-ribs winter fare.

As Evelyn gobbled down her food, she surveyed the room, and when her eyes settled on the flunky who was rushing from table to table with food and a pot of coffee, she felt a sense of relief settle in her—another woman. A rather nondescript girl was also working the tables. She looked extremely young, perhaps in her early teens. She was tiny and pale, with a mop of strawberry-blond curls. The older woman was extremely attractive and seemed dreadfully out of place in that rigorous world of men. Her dark auburn hair was kept in a tightly wrapped bun on the back of her head, and her fair skin made her look almost fragile. She had a slender build, and though she wore a long, heavy dress and an apron, Evelyn could tell she was well-endowed.

Evelyn watched the woman. She seemed to float around the cook shanty like a ghost, trying to go unseen as she skirted her way around the men. She spoke only rarely to the cook, his helper, and the other flunky, and she almost always avoided eye contact. Evelyn wondered what her story was, how she had ended up at the camp. Every aspect of her seemed to stick out amidst the mass of men, but her very presence at the camp somehow gave Evelyn comfort. Even though she was disguised as a man, the presence of two other females made her feel less alone, not so outnumbered.

Evelyn held up her cup just as she had seen the others do to signal for more coffee, and the older woman quickly strode over with a pot. Evelyn found herself taking in the woman's hands as she poured the steaming coffee. They were delicate, unblemished, with long fingers. She's not accustomed to hard labor, Evelyn thought. Her own hands were more manly—wide, with thick fingers, and calluses here and there from the drudgeries of farm work. As the woman went to fill another jack's cup, Evelyn watched her move across the room. She was at least a foot shorter than Evelyn, and Evelyn wondered if the flunky feared for her safety, engulfed by so many men. She knew more than one of these men would take advantage of the woman if they had the opportunity. Though she didn't know her, Evelyn admired her tenacity, whatever her circumstances—being willing to be surrounded by so many gregarious men. She didn't seem to be the woman for the part. She carried herself with a certain refinement, and Evelyn couldn't help but wonder if this was her first time at the camp, also. Realizing that her eyes were lingering on the woman longer than was appropriate, she quickly dropped them to her plate.

❖

Evelyn's first night in the bunkhouse was worse than any nightmare she ever could have imagined. The noise was boisterous, nonstop, and the tension was thick, with the men tightly wedged into the too-small space. Evelyn sat on the edge of her bunk and listened to the barrage of sound around her. The men seemed to have a penchant for badgering each other. The bantering was constant, oftentimes good-natured, but she knew it would take only one wrong look or word for it to escalate beyond that into a brawl. Whiskey Jack pointed out some of the jacks to Evelyn.

"The biggest fellow in the house is that jack over there," he said.

Evelyn easily spotted the man. He was, indeed, a humongous man, about three jacks in one.

"He's been coming up here for two years now," Whiskey Jack said. "We're still waiting for the day when a bigger jack shows up, but it hasn't happened yet. He's like our own Paul Bunyan. He's not the quickest man, but he can practically move a mountain if you need him to. We call him Windy because he blows more farts than the rest of us put together. The nights that we have bean hole beans are especially fragrant."

Evelyn felt doomed.

"Good to know," she said.

Whiskey Jack identified a jack named Poker Pete as one of the biggest troublemakers in the camp. He had a head of bushy brown hair and a shortly cropped beard. His most distinct feature was a rather large, very crooked nose, which Evelyn assumed might have been broken more than once in a fistfight or brawl. As Whiskey Jack continued to point out men, Poker Pete yelled out to the man Whiskey Jack had said was their finest fiddler.

"Hey, Tommy, who's your wife going to be warming up to this winter?"

"That's nothing I need to worry about," Tommy answered good-naturedly, not about to let Poker Pete ruffle his feathers. "We've already got so many kids that she won't even let me sidle up to her anymore."

The jacks sitting with Poker Pete laughed. Whiskey Jack had told Evelyn that Tommy Tune boasted eight children. Evelyn pitied the woman who was home alone in the winter with that many children. She glanced about at the other men. Some of them hunkered down near the grinding stone to sharpen axes, repair equipment, or mend socks and mittens. Others tossed conversations back and forth, and she began to attach names to faces. Tommy Tune and Big Mike moved to a corner and began playing their fiddles. The dry, whining tones filled the room as a few of the jacks sang along in gruff voices. Other men played cards; the shuffling of the decks sounded like flags flapping in the wind. Two men hovered over a crude checkerboard that they had set up on a small section of the deacon's seat. Gabbie, staying true to his name, held command in a far corner of the room as he told the story of a river walker named Billy Jonas.

"Billy Jonas was one of the best known rivermen in all the Northwoods, the cowboy of the mighty Wisconsin River. One season after Billy finished a long run down river, he went to Milwaukee and bought a secondhand suit. He boarded the train, but he drank and gambled away all his money, so they threw him off the train in Portage. From there he started to walk to his original destination, Black Rapids, but it began to rain and his suit started to shrink. By the time he reached Ashland, his pants were nearly up to his knees, and his jacket sleeves were up to his elbows. The rain continued to fall, and Billy kept on walking. By the time he was within miles of

Black Rapids, the suit had shrunk so much that he couldn't wear it anymore, and by the time he entered town, he was completely naked. The sheriff had no choice but to throw him in jail. And that was the last time Billy Jonas ever took a train."

The men sitting around Gabbie chuckled and slapped their knees in good humor, and as Gabbie began to tell another story, Evelyn turned her attention to a man who sat in another corner of the bunkhouse, whittling. Whiskey Jack had told her his name was Walking Willy, and that his reputation preceded him. Willy was shorter and leaner than most of the other men, but his stature served him well, as he was known to be an incredibly agile man, revered as one of the best river walkers in the entire territory. Evelyn's eyes traveled from jack to jack, as she wondered which ones she should be leery of. It was known that some of the jacks were running from the law, and a few others were fleeing from their families for one reason or another. Every logger had a story. Evelyn planned to keep her distance from most of them as much as possible.

With the noise rising around her, Evelyn's head began to pound. She knew the nights would be the hardest on her, with the cramped quarters immersing her in misery. She wondered if a group of women in those conditions would be as unruly as these men were. She somehow doubted it. I'm sure it wouldn't be pleasant, she thought, but I don't think it would be like this. She rummaged through her pack and pulled out the pipe, the pouch of tobacco, and a box of wooden matches. She pushed some tobacco into the pipe and pulled on her coat and hat.

"You heading out, George?" Whiskey Jack asked. "Sounds like the wind's whipping up a bit out there."

"Just going to take a few puffs off my pipe," Evelyn said. "It's going to take me a while to get used to these close quarters after being on the prairie."

"Understandable," said Whiskey Jack.

Evelyn weaved around the men until she reached the door. As soon as she stepped outside and away from the bunkhouse, she felt relief. The only sounds were the wind, the creaking trees, and a few screeches from the night creatures. Occasionally, the faint sound of laughter arose from the shed where the teamsters tended to the horses. Evelyn rested against a tree, took a deep breath, and for the first time that day, felt her body relax a bit. She lit the pipe and watched the smoke curl up toward the sky. She thought about her children, and she wanted nothing more than to escape right then and there and return home.

❖

When Evelyn returned to the bunkhouse, she went to the bunk, put her pipe back in her pack, and took out the calendar and pencil that Helen had given her. In the dim light of the potbellied stove, she marked off her first day at the camp. Turning the pages that followed, she felt an overwhelming sense of gloom. She removed her boots, lay down, and pulled her blanket over her.

By the time nine o'clock finally arrived and the kerosene lamps were extinguished, a layer of thick tobacco smoke hung over the bunkhouse in a low-floating cloud, and the sour smell of sweat and damp wool seemed to seep into Evelyn's skin. She felt as if she would suffocate, and she tried to catch her breath, burrowing beneath the cover and curling into herself. Even beneath her cover, the nighttime noise surrounding her was unbearable. Snores from the others rumbled through the bunkhouse like an approaching thunderhead. One man growled in his sleep, and another exhaled in a semi-whistle. On and off throughout the night, one logger or another would spurt out some garbled phrase. Outside, escalating winds seemed to knock on the walls of the bunkhouse. Despite her fatigue, Evelyn prayed for morning to come quickly so she could escape into the outside and the fresh air. Her last thought was of her children, at home, safely snuggled in warm beds. Her sacrifice at the camp was worth it for their comfort. They were all she had, and she was all they had.

❖

The loud, clanking sound of the flunky hitting the triangle with a metal beater seemed to fill the air as soon as Evelyn closed her eyes. In sync with the others, she rolled off her bunk; pulled on additional socks and her boots; grabbed her coat, hat, and heavy wool mittens; and headed toward the door. Loggers filed out ahead of her and behind. In the cook shanty, they all fell silent, focused on the food. Evelyn found herself glancing up as the older flunky filled the cup of the logger sitting across from her, and for a moment, she caught the woman's eyes with her own. They were a deep blue, like the spring sky when it has been scoured by a sudden storm. Evelyn watched as the woman strode across the room to serve another jack. She couldn't take her eyes off her. Realizing that she was paying too much attention to the flunky, she admonished herself. *Stop staring at the woman! What's wrong with you?* She felt her cheeks burning with embarrassment, but she had to admit that she was curious about this woman who seemed more fitting for a parlor than a logging camp. Evelyn had never really noticed women before. Her closest confidante was Helen, and she considered Jess to be more like a second sister. Beyond that the other women in her life were merely acquaintances that she saw only infrequently. They, like her, lived lives with little time to spare. Now, immersed in this world of men, she couldn't help but notice this woman.

Realizing that some of the loggers were already getting up from the table and heading outside to return to the bunkhouse and gather their tools, Evelyn took one last bite of food and one last gulp of coffee and followed suit. The air was crisp, cold, just below freezing, but the snow on the ground had not yet accumulated enough to be a deterrent or hardship. Evelyn knew that would not be the case for long. She hurried into the bunkhouse to get her ax, rested it on her shoulder, and followed the others into the woods. Whiskey Jack caught up with her and they walked in unison.

"You a sawyer, George?" Whiskey Jack asked.

"Sure am," Evelyn said.

"Good enough. I haven't teamed up with anyone yet. You can be my chopping mate and my bunkmate."

"Fine with me," Evelyn said.

"We'll be heading about a mile in," Whiskey Jack said.

"You been here long?" Evelyn asked.

"Got in four days ago. You a family man, George?"

Evelyn gathered her thoughts before she spoke.

"I've got three children—two boys and one girl. My wife passed away a few months back."

They fell silent for a moment, and Whiskey Jack finally cleared his throat.

"That's a hard row to hoe."

"Yeah," Evelyn said. "That and a bad year of farming's what brings me here. I'm just trying to make ends meet."

"Sorry for your loss, George," Whiskey Jack said.

Evelyn nodded and they continued to trudge beneath the cathedral of trees—poplars, paper birches, elms, maples, oaks, balsams, jack and Norway pines. They pushed deeper into the woods, the mottled grays, browns, and blacks of the different barks melding into a mirage. The cutting wind was so icy that sharp pains smacked Evelyn between the eyes, just above the bridge of her nose. She winced.

"What about you, Whiskey?" she asked. "How long have you been logging in these woods?"

"Longer than I can remember," Whiskey Jack said. "Started coming up as a kid, just like that greenhorn. Came from a big family, and my father was a brute. I escaped the day after he nearly choked me to death for talking back to him. I was fourteen. My mother couldn't save me. Hell, she couldn't save herself. I took off and never looked back."

"That's harsh," Evelyn said.

She imagined him as a young boy, scrawny and frightened, striking out on his own. That took a lot of gumption, and she knew that more than one of these men had stories of abuse and strife. As she and Whiskey Jack moved deeper into the woods, a rabbit bolted across their path.

"That would make a tasty dinner," Whiskey Jack said. He pointed at the two jacks ahead of them. "See those two up there?"

"Sure do."

"Stay clear of them. The one on the left is Stinky Joe. He's a known troublemaker. He abandoned his wife and children early on and spends most of his time working in the woods, avoiding the law. Don't trust him, especially not with your life. The other one there, on the right, we call Stumpy. He starts most of the fights—him and Poker Pete. He has only one toe on his left foot. He was attacked by another jack with an ax about four years back. He felled a tree without giving a warning shout. As you know, that's some damn serious business up here. The jack who attacked him was the one who had to jump out of the crashing tree's way just in time."

"I'll keep an eye out," Evelyn said.

The rest of their trek was silent, and as the loggers moved deeper into the woods, they began to fan out within the boundaries marked by the cruiser, targeting the pine and hemlock trees that were light enough to float downriver. Evelyn took in the magnificence of the trees as she and Whiskey Jack walked. When they were about a mile in, Whiskey Jack stopped and examined a tall pine before them.

"This one's leaning a bit west, into the wind," he said. "Should be easy enough to take down."

Wanting to take the lead to prove herself, Evelyn swung her ax and began to cut a V-shaped notch about waist high on the tree's west side. When she had chopped through nearly a third of the way, Whiskey Jack took over and cut another notch about a foot above that, on the opposite side. They worked back and forth until they had created a hinge that held the tree in place as it began to fall. Whiskey Jack and Evelyn let out a warning shout and quickly backed away from the tree in the direction opposite from which it would come down. They continued like that, tree after tree, and halfway through the day, Evelyn thought she might collapse. When she wasn't chopping, she would look at the snow longingly. It looked like a soft bed of feathers, and she longed to lie down. After what seemed like an endless amount of time, dusk finally began to descend like a gauzy veil over the woods. By the time the men started to head back to camp, Evelyn felt as if she was in a daze of bone-deep weariness and numbness.

That night Evelyn didn't think she would be able to last another day. When she finally stretched out on her bunk, she realized how much her body ached in every place. As strong as she wanted to be, she had never felt weaker, and under her covers, she silently cried. She wanted her own bed, her home, her children, and they seemed a world away.

CHAPTER FOUR

Sarah had cried herself to sleep every night her first two weeks at camp. Sorrow over her loss of Abigail still coursed through her, and she could not help but think that only one month earlier, her life had been full of hopes and prospects—love. Now her life seemed only to echo loneliness and despair. By the end of November, with all the loggers in place and ready to work, she had determined that she would never return to the camp again and would find some other way to support herself. The loud gruffness of the jacks made her jittery, and she dreaded every day that she awakened.

Her fears about being surrounded by so many jacks were substantiated on the third night that the loggers were in camp, with the men huddled into the crowded cook shanty. On that night, the jack named Poker Pete firmly planted a hand on her buttocks as she filled his coffee cup. For a moment, she was startled, her body prickling. The jack sitting beside him had defended her and smacked Poker Pete's hand away just as Sarah instinctively poured steaming coffee on it. Poker Pete released a deep grunt and promptly removed his hand from her.

"Don't get in my way again, Bauer," Sarah had heard Poker Pete snarl at the jack who had intervened.

"She deserves some respect," the jack named Bauer had said.

"No talking in the shanty," Sam had yelled from the other side of the room.

Sarah was surprised that the jack had stuck up for her. She never would have expected that from any of the men. *At least I know one* of these men has a decent streak, she thought. From that point on, she moved past the men as quickly as possible, always keeping her eyes on those nearest to her. She did feel somewhat protected by Sam. He watched the loggers closely whenever she was around, but the way he sometimes looked at her made her uncomfortable and self-conscious. A part of her wished that he knew what her relationship with Abigail had been. She thought she might feel more able to confide in him and feel some sense of trust. She also knew that might make matters even worse, as she thought that perhaps Abigail had been right in thinking that Sam had his sights on her.

The living conditions were no consolation to Sarah, either. The constant manual labor made her feel as if she might lose her mind. Her hands were sore, with cuts and bruises from her daily chores—collecting the wood and starting the fire, carrying buckets of water from the river to the shanty in the freezing cold, and the endless chopping and cutting of food. One of her worst dreads, the one thing she thought might push her to the edge of insanity, was the lice. She found herself checking for them during any idle moment, scratching itches that weren't even there, and each night she took down her hair and rigorously brushed it before putting it back into a tight bun. She would then scour herself for any sign of bites in the dim kerosene light. On Sundays, she would make sure the water she washed her clothes and bedding in was boiling, hot enough to scald the insects. Even with that, she had the constant feeling of the creatures scaling her skin.

Sarah's life with Abigail had been a docile one, free of the drudgery she now faced daily. They didn't live in luxury, but they'd had all the comforts that anyone could desire and a sense of solitude that was never present at the camp. Their days were spent sewing and tailoring, and their evenings were quiet times—cooking dinner and settling in the parlor to read to each other. That world seemed a lifetime away, and Sarah didn't think she would ever adapt to the logging camp.

Without anyone to confide in or befriend, besides Annie, Sarah was isolated among the many men. Mack kept Annie close to his side, which Sarah understood, but she wished the young girl could provide some kinship, someone to whom she could speak. Their conversations were short-lived, though, and clipped—partly because of the young girl's shyness, and partly because the endless work left little time for chatter. Her conversations with Sam, beyond the needs of the kitchen, were strained and stilted. He never really spoke of Abigail, and the few times that Sarah brought up her name, he grew even quieter.

Besides meal times in the cook shanty, Sarah had the most exposure to the jacks on Sundays, the one day the loggers didn't go into the woods. At the camp, every day was the same day, and the days seemed to blur together—Monday, Thursday. The only different day, the one day that stood out, was Sunday. Sarah and Annie did their laundry on that day, and the jacks devoted the day to cleaning the bunkhouse, and washing and boiling clothes in huge iron kettles that sat atop fires outside. Some of the jacks would give each other haircuts and others tried to mend their clothes as best they could. The roughhousing was endless, as a good number of the lumberjacks were obnoxious brutes, while the others were just loud and raucous.

The quietest of the loggers, the man named Bauer, who had stuck up for her in the shanty, did catch Sarah's attention. She had seen him outside alone in the evenings, smoking his pipe, when she had gone out to gather wood for the next morning or taken a peek out of the small window in her shed. On Sundays when she was outside boiling her clothing, she had noticed him being rather aloof, interacting with only a few of the other men. He seemed different somehow, more subdued than the others. Sarah had heard some of the other loggers call the man George.

She had never before had any interest in any man, but this one in particular…Besides the fact that he had defended her, he also had a certain quirkiness about him. He had striking features—a nose with a prominent bridge, jutting cheekbones, and a sturdy jawline. She had observed early on that even though he kept his distance from most of the men, the others seemed to like him well enough. He was, without a doubt, the best darner among the loggers, and she often witnessed some of the other jacks asking him to do a mending job for them. He was quick, nimble with his fingers. That piqued Sarah's curiosity even more, for she knew few men would be as comfortable as he was with a needle and thread, especially those who boasted being lumberjacks, though this man didn't seem to take to boasting. The darning was her one opening with the jack.

One Sunday afternoon when the sun glared off the snow and almost seemed to warm the air, she saw George sitting on a stump, mending socks and mittens. Sarah, who had her own articles of clothing she needed to fix, walked over to him and observed his stitchery. She had to admit he did surprisingly fine work.

"You're really quite good at that," she said. "Who taught you how to darn?"

George looked up at her and cleared his throat.

"I often helped my wife with the children's clothes back home."

"How many children?" Sarah asked.

"Three."

"Boys or girls?"

"Two boys and a girl," George said, dropping his eyes to focus on his darning.

"I can't imagine many other men do the same," Sarah said.

George shrugged.

"She helped me plenty with the farm. On the farm you learn to fix whatever needs fixing."

Sarah found it odd that he spoke in the past tense when he mentioned his wife, but she didn't want to pry. As much as she wanted to keep the conversation going, she could think of nothing else to say, and George kept his eyes focused on his darning. As Sarah left his side to return to her kettle of boiling water, she saw Sam watching her and averted her own eyes.

❖

When the flunky walked away from Evelyn that day, she realized that as curious as she was about the flunky, she was leery of her and her questions, fearing that she might somehow sense that Evelyn was not as she appeared to be. I should never have started with the darning, she thought. Her next encounter with the older flunky was a day in mid-December when the greenhorn Henry Jankowski, who had ridden into camp on his horse, paired up with Poker Pete. Evelyn had her concerns about Henry working with that jack in particular, as he was every bit as nasty as Whiskey Jack had said he was, and Evelyn already had a soft spot for Henry. As a greenhorn and the only Polish logger at the camp, he was the butt of most of the German and Norwegian loggers' jokes and pranks.

Poker Pete and Henry were working a tree within sight of where Evelyn and Whiskey Jack were that day. At one point Evelyn looked over their way and noticed that Poker Pete had left Henry alone. Ten minutes later, when she looked again, she realized that the tree Henry was working on had begun to topple earlier than he had expected. Backing away as quickly as he could, the boy hollered out a warning to the other loggers. The tree went down with a boom and a crash, with Henry still not fully clear of it, and then a piercing scream rose from Henry and rang through the woods.

"Jankowski's down," Evelyn told Whiskey Jack.

She dropped her ax and made her way to him as fast as she could, trudging through snow that was almost knee-deep. When she reached the young jack, he was crouching over, his face, neck, and hands covered with the quills of a porcupine that had been nesting in the top of the tree. It had charged Henry after the tree came down. Evelyn quickly looked around. Poker Pete was still nowhere in sight, and Evelyn suspected that he had known the porcupine was in the tree all along.

"What's going on over there?" Whiskey Jack yelled out.

"Porcupine," Evelyn hollered back. "We've gotta get him back to camp. We need to get these quills out or he's going to have trouble."

Whiskey Jack joined her, and they helped Henry up and walked him back to the camp. When they reached it, they helped him into the bunkhouse and sat him on the deacon's seat.

"You'll need to stay calm, Henry," Evelyn said. "If you move around while I'm doing this, the quill tips might break off and lodge deeper."

"You sure you know what you're doing, George?" Whiskey Jack asked.

"My eldest tried to chase down a porcupine last summer," Evelyn said. "Reckon he learned his lesson."

"All right, then," Whiskey Jack said.

"I need some kind of tool—flat head pliers or something of the sort," Evelyn said.

Whiskey Jack rifled through the small box of tools kept near the grindstone, pulled out a crude pair of pliers, and handed them to Evelyn.

"I'm going to have to clean these before I use them," Evelyn said, examining the pliers. "I'll head to the cook shanty. They'll at least have some boiling water, maybe a little whiskey on hand. Keep him calm while I'm gone."

"Will do, but then you're on your own," said Whiskey Jack. "If I don't head back, we'll all be in trouble with Johnny."

"All right," Evelyn said.

She looked at Henry, who sat statue still, with a pained and terrified look on his face.

❖

Evelyn hesitated outside the cook shanty and then knocked. She didn't want to barge in. She wanted to respect the little privacy that the women who worked in the shanty had. She toggled from foot to foot and rubbed her hands together as she waited at the shanty door, the cold biting at her. The door finally opened and Evelyn stood face-to-face with the older flunky.

"Yes?" the woman said, her voice quiet compared to all the booming voices Evelyn was usually surrounded by.

Evelyn suddenly felt self-conscious, standing before the flunky while dressed as a man.

"One of the loggers disturbed a porcupine. We need to get the quills out. We've got pliers, but they're awfully dirty. Could you boil some water for us?"

"I've got some on the stove right now. It should be ready

shortly," the flunky said. "You might as well come in and wait, and then you can take some back in a pot."

Evelyn stepped aside.

"Thank you," she said.

"You can sit," the flunky said. "It'll be a few minutes."

"We could use some whiskey, too, if you've got any," Evelyn said. "Just to clean the wounds."

"As you know, whiskey's not allowed in camp," the flunky said. "Though I do suspect Sam has a bit stashed away for himself somewhere, I'd have no idea where to look."

"Then we'll do with what we have," Evelyn said.

She took a seat at one of the long tables, empty of food and men. She was grateful for the warmth, and her fingers and toes began to tingle as it seeped in.

"I didn't introduce myself when we first spoke," the woman said. "I'm Sarah. I'd offer you something to eat, but I'm just about to start putting dinner together."

"No need. I've still got my lunch pail waiting for me in the woods," Evelyn said. "I'm George Bauer."

"You up here every winter, George?" Sarah asked.

"Only when necessary," Evelyn said. "A couple bad years of farming does the trick."

"Where is the farm?" Sarah asked.

"Outside Maple Grove."

"I'm from Pine Creek. This is my first time in a logging camp."

"You taking a liking to it?"

"I think I need to find another line of work," Sarah said.

Evelyn released a low chuckle.

Sarah hoisted the pot off the woodstove and poured some water into a smaller pot.

"The water's ready," she said. "Is there another jack to help you?"

"Whiskey Jack helped me get him here, but he's heading back to the woods as soon as I return."

"You'll need another set of hands, then," Sarah said. "I can help."

Evelyn grabbed the pot of boiling water and they headed to the bunkhouse. Inside, Whiskey Jack politely nodded at Sarah and promptly left. Evelyn put the pliers in the bucket and rested a hand on one of Henry's shoulders.

"You're going to have to sit on this crate here, Henry," she said. "We'll need to have a second set of hands on you while I do this."

Henry moved from the deacon's seat to the crate, and Evelyn stationed herself before him.

"Take a hold of his shoulders," she told Sarah. "Make sure he stays still."

"Okay," Sarah said.

She positioned herself behind Henry and pressed down on his shoulders.

Evelyn began to carefully remove the quills. She grabbed each one as near to the skin as she could, carefully pushing down the skin around it. She pulled each quill out as firmly and quickly as possible, trying to extract them at the same angle at which they had entered. Every time she removed one, she examined that patch of skin to make sure the tip hadn't broken off. Sarah watched closely as Evelyn worked.

"You've done this before," she said.

"I told you I've got three children back home."

"That's right," Sarah said. "The children whose socks you darn. Your wife's alone with them for the winter?"

Evelyn hesitated, then said, "Wife's dead. Died this past autumn."

"I'm sorry," Sarah said. "That's a lot to handle. I recently lost…"

Her voice trailed off.

"That it is," Evelyn said. "My sister's with the children while I'm here. You were saying you…"

"Never mind," Sarah said. "It's a long story."

More than half an hour passed before all the quills were removed and a look of relief made its way over Henry's face.

"You'll want to keep those wounds clean," Evelyn told him.

"Use plenty of soap and water. Be as thorough as you can. You don't want to get sick while you're stuck up here."

"Okay," Henry said. "I can't thank you enough."

"I'll check in with you at dinnertime," Evelyn said. "Gotta head back to the woods. I'll let the foreman know where you are when I get back to the site."

Both she and Sarah turned to leave the bunkhouse, Sarah heading to the cook shanty and Evelyn toward the forest.

"Thank you for your help," Evelyn said as Sarah strode away.

Sarah turned around, smiled, and pressed on.

When Sarah returned to the cook shanty from the bunkhouse, Sam was waiting for her at the door. His jaw was firmly set, taut with tension, and his bushy eyebrows seemed to push against each other.

"You've got no place in the bunkhouse," he said gruffly as he followed Sarah into the shanty. "What were you doing there?"

Sarah was startled by the rage in his voice.

"There was an accident," she said. "I had to help a jack remove some porcupine quills from another jack."

"That so," Sam said. "And which jack was that who needed the help? Did he come here to get you?"

Sarah felt as if she had to defend herself from Sam's accusatory tone. "Bauer," she said. "He needed some boiling water."

"And you just offered your services, even with the work you've got to do here?"

"Well, yes, I—"

"You shouldn't be fraternizing with the jacks," Sam barked at her.

Sarah felt a sense of desperation.

"He needed help," she said.

Sam abruptly turned away and walked out of the shanty, slamming the door behind him.

❖

That night as the loggers headed to the cook shanty, Evelyn spotted Poker Pete and hurried to catch up to him.

"That prank you pulled today could've taken a nasty turn," she said. "You knew that porcupine was in that tree. You knew the damage that could've been done. That greenhorn could have been badly injured."

Poker Pete looked at her and grimaced. "What does it matter to you?"

"I'm the one who took the time out to help him," Evelyn said.

Poker Pete took a step toward Evelyn and pushed her back against a tree.

"You did that of your own accord," he said as he pressed against her. "You should mind your own business, Bauer."

Evelyn pushed him off her, and just as Poker Pete lifted an arm and fisted his hand, Whiskey Jack came up from behind and grabbed him.

"Back off, Pete," he said. "Bauer's right. Next time you want to mess with a jack, pick someone other than a greenhorn."

Poker Pete broke away from Whiskey Jack's grasp, glared at Evelyn, and stalked off toward the shanty.

"You all right, George?" Whiskey Jack asked Evelyn.

"I'm fine," Evelyn said. "Just fine. And I appreciate your help, Whiskey, but I can fend for myself. Don't want you getting into any trouble on my account."

Evelyn had surprised herself. She had felt no fear in that moment. Instead, she had a surge of anger she had never before experienced. She had been willing to fight Poker Pete.

"You'd do the same for me," Whiskey Jack said. "Come on. Let's go get some grub."

They walked side by side to the shanty, Whiskey Jack whistling some tune.

❖

When Evelyn entered the cook shanty for dinner, she stood in the doorway and scanned the two long wooden tables for Henry. When she spotted him, she moved through the crowded room and squeezed in next to him. They nodded at each other in greeting and grunted their helloes. They filled their plates and started to eat. Evelyn looked up from her plate now and then to steal glimpses of Sarah whenever possible, without drawing attention. The more interaction that she had with her, the more intrigued she was. She wanted to know more about her. Evelyn raised her cup in the air to signal for coffee. Sarah hurried over to the table with a steaming pot. For no reason at all, Evelyn felt herself reddening and dropped her head. Sarah topped off Evelyn's cup, and Evelyn nodded in gratitude. As Sarah turned to address the other table, she momentarily rested a hand on Evelyn's shoulder, and Evelyn's breath snagged in her throat. She felt as if she was being branded where the hand rested.

That night in the bunkhouse, Evelyn sat quietly on the edge of her bunk, listening to the sliding songs of the fiddle. Whiskey Jack and Gabbie were playing cards and talking near the wood stove, and Evelyn heard George's name come up in conversation.

"George there was the one to remove the quills."

"You did that single-handedly, George?" a jack named Rusty leaned over and asked.

"The flunky helped," Evelyn said quietly.

"Ah, the flunky," Rusty said. He nudged Whiskey Jack. "Now, she's a looker, that one is. I'd dream about her at night if I wasn't so damn tired."

"I'd do a bit more than dream," Whiskey Jack said. "When it came to giving out breasts, God was very generous with that woman."

"The women who work the cook shanties are usually eyesores, but this one here, she's a sight for sore eyes," Gabbie said. "What do you think, George?"

"Got my own family back home," was all Evelyn said.

Evelyn had never really paid attention to the physical attributes of other women, and she had to admit the men were right. She couldn't hold the discourse against them when she found the woman fetching. She was striking, with feminine traits that Evelyn had never harbored—a certain grace and quiet style that Evelyn found to be appealing. She had never looked at a woman that way before and thought maybe it was because of the man clothes. She didn't understand the feelings she was experiencing, what she could only describe as an attraction of sorts. Earlier, at dinner, when Sarah had briefly touched her…Evelyn had never felt her body respond in that way to a touch. What is wrong with me, she had silently questioned herself. She thought that working as a man, being constantly surrounded by them, was having some strange effect on her. Maybe it was making her more…like them. She didn't know.

Evelyn had never really thought before about what made men and women different, besides the evident physical attributes. Many believed that a woman was simply a man turned within, and vice versa—the man's genitalia on the outside and the woman's on the inside. Though men and women did have separate roles, she had always assumed that was simply the necessary division of labor, a way to get things done. She never thought it had anything to do with a woman's ability or aptitude. She also thought that she might be drawn to Sarah because she was the only other woman at the camp besides the younger flunky, and Evelyn shared a certain sense of sisterhood with her, though Evelyn was presenting as a man.

Whiskey Jack smacked his hand of cards down on the floor and let out a hoot, startling her out of her reverie.

"Game's mine," he said joyously. "You owe me a pint when we get back to town, Gabbie."

"Yeah, yeah, yeah," Gabbie grumbled. "That's enough for me. Why don't you tell us a story, George? I'm feeling all told out tonight."

"What do you say, George?" Whiskey Jack said. "You must have a tale or two that you tell your kids."

Wanting to steel some sense of camaraderie with the jacks, Evelyn conceded.

"My kids like stories about Paul Bunyan."

"That works for me," Gabbie said. "You got one we haven't already heard?"

"I reckon I do," Evelyn said.

"Let's hear it," Whiskey Jack said as he pushed the deck of cards into his pocket.

Evelyn started to speak in a low voice.

"One summer long ago, the air was so hot and stale that there was no relief to be found, not even up here in the Northwoods, where the weather tended to be a bit cooler. Paul Bunyan reportedly sweated so much that summer that lakes and ponds were created where his sweat fell and gathered, and Babe the Blue Ox moaned in misery. One particularly humid and sticky day, Paul was worried about Babe, so he led her over to Lake Superior, hoping she could cool off in the frigid waters. As they reached the lake, massive storm clouds the color of charcoal began to roll in. Babe walked into Lake Superior, but she was so big that she got relief for only her lower quarters. Unsatisfied, Babe finally reared up on her hind legs, and she jabbed at the thick clouds with her front legs until they busted open, a torrent of rain finally cooling down the big Babe. So much rain fell that day that the tiny town of Wabash was washed away."

"Never heard that one before," Whiskey Jack said.

"Good one," said Gabbie.

"That's all I've got for now," Evelyn said. "Think I'll step out and smoke a bit before lights out."

Whiskey Jack and Gabbie headed toward their bunks, and Evelyn filled her pipe with tobacco.

Later that night, after the men were bunked down, the winds screeched and slammed against the bunkhouse so ferociously that Evelyn thought it might collapse. She lay in her bunk and marveled at how sore her body was. She had thought she would adapt over time, but the work of a sawyer was strenuous and tiring. Every night, her back felt as if it was twisted into a tight knot. She could feel the strip of cloth that flattened her breasts cutting into her skin, bruising her deep down. Her arms felt as stiff as the ax she wielded to cut down the trees, and her legs sometimes felt like logs themselves, incapable of movement.

She took out her calendar and crossed off one more day. They were nearing the end of December. Evelyn was amazed at how painstakingly slow time was passing. Her thoughts settled on her children. She knew the fact that she hadn't heard from her sister meant everything back home was fine, but she missed them and wanted them near. She thought many of the men must feel the same way, being away from their children, though none of them voiced their emotions. Christmas was three days away, and though their holiday at home over the years had always been simple—toys crafted by George, a rare pheasant or rabbit dinner cooked by Evelyn, carols and stories shared by the fireplace—it was always acknowledged and celebrated. At the camp, she knew the day would pass like any other day with only a few of the jacks pausing to share holiday greetings. Maybe Tommy would play a Christmas tune or two in the evening.

Evelyn gathered her blanket around her more tightly as the winds grew even stronger and the cold crept through the bunkhouse walls. It seemed to settle on her skin and burrow into her bones. She hadn't been warm since the day she arrived at the camp.

Chapter Five

The dark days of January found Sarah slipping even further into despair. On one especially frigid night, sleep evaded her, partly because the winds outside were reaching shrill howls, and partly because Sam had started to pace outside her shed some nights, back and forth, mumbling to himself, the snow crunching beneath his feet. Sarah suspected that he was stepping out of the cook shanty, away from Mack and Annie, to sneak a few snorts of whiskey on those nights. He was out there that night. At moments, Sarah held her breath and listened closely, thinking she had heard him stop outside her door. She glanced at the small pocket watch Sam had given her to ensure she was up early each morning and released a sigh of irritation. In only a few hours, she would have to wake to fetch the water. She burrowed more deeply under the two blankets on her cot; the rising winds slipped through the cracks in the walls.

Sarah had noticed a shift in her dynamics with Sam after she had helped George Bauer remove the porcupine quills from the young jack. Three weeks had passed since the incident, and Sam's behavior seemed to be getting stranger. Sarah had seen him glaring at George Bauer for no reason from across the shanty, and any time she served George, she would nearly always turn to another logger only to find Sam's eyes settled on her. Deep down Sarah knew Sam was jealous of George, though for no reason at all. Sarah was drawn to the gentle jack, but they had barely interacted. Sarah did find herself watching him, though, trying to catch the few words he mumbled. She thought maybe Sam was sensing that.

As much as she was growing to distrust Sam, she felt dependent on him, still believed he might protect her, if necessary. Her greatest worry was that if he did have to fight for her one day, he would want to claim her as his prize, which made her feel increasingly uncomfortable around him. She often found him edging into her more closely than necessary as they worked, commenting on her appearance, keeping an angry eye on any jack who paid her extra attention. Her only consolation was that she could avoid him at night.

Even Sarah was puzzled by her own attentiveness toward George and confused about the feelings nudging within her. She found herself wishing for more encounters with him, though she knew the opportunity for that was slim. She thought that her longing was due to the daily isolation that she faced at the camp, surrounded but alone, or her lingering sorrow over her loss of Abigail. She had sunken into even deeper despair after Christmas, or the lack of Christmas, which had passed like any other day at the logging camp. Sarah knew of its presence only because of the tick on her calendar. The snow was thick on the ground, and icicles hung from the low roofs of the bunkhouse and shanty like crystallized stalagmites, glinting in the sun. The woods were awash in glittery whiteness, a beautiful spectacle, but Sarah felt only gloom, remembering her past Christmases with Abigail. They had been filled with warmth—visits from friends, gleeful decorations, Christmas carols, and ringing bells. She had always felt so safe and secure with Abigail, a true sense of belonging, and now she felt only gnawing emptiness. Even physically she felt as if she was starving and might simply fade away.

Perhaps that was why George Bauer seemed like some kind of lifesaver. He was a handsome man, and he seemed to have a calmer, kinder side that few of the other loggers displayed. She thought that perhaps it was because he had children, but she knew many of the other loggers also had families. Still, this man stuck out in the crowd of boisterous men, if for no other reason than he seemed to be most content when he could quietly keep to himself, and he didn't pull pranks or roughhouse like the others did. Those nights when Sarah went out to get wood for the morning fire and glimpsed George outside alone, leaning against a tree, smoking a pipe and staring up at the stars, she had wanted to approach him, just for conversation, but she never did. She didn't want to incur Sam's wrath any more than she already had.

When Sam's footsteps finally faded away from her door, Sarah took a deep breath and burrowed even farther beneath her bedding. Her eyes fluttered shut and she eventually escaped into sleep, until she woke and checked her watch. She groaned: *Time to fetch the water.*

❖

When the bunkhouse finally filled with snores and the sharp winds outside, Evelyn rummaged through her pack and crawled out of her bunk, taking with her a bundle of rags, which she shoved in her coat pocket. She quietly walked across the bunkhouse to the door, stepped outside into the cutting cold, and quickly made her way to the outhouses. She lowered her pants and long johns and unpinned the soiled rags that were attached to her drawers. She removed the rags and replaced them with the ones in her pocket, creating a thick pad. This was one of her biggest hardships in the camp, and her only consolation was that the odors of the bunkhouse were so overwhelming that she didn't worry about her own feminine scents being detected by any of the jacks. Holding the soiled rags, Evelyn emerged from the outhouse and found herself face-to-face with Sarah, who was carrying a bucket of water back to the cook shanty. She had a startled look on her face.

"George, are you hurt?"

Her voice had a sense of urgency, her eyes focusing on the bloodied rags in Evelyn's hand. Stunned, Evelyn remained silent for a moment, trying to gather her thoughts.

"You're bleeding," Sarah said. "Can I help you? Did you get hurt in the woods yesterday?"

"No," Evelyn said, "I'm fine."

"But…"

"Things aren't as they appear," Evelyn said in a hushed voice, looking around to ensure no one else was nearby.

"I don't understand."

"Let me get rid of this and I'll explain," Evelyn said.

With Sarah trailing behind her, Evelyn walked a good distance back behind the outhouses and began to dig deep into a snowbank, where she buried her soiled rags. She was afraid that if she dumped them in the outhouse they might be spotted. The second week in camp, a jack accidentally dropped his watch down the hole and had used a lantern and a stick to fish it out. Sarah watched with a puzzled look on her face. With the rags well hidden, Evelyn stood to face Sarah. She still didn't know what to say to her, how to keep her secret any longer. She finally leaned over and whispered in Sarah's ear.

"I'm menstruating."

"You're…But…How can that be?"

"It wasn't my wife who died," Evelyn said. "It was my husband. I had no choice but to take his place."

This time Sarah was the one caught without words.

"I thought…Hmm…That explains your fine job of darning," she eventually said.

She studied Evelyn closely, with a puzzled look on her face.

"Well, you're right about that," Evelyn said.

"So, your name is really…?"

"Evelyn."

"Evelyn," Sarah repeated.

She stared at Evelyn.

"Is something wrong?" Evelyn asked.

"No," Sarah said. "Not at all. I'm just trying to envision you as a woman, as Evelyn. I'm used to seeing you as…George."

"My hair used to be long, down to the middle of my back, and I have my breasts bound."

Sarah giggled slightly.

"I'm sorry," she said. "I must admit I'm a bit relieved."

"Relieved?" Evelyn said.

"It's just that you seemed different from the others somehow, nothing I could really put a finger on, but…I never would have guessed this."

"Ah," Evelyn said. "You don't think the others suspect anything, do you?"

"Goodness no," Sarah said. "As it is, Sam dislikes you because he thinks you and I…Wouldn't he be surprised?"

"I'm sure everybody would," Evelyn said.

"How are you able to keep up with the work?" Sarah asked. "I can barely manage my kitchen duties."

"I'm accustomed to a hard day's work," Evelyn said. "The work on the farm has prepared me in many ways. I've chopped plenty of wood in my day. I just focus on my children. If I fail here, I fail them. George passed away suddenly, with no warning, and we were strapped for money. Coming here seemed to be my only feasible option."

"That's very honorable," Sarah said.

"It's a matter of necessity."

"I understand."

"So, my secret's safe with you?" Evelyn asked.

"Of course," Sarah said. "I would never do anything to put you in harm's way. But maybe if they knew you were a woman, if they knew of your circumstances, they would let you work in the cook shanty, instead of sending you into the woods."

"I can't risk it," Evelyn said. "Besides, you already have a full house in the shanty, and as you said, Sam doesn't particularly like me. Johnny would most likely just send me back home."

"I guess you're right," Sarah said.

Evelyn turned toward the bunkhouse.

"I should get going," she said.

Sarah quickly snagged one of her hands with her own.

"It's a pleasure to meet you, Evelyn," she said.

Evelyn smiled and Sarah released her hand and headed toward the shanty.

When Evelyn returned to the bunkhouse and settled back down, shivering beneath her blankets, she felt a sense of excitement, her truth finally revealed. She also found herself wondering even more about Sarah and wishing they had more opportunity to talk and confide with each other, but Whiskey Jack had forewarned her about Sam not long after the porcupine incident. They had been trudging through the snow, scouting a spot to work in that day.

"I've noticed Sam's been keeping a keen eye on you lately," Whiskey Jack had said.

"Yeah?" Evelyn said.

"Ever since that flunky helped you out with Henry."

"That's nothing for him to worry about."

"Doesn't matter if you've got intentions or not, George. It's about what he thinks might be going on, and he's clearly smitten with the woman."

"Nothing I can do about what he's thinking," Evelyn had said.

"I just think you should watch your back around him, and around her," Whiskey Jack had told her. "I reckon Sam has a jealous streak."

"I don't think there's anything to fret about," Evelyn had said. "I'll heed your warning, though."

As much as she didn't want to create any additional hardships for herself at the camp, Evelyn craved some personal connection, and now that Sarah knew her truth… Evelyn closed her eyes and envisioned Sarah. She wondered how old she was. She was certainly younger than Evelyn. She had mentioned a loss, and Evelyn wondered what that loss was. With Sarah on her mind, she drifted off to sleep.

Back in her shed, Sarah paced back and forth. She was shocked by her discovery. George was Evelyn. Evelyn was George. No wonder she had been drawn to the strange jack. He was a woman. George was a woman. Sarah had to admit that Evelyn was doing a grand job of melding in with the other jacks. She had found her attraction to George Bauer odd and somewhat disconcerting, but she had never considered that this might be the case. When she finally settled down, she realized it was time to head to the cook shanty. She stepped out of the shed and grabbed the bucket of water that she had fetched. She walked to the shanty, snow crackling beneath her boots. She took a deep breath of the crisp air. Soon she would see George—Evelyn—again, and she had to admit that the small attraction she had harbored before had suddenly become more amplified.

❖

Evelyn rose with the rest of the jacks and headed to the cook shanty. She was anxious to see Sarah. She entered the shanty and glanced about the room; her eyes settled on Sarah, then shifted away. She sat down, filled her plate, and lifted her empty coffee cup in the air, her hand slightly shaking. She kept her eyes focused on her plate while she waited for one of the flunkies to come to her table. When Sarah reached her side, Evelyn felt her cheeks flush with heat, and she grew so nervous that she found herself holding her breath. Sarah fleetingly rested a hand on her shoulder before moving on to refill another jack's cup, and Evelyn felt the same warmth she had felt the first time Sarah touched her. When she did finally look up, she saw Sam, glaring at her from across the room, with a disgruntled look on his face. He then turned his attention to Sarah.

Evelyn returned to the bunkhouse with the others after breakfast to retrieve her ax, only to find it missing.

"Let's get going, George," Whiskey Jack said as he lifted his ax to his shoulder.

"Can't find my ax," Evelyn said. "Left it right by the bunk, just like I always do."

"My guess is Poker Pete's got that ax," Whiskey Jack said. "He's known for ruining his own equipment and taking what he needs from the rest of us. That man would steal from himself if he had anything worth taking. Besides, he's got a bone to pick with you."

Evelyn quickly turned around and headed outside, scanning the dispersing crowd of lumberjacks until she saw Poker Pete. She hurried over to him with Whiskey Jack following closely behind.

"I think that's my ax you've got there, Pete," she said.

"I'm thinking you're wrong, Bauer," Poker Pete said. "You know all these axes look alike. This one here is definitely mine. You must've misplaced yours."

"Not likely that I'd lose track of my ax," Evelyn said. "I put it in the same place every night."

She reached out to take hold of the ax Poker Pete was carrying.

"Mine's got my initials carved into the bottom of the handle," she said.

She firmly grabbed the ax, and Poker Pete pushed her away. Evelyn moved in again to claim the ax, and Poker Pete took a swing at her. Evelyn ducked, but Poker Pete's fist landed squarely on her left cheek. She reeled backward, then regained her balance and rushed Poker Pete, head butting him in the belly. A surge of rage traveled through her. That was it. She had had enough of Poker Pete. She grabbed his legs behind the knees, just as she had seen the other jacks do while Indian wrestling, and took him down. She was about to deliver her first blow to Poker Pete when Whiskey Jack pulled her off him.

"Don't do it, George," he said. "You'll get in as much trouble as he will. Johnny won't care who started the fight. He'll send both of you home."

Evelyn released Poker Pete and grabbed the ax that was lying on the ground. She looked at the bottom of the handle and showed it to Poker Pete.

"Just like I said—GB."

Still on the ground, Poker Pete grunted. "I'm not forgetting this, Bauer," he snapped.

Whiskey Jack steered her away from Poker Pete, and they headed into the woods. Evelyn knew that Poker Pete was her biggest foe at the camp, besides Sam, and she knew he was not to be trusted. She ran a hand over her cheek, which still stung from the impact of Poker Pete's punch. Evelyn had never been in a fight before, with anyone, but she felt no fear. She couldn't afford to. She thought that some of the men at the camp might be posturing, transforming into kinder, gentler men when they returned home, but she knew that most of them were incapable of anything else. She was just grateful to have aligned with Whiskey Jack and Henry. They were the only jacks she trusted, and she had to always be prepared to defend herself. Her life at the camp was all about survival.

"He's really going to have it out for you now," Whiskey Jack said as they tramped through snow.

"Not my problem," Evelyn said. "He's had it out for me ever since I helped Jankowski and questioned him about the porcupine."

"Well, you'll have to watch your back," Whiskey Jack said.

Evelyn knew he was right.

"Maybe he should watch his," she said.

She now would have to be vigilant of both Sam and Poker Pete. She and Whiskey Jack pushed deeper into the woods, walking the rest of the way in silence. Snow began to fall, lightly at first, and then heavier, a gauzy white curtain descending over the woods. Evelyn gazed up at the crystalline flakes and licked her lips. She yearned to be back at home, with her children, and her heart felt dark and heavy. Back home, Helen would be rousing the children, getting the boys ready for their chores and then school, with little Louise by her side.

CHAPTER SIX

The Sunday after Sarah discovered the truth about Evelyn, she woke with a sense of relief that she had never before experienced since her arrival at the camp. The jacks would be at camp for the day, and she would be able to see more of Evelyn than she did on any other day. They hadn't had a chance to speak since their encounter at the outhouse, and Sarah was determined to find some way to connect with her, away from the others. She pulled on her clothes and coat and went to the cook shanty to stir the coals in the fireplace. The embers that remained after a night of burning were a luminescent blue that suddenly flared into a bright orange-red. Sam and Mack were still asleep, snoring in their bunks. She moved to the other side of the shanty and built the fire in the woodstove. The smell of pine filled the cook shanty, and she took a deep breath. A cloud of frost escaped when she exhaled, and she shivered in the cold. The day would not begin to warm until the sun climbed up above the tree line.

As the fires slowly began to warm the shanty, Sarah began to prepare the breakfast for the day, first filling the coffeepots with water and grinds and putting them on the woodstove. The door to the small room in the back opened and Annie walked out. She sniffed the air.

"You already started the coffee?" she asked.

"Got the first four pots on," Sarah said. "You can set the tables while I check on the beans I put in the fireplace last night."

"Okay," Annie said.

Sam roused from his sleep, mumbled a good morning, put on his coat, and went outside, nudging Mack on his way. Mack sat up, pulled on his boots and coat without saying a word, and followed Sam outside. Sarah returned to the fireplace and carefully pulled the pot of beans from the coals. She removed the lid, grabbed a large spoon, and stirred. The smell of molasses rose from the pot. Sarah took a small taste of the beans, put the lid back on the pot, and carried it over to the large counter near the woodstove. She turned her attention to the salt pork and began to hum.

"You seem to be quite happy this morning," Annie said.

"I slept well last night," Sarah said. "And it's Sunday—the one day we get a bit of a break."

"It is strange having the jacks around during the day, but it does bring the camp to life," Annie said. "When they're in the woods, everything here seems so quiet and desolate."

Sarah glanced at Annie. She knew the girl must feel as isolated as she did, and she had caught her settling her eyes on Henry Jankowski more than once.

"Perhaps you can find an opportunity to chat with that young jack you've had your eyes on."

She watched Annie's cheeks redden.

"Is it that obvious?" Annie asked. "I'd hate to get in trouble with Father."

"I'm sure he's never noticed," Sarah said. "Too much hubbub going on in here, and his eyes are almost always on the stove."

Annie sighed.

"Do you know his name?" she asked coyly.

"Henry Jankowski," Sarah said. "He seems to be a nice young man. A bit timid."

"I think he's quite handsome," Annie said.

The door to the shanty slowly pushed open and Mack entered. Sarah wished that Sam's temperament was more akin to his, as he was good-natured, always humming and whistling as he performed his chores, and he treated his daughter with patient kindness.

"Good morning," he said as he headed to the stove.

Both Sarah and Annie greeted him, then their conversation fell flat as they began to bustle about the shanty.

❖

Sarah grew excited as the last of the loggers filed out of the shanty after breakfast. The sun was finally perched up in the sky, and she looked forward to spending some time in its bright warmth after they cleaned up the mess remaining from breakfast. Sam and Mack left to take the pot for the beans out for a soaking in the river. Sarah and Annie gathered up the tin cups, plates, and utensils and began to scrub them in the basin. They then tackled the pots and pans. The lunch for the day was simple, prepared the day before—sandwiches, pies, and coffee. The coffee never ceased to flow at the camp.

By the time they finished with their chores, they could hear the shouts and guffaws of the loggers gathering outside. Annie went to her room to collect the clothes she needed to wash, and Sarah quickly swept the shanty floor. She looked out one of the tiny windows to search through the crowd of jacks, checking to see if Evelyn had emerged yet. When she spotted her, she felt a sense of urgency. She turned from the window and left the shanty to go to the shed to grab her laundry and a few items she needed to mend. She reached into a small bag in her satchel and took out a darning needle and a nearly empty spool of thread, which she put in her coat pocket. She needed some reason to approach Evelyn without stoking Sam's ire too much.

Outside, the sun hit the icy snow with a blinding glare, but its warmth felt like a welcome caress. Sarah headed to the kettle that she and Annie used for washing and turned it over. Annie joined her and they walked to the river to fill buckets with water. When they returned Sarah noted that Evelyn had already situated herself on the stump she usually occupied while mending clothes. Sarah built and lit the fire beneath her and Annie's kettle, and they filled it with the water they had fetched and waited for it to begin to boil. When the water was finally hot enough, they both plunged their clothes into the kettle. Unable to wait any longer, Sarah stirred the kettle of soaking clothes with a long wooden paddle. She then turned to Annie.

"I need to see if that jack over there has some thread I can borrow," she said. "I'll have to add that to the list of provisions that we need when Sam next travels to town."

She walked over to Evelyn, carefully glancing over her shoulder to see if she spotted Sam. He was nowhere in sight, and she suspected that he and a few of the jacks had escaped into the woods for an illicit game of poker, perhaps a drink or two of whiskey. Standing beside Evelyn, Sarah cleared her throat and spoke quietly.

"Sorry to interrupt you, George," she said.

The name caught in her throat.

She waited for the moment when Evelyn's eyes would lift and meet hers. Evelyn raised her head.

"Morning," she said.

"It's a beautiful day, isn't it?" Sarah said. "The sun feels so good."

"Does, doesn't it?" Evelyn replied, awkwardly shifting on the stump.

"I seem to be running a bit low on thread," Sarah said. "I was wondering if you could spare some until Sam goes for more supplies."

"I think I have half a spool that I can let you use," Evelyn said.

She dug into one of her coat pockets and pulled out a spool, then handed it to Sarah. Their fingers met for a moment, and Sarah wished the moment could linger, but Evelyn quickly retracted her hand. Sarah studied the spool of thread. No part of her wanted to leave Evelyn's side.

"I'll be fetching water from the river after I clean up the dinner mess tonight," she said quietly. "Perhaps you'll be stepping out for a smoke around then."

Evelyn didn't say anything initially, but just as Sarah turned to walk away, she spoke.

"I reckon it'll be a good night for a smoke."

Feeling a quiver of joy, Sarah headed back to Annie and their kettle. Annie was smiling at her shyly.

"Are you taking a liking to that jack?" she asked.

Startled, Sarah felt herself blush. She opened her hand to reveal the spool of thread.

"Of course not," she said a bit too earnestly. "I told you. I needed to borrow some thread for today's mending."

"He's the jack who helped Henry, isn't he?" Annie asked. "He seems different from the others—quieter."

"He does seem to be a rather mild man compared to the others," Sarah agreed.

"So?" Annie said in her young, schoolgirl voice.

Sarah wanted to put an end to Annie's speculations.

"He's a married man," she said. "I think he said he has three children back home. Besides, I'm not looking for a man. I'm perfectly content with my life back home. I just have to make it through the rest of my days here so I can finally return."

"I live for the day I can meet the right man and get married," Annie said. "That's the only way I'll ever be able to leave my folks' farm."

Sarah felt a certain sadness for the young girl, as she knew she spoke the truth, the truth of most women. Annie and so many others like her would never think about venturing out into the world alone. The world, as it was, didn't seem suited for that. Those very realities made Evelyn even more intriguing to her. She could not imagine the strength and tenacity it must take to pull off such a masquerade.

Sarah never thought the night's cleanup after dinner would end. When she and Annie finally finished the dishes, complete darkness had descended and the winds were creeping in through the shanty wall's chinks. Mack had gone out to use the outhouse before bedding down, and Sam had already passed out in his bunk.

"Do you need me for anything else?" Annie asked.

"I think that's it for the night," Sarah said. "I'll head out soon to fetch the water for the morning."

Annie turned toward her room.

"All right," she said. "I'll see you tomorrow, then."

"Sleep well," said Sarah.

Carrying two empty buckets, Sarah stepped out of the shanty. The wind had escalated. She set down the buckets to pull her coat more closely around her and fumbled with the buttons in the cold. Mack, returning from the outhouse, picked up the buckets and handed them to her.

"Thanks, Mack," she said.

"Just leave them inside the door after you fill them up, and I'll take care of them," Mack said.

He disappeared into the shanty. Sarah began her trek to the river and saw Evelyn's silhouette. She was leaning back against a tree beyond the bunkhouse. Sarah eagerly headed toward her, and when she reached her, she spoke.

"Can you come with me to the river?" she asked softly, well aware of how noise carried at night in the woods.

Evelyn quickly looked around.

"Is Sam inside?" she asked.

"He's in the shanty, already passed out on his bunk," Sarah said. "I reckon he downed a bit too much whiskey today."

Evelyn grunted and fell in step with Sarah. They didn't speak at first, and the silence made Sarah feel uneasy.

"Is everything okay?" she asked.

"Back's been acting up more and more lately," Evelyn said. "The binding is taking a toll. It feels like it's cutting into me more deeply, and the pains are getting sharper. It's making the days more strenuous."

"Your wrap might be too tight," Sarah said.

"Nothing I can do about that," Evelyn told her. "Hopefully, this will pass."

"I wish I could help," Sarah said.

"Nothing you can do," said Evelyn.

"Well, I'm hoping we have less than three months left in this godforsaken place," Sarah said.

Evelyn chuckled.

"I couldn't agree more," she said. "At least we made it through January. I can't wait to get back to my children again, and the farm. That life will seem so simple after this. And what do you go back to?"

Sarah fell silent. *What do I return to?* She hadn't really had the time to contemplate that since arriving at the camp, and when the thought did creep into her mind, she pushed it away. She pictured the small, modest house in Pine Creek in her mind—empty now, absent of Abigail. In her mind she could see Abigail as clearly as if she were standing directly before her, and every part of Sarah ached and quaked. She felt herself struggling to hold back tears, one of which slid past an eyelid and froze halfway down her cheek.

"Sarah, are you…? What's wrong?" Evelyn asked.

Sarah quickly swiped a hand over her cheek.

"I'm okay," she said quietly. "I just…I'd not thought about that since my arrival here. No time. Sheer avoidance. The woman I lived with in Pine Creek, Abigail, took me in from the orphanage when I was seventeen. My parents both died when I was young—typhoid fever. I'd lived in the orphanage from the time I was eight. After I'd been living with Abigail for some time, we became…"

"Lovers?" Evelyn asked, the word nearly getting stuck in her throat.

Sarah nodded.

"You don't have any family—no aunts or uncles, distant relatives?"

"Abigail was my only family," Sarah said. "She was my life."

"Was?"

Sarah's eyes again brimmed with tears.

"She passed away at the end of October. That's why I'm here— to supplement my income. Abigail was Sam's sister. I thought I was going to lose my mind the first week that she was gone. I just felt so lonely, so empty. I missed her arms around me, her closeness, so much that I felt physical pain. For a while, I must admit, I wasn't sure I wanted to continue on without her. I can only imagine how much you miss your husband."

She stopped speaking again, afraid she might choke on her words.

"I'm so sorry for your loss," Evelyn said. "I don't know what to say. It seems we're both in the same situation."

"A crossroad," Sarah said, fear making her voice tremble.

"A crossroad," Evelyn echoed.

She took one last drag off her pipe, then tapped it against the tree.

"We should get back," she said.

"Wait," Sarah said. "When can we talk again? I find the thought of an ally consoling. I feel so alone out here."

"We have to be careful," Evelyn said. "We can't afford to draw anyone's attention, especially Sam's."

"But we need some way to signal one another, if one of us wants to meet, if there's a problem."

Sarah could hear the urgency in her own words as she spoke.

"Is there something that worries you?" Evelyn asked.

"No," Sarah said. "It's just... One never knows. We're so far from anywhere, and I think Sam's been drinking more and more. The liquor changes him."

Evelyn did not immediately reply, but eventually asked, "What do you suggest?"

"I have two different aprons," Sarah said. "One white and one blue. If I wear the blue one, I need to see you. Is that all right with you?"

Evelyn nodded.

Sarah felt a bit more at ease.

"Good," she said. "Good."

With that the conversation ended, and Evelyn and Sarah took a few steps together toward the camp, and then they parted ways.

Chapter Seven

A week had passed since Evelyn and Sarah had talked, and Evelyn had been preoccupied with their conversation every waking hour since. She couldn't get it out of her mind. The information that Sarah had divulged surprised her. She had so many questions. *Who was this Abigail? How long did they live together?* Sarah seemed young. She was definitely younger than Evelyn. *How did they, Sarah and Abigail, know they wanted to...were meant to...? Did things just somehow happen between them?* She had often wondered the same thing about Helen and Jess. *How do two women find each other, find a way to spend their lives together?* Then, the one question she avoided: *What do two women do together...sexually? How do two women pleasure each other?* The idea of sex without the purpose of procreation was an unfamiliar concept for Evelyn. Then again, she had learned how to please herself, if even momentarily, during her life with George.

Two women owned and worked a farm together about forty miles from Evelyn and George's farm. Evelyn had seen them occasionally when she had gone to the feed store in Maple Grove with George. Their names were Harriet and May. Harriet was rather masculine, bulky and boisterous, with shortly cropped hair, and she wore men's clothing. May, on the other hand, was very feminine, soft looking, and she usually wore a flower-patterned dress. When Evelyn and George were making the journey back to their farm one day, Evelyn had asked George about them. George had laughed quietly. He told her that for years folks had speculated that the ladies were lovebirds, though they always told people they were *cousins*.

Evelyn wondered if Sarah's Abigail had been as pretty as Sarah. She thought of herself, of how she was presenting, and she felt a wave of embarrassment. My God, the woman must think I'm a manly mess, she thought. Even Evelyn was so immersed in her role as George that she sometimes forgot her true self—her long hair, the soft place between her legs, her breasts.

She didn't speak as she and Whiskey Jack walked farther into the woods, seeking a spot to work in for the day. Whiskey Jack finally interrupted her thoughts.

"See that sky?" he asked. "Notice the quiet?"

Evelyn glanced up at the sky, the opaque aqua quickly being covered by a dense blanket of gray-white clouds. The wind hastened around them with a steely bite. Whiskey Jack took a deep breath.

"The squirrels and birds seem pretty scarce," Evelyn said.

"They're already scrambling for shelter. We've got a storm on the way. Maybe a blizzard. Definitely by the time the weekend hits."

"I was hoping we'd avoid that, though I know the chances of that are slim. It wouldn't be a Wisconsin winter without at least one brutal storm," Evelyn said. "We're halfway into the month of February, though, so we nearly made it."

"Well, I'll be keeping an eye on the sky," Whiskey Jack said. "We don't want to get stuck out here when it hits."

Evelyn thought about her children and Helen, back home. They were no strangers to the weather, and they were probably already preparing the farm, readying the animals, bracing for the worst and hoping for the best. She could imagine how happy they would be as the snow fell and gathered, creating for them a playground for building snowmen and sledding.

That night, when Evelyn entered the cook shanty, Sarah caught her eye. She was wearing her blue apron—their signal to meet. Evelyn's stomach quickly flipped with both excitement and a sense of danger. Their encounters were so rare. They could only watch each other from afar. She ate as fast as she could, anxious to get back to the bunkhouse. She was soon joined by the others, most of whom were talking about what they thought was a blizzard closing in.

"Remember that whiteout in 1847?" Gabbie asked Whiskey Jack.

He sighed. "Oh yeah. That was the winter we lost Smoking Joe. Man got so turned around in the woods that he never made it back to the bunkhouse. We never found his body until the thaw set in and we were about to put the lumber in the river."

"That's right," Gabbie said. "Let's hope we don't have a repeat."

Evelyn waited until it was almost time for lights out, then took out her pipe and packed it with tobacco. Whiskey Jack leaned over the side of his bunk.

"I don't understand why you step out to smoke while all the other jacks smoke inside, George," he said. "It's cold as hell out there at night."

"It is, but it's so loud in the bunkhouse I can't even think sometimes," Evelyn said.

"Well, what are you thinking about, George?" Whiskey Jack asked.

"Back home, the farm and my kids," Evelyn said. "This storm will be heading their way too. I worry about them every day, Whiskey Jack, and you know the noise in here gives me a headache sometimes."

"I know," Whiskey Jack said. "I'm sorry, George. I'm sure your kids will be fine. Who's tending to them, anyway?"

"My sister," Evelyn said.

"Well, then they're in good hands."

Evelyn nodded. She pulled on her coat, grabbed her hat and mittens, and headed to the door; the swirl of conversation became muffled as she shut the door behind her. The wind was growing gruffer, icier. She walked over to the tree she usually used as her smoking spot, huddled into it to light the pipe, and breathed in the semisweet smoke of the tobacco. The smell reminded her of a campfire. She looked up at the sky devoid of stars, and then she heard footsteps. She turned to see Sarah with a water bucket in hand. They nodded at each other. Evelyn felt tongue-tied. *Why does she want to see me?*

"You wore your blue apron," she said.

"Yes," Sarah said.

"What is it? Is something wrong?"

Evelyn felt self-conscious and hypervigilant, constantly shifting her eyes around to ensure no one was wandering their way.

"Nothing's wrong," Sarah said. "I wanted to let you know that Sam is planning to head out to town for supplies before breakfast on Saturday. He won't be back until later Sunday."

"That's assuming he even makes it out of the camp," Evelyn said. "A lot of the jacks think a blizzard's heading our way."

She wasn't sure what Sarah was trying to say, and she didn't want to assume anything.

"If he does go, I want you to try to come to my shed after dinner. I can help you with your wrap. Your gait and posture seem more strained every day."

"The pain is nearly constant now," Evelyn admitted. "I feel like it's slicing into me."

"We can talk, steal a little time away from the others," Sarah said, a slight urgency in her voice.

Evelyn hesitated.

"I'm not sure that's a good idea," she said. "It would take only one jack to see me heading to that shed and begin wondering about us for trouble to set in."

"We barely even acknowledge each other, and we haven't had any problems yet," Sarah said. "Please. I feel as if I'm losing my mind. I can't help but look at the calendar, count the days, and it's still only February. I just… It's our one chance to have some time, a normal conversation."

"Okay, as long as it seems safe," Evelyn conceded.

She wanted some time with Sarah, to speak more with her, learn more about her, her life. She could use a confidante. Evelyn treasured her few moments alone with Sarah, away from the jacks.

They afforded her a bit of time during which she could step back into her true self, Evelyn, and remove her mask. She also needed some help with the binding, anything that might make it more tolerable.

"Thank you," Sarah said.

She felt relief. Without saying another word, she left Evelyn's side and headed toward the river. Evelyn took a few last puffs off her pipe. She knew she was taking a chance if she did, indeed, visit Sarah, but a part of her couldn't resist.

❖

On Saturday morning, the snow was falling before the jacks even headed into the woods. The wind began with a whistle, whipping through the tree limbs. The jacks ate breakfast more quickly than usual, wolfing down some sustenance before heading out. By the time they were well in to the forest, the wind became a gushing roar, and the snow swirled around Evelyn and Whiskey Jack in funnels.

"We'll be lucky if we get one tree down before Jones calls everyone back in," Whiskey Jack said. "He won't want to risk losing a man, and it's too easy to get lost in a whiteout in these woods. You can barely see ahead of you. You lose your bearings."

"Where do you want to head to, then?" Evelyn asked.

"Let's go west, try to find that poplar patch we were working yesterday," Whiskey Jack said. "It's not that far from here."

As Evelyn and Whiskey Jack pushed on farther into the woods, the snow that first fell like light feathers became a thick, churning froth, and Evelyn and Whiskey Jack could barely see twenty feet ahead of them. The wind became icy and the snow, driven horizontally by the wind, pelted their faces like handfuls of sand. With it stinging and burning her skin, Evelyn put her forearm across her forehead as a shield and found relief only when she walked backward in intervals. Whiskey Jack rested a hand on a good-sized tree.

"Let's go for this poplar here," he said.

"Okay," Evelyn said.

Whiskey Jack hoisted up his ax and swung it, and the sharp head sliced into the trunk. He worked vigorously, and just as Evelyn was about to take over, they heard a muffled banging and distant voices.

"Hold on there a minute, George," Whiskey Jack said. "You hear that?"

Evelyn stood in place, and she and Whiskey Jack strained, trying to separate the rush of the whining winds from any other discernible sound. They heard it again, a metal clanging, like two pots being banged together, and loud shouts.

"Jones is calling everyone in," Whiskey Jack said.

"Shouldn't we finish taking this down?" Evelyn asked.

"I don't think so, George," Whiskey Jack said. "That's another forty minutes or so of chopping. If Jones is calling us in this early, it means he thinks things are going to get bad real quick. We'll need to ready the camp before the brunt of the storm hits."

"All right," Evelyn said.

She and Whiskey Jack lifted their axes to their shoulders and headed back in the direction they came from. Each new gust of wind felt like a fresh slap to the face. As they neared the camp, they began to hear voices, and eventually, Evelyn could make out the blurry images of other jacks moving through the heavy curtain of snow. When they reached the camp, Johnny Jones was screaming out commands.

"You teamsters need to get those horses fed and secured in the shed."

The teamsters were just leading the horses out of the woods as he spoke.

"You all know the drill," Jones continued. "We need safety lines going from the bunkhouse to the cook shanty and the sheds, and from the cook shanty to the outhouses. Tie them down good and tight, men. They won't do us a damn bit of good if they come loose in the wind."

The lumberjacks scrambled instinctively.

"Follow me," Whiskey Jack said to Evelyn.

She went with him to the bunkhouse, where Johnny Jones had taken a command position and was handing out coils of rope to the jacks. Whiskey Jack grabbed one, and he and Evelyn went to a tree close to the bunkhouse door. Whiskey Jack began to wrap the rope around the tree at about chest level. He knotted it as tightly as he could. Holding the rest of the rope, Evelyn proceeded to the next tree, which they also wrapped the rope around. As she and Whiskey Jack went from tree to tree, fastening the rope, Evelyn thought about the farm and the children, and she felt a surge of panic. She tried to calm herself. *The farm will be okay. The children will be all right. Their uncle will surely go to them, and Helen will be there. Maybe even Jess. Still, they'll wish that I was there, and I'm not.* She wanted to cry, but that was no time for tears. She sucked in the bitter air and kept moving, she and Whiskey Jack traveling from tree to tree, until they had a line of rope that led from the bunkhouse to the front of the cook shanty. The other loggers did the same, and by the time the blizzard was fully upon them, roaring like a locomotive, visibility nearly nil, there was a rope that led from the bunkhouse to every other structure in the camp, including the outhouses. The air had become so frigid that frost gathered in the jacks' beards and on their mustaches.

Whiskey Jack and Evelyn returned to the bunkhouse to see if Jones had anything else for them to do. Jones had Whiskey Jack join a few of the other men inside to try to stuff the chinks in the walls with whatever they could find.

"Bauer, I want you to go to the cook shanty and see if Mack and the flunkies have enough wood to make it through the night and into the morning. If they don't have heat, we won't have food. Help them pull together what they need."

"Will do," Evelyn said.

She grabbed on to the rope that led from the bunkhouse to the shanty and pulled herself through the driving snow. When she reached the cook shanty, she pounded on the door. Within a few minutes, she found herself face-to-face with Sarah.

"George, what is it?" Sarah asked, her voice barely audible over the howling wind.

"Jones told me to check with Mack and see if you need any more wood here for tonight and tomorrow," Evelyn said.

"He just went with Annie to the cellar to get the provisions we'll need for breakfast before the weather worsens," Sarah said. "I think we're set for wood. We started to pile it up in here last night, and I've got plenty in my shed."

"The bad weather could go on for a few days," Evelyn said. "You sure?"

"Well, maybe another bundle or two," Sarah said. "I'd go with you, but Mack wants to get dinner going early tonight since the jacks are already in from the woods, and we're a bit behind."

"You start your work here," Evelyn said. "I'll go grab a couple more armfuls. Are you doing okay, otherwise?"

"I am," Sarah said, her eyes meeting Evelyn's. "I can't tell you what a relief it's been just having Sam away for a day, even with the storm coming. I haven't had to feel so guarded. I didn't realize how much his presence weighs on me."

"Unfortunately, your break won't last long," Evelyn said. "Anyways, I better get going. Soon I won't even be able to find the woodpiles. The snow's falling harder now, and the winds are so violent that the drifting is covering any tracks."

Evelyn turned to go, and Sarah caught her hand in her own.

"Be careful out there," Sarah said. "And don't forget tonight. Come after everyone eats and settles down."

"I'm not sure it's a good idea with this storm setting in," Evelyn said.

"No one will even notice. Everyone will be distracted," Sarah said with earnest desperation in her voice.

"Okay," Evelyn said. "I'll do what I can. I'll be back with the wood in a bit."

"Thank you," Sarah said.

She finally released Evelyn's hand.

❖

As soon as everything in the camp was secured and the safety ropes were in place, the jacks returned to the bunkhouse where Jones did a headcount to make sure all the men had made it back from the woods.

"You're going to have to make sure you keep the fire stoked tonight," he told the jacks. "It'll be colder than a witch's tit, and you'll be lucky if you don't wake up to an inch or two of snow in here tomorrow morning."

Some of the jacks crawled into their bunks, while others hunkered down on the deacon's seat. A few of the men continued to fill whatever chinks they could find, hoping they would not wake to snow in the bunkhouse the next morning, as Jones predicted. Before long, the dinner triangle sounded, barely rising above the winds, and the jacks filed out of the bunkhouse, one at a time, grabbing hold of the safety line that led to the shanty.

The jacks seemed more rambunctious than usual that night after dinner, with the men wondering what the blizzard might bring and how long they might be holed up before it ended.

"What if Sam didn't make it to town before the brunt of the storm hit?" one of the men asked.

"When did he head out?" another asked.

"He headed out in the middle of the night, long before we even woke," said Poker Pete. "Chances are good that he made it to town before things got too bad, but he definitely might be delayed if he tries to return tomorrow."

Poker Pete spent more time with Sam than any other jack. Some of the jacks guessed it was their mutual passion for cards and whiskey that cemented their camaraderie. They both also had a bully streak running through them.

The wind slammed against the bunkhouse in intervals, howling so ferociously that it seemed as if the entire forest was screaming. About an hour before lights out, when Evelyn figured that Sarah would finally be alone in her shed after the nighttime cleanup, she rose from her bunk and pulled on her outer clothing, then retrieved her pipe and tobacco from her pack. Whiskey Jack leaned over the top bunk.

"You're going out in this weather, are you, George?" he asked.

"Feel everything closing in, Whiskey," Evelyn said. "I've got to get some air before I bed down for the night."

"Well, if you've got to go, you keep a tight grip on those ropes out there," Whiskey Jack said.

"Will do. From the sound of those winds, they could pick up any one of us and carry us away."

Evelyn bundled up with layers, pulled on her mittens, and walked toward the door. The other jacks were accustomed to her stepping out at night, but that night, she caught the attention of many of them.

"You're going to freeze your balls off out there, Bauer," Poker Pete yelled from the other side of the bunkhouse.

The others jacks laughed loudly. If they only knew, Evelyn thought.

"Well, it's not like that equipment is doing me any good up here," Evelyn said. "If you know what I mean."

The jacks broke into laughter again, and Evelyn pushed the door open, the wind on the other side pushing back. She secured the door and grabbed on to the safety rope that led to the shanty. The snow had already blown into drifts, some nearly thigh high, and the visibility was zero. Evelyn carefully pulled herself along and, after what seemed like forever, she finally made it to the shanty. She latched on to the line that led to Sarah's shed, and when she reached it, she pounded on the door. No answer. She pounded again, hoping the trip had not been in vain. The door opened, and Sarah pulled her in out of the cold.

"I was wondering if you'd come," she said.

Evelyn wiped a hand over her face, wet with snow.

"The other jacks think I'm crazy," she said. "I can't dawdle here too long. I don't want them to think I got lost out there."

"It's almost time for lights out," Sarah said. "They'll be conked out before they even realize you're still gone, but I won't keep you long. Sit down here and warm up, and then I'll redo your wrap for you. I've got some salve that might soothe the wound some."

Evelyn sat down and removed her coat, and she felt a fluttering in her stomach, realizing that Sarah would be...seeing her.

"Are you all right in here alone tonight?" Evelyn asked.

"Sounds like the winds are going to blow down these walls at times," Sarah said. "I've got plenty of wood, though, and at least I don't have to deal with Sam pacing back and forth in front of my door all night." She sighed.

"He does that?" Evelyn asked.

"Some nights," she said. "I keep the chair jammed up under the doorknob, in case he ever tries to enter. Not that I think he would do anything to cause me harm."

"Has he ever tried to come in?" Evelyn asked.

"No, but the extra measure reassures me. At least I would have some warning. Let me stir the fire and we can get started. You can take off your coat and sit."

Sarah gestured toward her cot. Fluttering filled Evelyn's stomach once again.

"All right," she said.

Sarah picked up a metal poker near the woodstove, opened the stove's door, and stirred the coals.

"That should do for now," she said.

"This place is so small," Evelyn said. "I thought the bunkhouse was cramped."

"At least I'm not stuck in the shanty with Sam," Sarah said. "Take off your shirts and I'll help you remove your wrap."

Evelyn removed her mackinaw. Sarah searched through her few belongings until she found a tin of salve, and when their eyes met, Evelyn quickly dropped hers, feeling shy. She took off her long john shirt, and a shiver crawled over her. Sarah looked at her unabashedly and reached over to gently and carefully unfasten the pins that held Evelyn's wrap in place. The panel of linen was dirty and soiled with sweat from the long days of work, and it smelled as if it had absorbed all the odors of the bunkhouse.

"It's so tight," she said. "I don't know how you can even breathe with it on, furthermore do the work that you do."

"I knew the work up here would be hard, but I never could have imagined this," Evelyn said. "George never really went into detail about what it's like up here. Every part of my body aches."

"Life on the farm must be a dream compared to what it is here," Sarah said.

"It's a difficult life, don't get me wrong. But we get our breaks, our moments of relief," Evelyn said. "This is nonstop."

"My life with Abigail was so simple and easy," Sarah said. "I'm almost embarrassed."

"You shouldn't be," Evelyn said. "That was your path, just as the farm is mine."

"It must have its charms," Sarah said. "Doesn't it?"

"Ah," Evelyn said. "Folks do like to romanticize about farming, and it does have its perks—the self-sufficiency, the beauty of the land. The most difficult aspect is being in a position where one's livelihood is so dependent on nature. No one controls nature."

"I know," Sarah said. "Compared to that, my life up until now has been so routine, commonplace in a sense. Can you raise your arms?"

Evelyn felt so self-conscious in that moment that a wave of panic surged through her, and she felt as if she was burning up. She raised her arms. Sarah was so close to her, before her, that she could feel the warmth of her breath. Evelyn's entire body tingled. Sarah slowly unraveled the wrap until it was completely removed, and she dropped it to the floor.

"Well, you are a woman, indeed," she said to Evelyn, taking her in. "I never would've known, under all the male clothing."

Evelyn sat speechless as she felt herself blushing to crimson. She felt so foolish, sitting before this attractive, young woman, half undressed.

"I'll make you a fresh wrap," Sarah said. "Not fully actualizing what this place might be like, I packed a few linens, as if I'd actually need bedding."

She giggled a bit. She rested a hand on one of Evelyn's shoulders, and Evelyn stopped breathing for a moment, sitting still, in silence. She raised her head, her eyes meeting Sarah's, and she then quickly looked away. She felt like such a klutz in that moment, compared to Sarah, and she had to admit that she was attracted to her in a way she never felt possible. She found her feelings so confusing. Part of her thought that the feelings were arising because of the role playing—George, Evelyn. It's as if I'm confusing myself with someone else, she thought.

"I don't like the look of these bruises," Sarah said matter-of-factly. "I want to wash you down before I use the salve."

She sat beside Evelyn on the bed, dipped a cloth into the small bucket of water, and began to rinse off Evelyn's back. Her touch was soft, gentle.

"I'm sorry if it's cold," she said.

"Don't worry," Evelyn said. "I've been cold since the day I got here."

Sarah smiled and put the cloth in the water again, wrung it out, and softly scrubbed Evelyn's neck. She then moved to Evelyn's breasts. Evelyn stiffened, and the surge that she felt, between her legs... An unfamiliar warmth traveled through her. Initially, she thought it was only because she had gone without any touch except for that of her children since George's death, but even with George she had never experienced what she was feeling in that moment—a surge of titillation. Without thinking, she pulled away from Sarah.

"Are you okay?" Sarah asked. "Did I...?"

"I just caught a chill," Evelyn answered quickly, not wanting Sarah to suspect anything else.

"I'm done anyway," Sarah said. "I'll just dry you off."

They sat beside each other, surrounded by the noises of the blizzard outside—the crescendo of the wind rising to a roar and shaking the shanty. After she dried Evelyn's back, Sarah reached for the tin of salve and scooped some out. She first rubbed it onto Evelyn's back using solid, firm strokes.

"When you and Abigail met, how did you know...? What made you...?"

Evelyn felt herself stuttering, at a loss for words. Sarah looked at her.

"I discovered that I was attracted to girls, well, women,

eventually, when I was in the orphanage," Sarah said. "When Abigail took me in, she was so kind, and beautiful... My feelings for her took root in no time, and from there everything just seemed to happen naturally. She had been with a woman before me, but that ended when that woman's parents pressured her into marriage. Have you always been drawn to men?"

"There was never any actual thought process," Evelyn said. "Being with a woman would never have entered my mind. My relationship with George was formed more of necessity than passion," Evelyn said. "He was a good man. We'd known each other since youth, but... By the time both of my folks were gone, my sister Helen was already living and working in the small town nearby. She's been living with another woman for years, in a relationship like the one you had with your Abigail. I had always suspected it, but we only recently talked about it."

"Do you think you would marry again?" Sarah asked.

"I don't think so," Evelyn said. "I can't see myself seeking out a man."

"If you could have any life that you wanted, what life would that be?" Sarah asked.

"I wouldn't be here," Evelyn answered.

They leaned into each other and laughed.

"Beyond that, I never contemplated having a life any different than the one I have now. I wouldn't give up the children or the farm for anything, but I don't think I will want another man in my life. I assume I'll spend the rest of my life alone."

"I am beginning to have that same fear for myself," Sarah said. "What are your children's names?"

"Peter is the oldest," Evelyn answered. "He's ten. Karl is seven, and little Louise is four, soon to be five. I think about them all the time. I'm sure everything is okay on the farm, or my sister would have contacted me, but...I've never been away from them before, even for a day."

"They're fortunate," Sarah said. "You obviously would do anything for them that you had to."

"Anything, any time," Evelyn said.

"I admire your loyalty," Sarah said. "It's a most attractive trait."

Evelyn couldn't stop looking at Sarah's lips—full, rose-colored, delicately curving.

"I should get ready to go back," she said, though she regretted having to leave when she felt so at ease, when she and Sarah were just beginning to know each other.

"I wish you could stay," Sarah said. "I wish we had more time."

Evelyn wished the same thing but knew it was impossible. She sat quietly while Sarah tore a strip for a new wrap from a sheet.

"I don't want to make this as tight as it was before," she said.

"You're going to have to," Evelyn said. "I can't take a chance of it coming undone."

Sarah sighed.

"Okay," she conceded. "Lift your arms."

Evelyn raised her arms and Sarah began to wrap the strip of cloth over her breasts. When it was firmly in place, she fastened it with the pins.

"That should hold," she said. "Say good-bye to Evelyn and hello to George."

Evelyn rose to put on the rest of her clothes, dreading her return to the bunkhouse.

"I wish we could do this more often," Sarah said. "This is the first real conversation I've had since arriving here."

"We have to be careful," Evelyn said. "I worry that Sam already has his suspicions, and I've already had a few quarrels with the jack they call Poker Pete. I imagine he'd like nothing more than to see some trouble come my way."

"I understand," Sarah said.

"You sure you'll be okay in here tonight?" Evelyn asked as a gust of wind rattled the shed. "Maybe you should stay in the shanty for the night."

"I'll be fine," Sarah said. "I'll see you in the morning."

"That you will," Evelyn replied.

Sarah cracked open the door, and Evelyn ventured out into the storm as a swirl of snow spun into the shed. Evelyn grabbed on to the rope that led from the shed to the cook shanty. She could see nothing ahead of her but the blowing whiteness. Each step against the wind was a struggle, the wind most often winning—one step forward, two steps back. At the shanty, she snagged the rope that led to the bunkhouse. When she finally reached it, a drift of snow banked the door. With one hand still on the rope, she laboriously cleared a small opening before the door with her free hand, then, using all the strength she had, she pulled the door open.

She didn't think she had been absent for much more than half an hour, but the bunkhouse already felt frigid. With the lights out, the faint light that emanated from the woodstove lit the room only slightly. She made her way to the stove and put in two more logs of wood. When the fire flared, she saw that a light layer of snow was, indeed, covering the inside of the bunkhouse, just as Jones had warned that it would. Evelyn made her way to her bunk, kicked off her boots, removed her coat, and crawled beneath her cover. The snoring of the jacks mixed with the sounds of the whining wind. Whiskey Jack hung his head over the top bunk.

"Was beginning to worry about you, George," he said.

"Got a bit turned around out there," Evelyn said, startled that he was still awake. "Storm's not slacking up at all."

"Sure you didn't stop by that shed for some warming up with the flunky, Bauer?" Poker Pete piped up from the other side of the room.

Evelyn had a moment of panic. *Did Poker Pete follow me out? Did some of the other jacks have their suspicions, also?* That would be the one thing that could make her remaining time at the camp more difficult. She studied Whiskey Jack's face for some sign of concern, but saw none.

"Told you before," Evelyn said. "I'm a family man."

"Lots of us are family men, Bauer," Poker Pete said. "But it's February, and we've been up here for nearly four months or so now. A man's got needs."

"Sounds like you're talking more about yourself than me," Evelyn said, and a few of the men who were still awake chuckled.

"Whiskey was thinking about heading out to look for you,"

Poker Pete said, with the scratch of irritation in his voice. "I told him you weren't worth it."

A number of the jacks laughed. Apparently, more than a few were having a hard time sleeping through the noise of the brutal winds.

"That's all right with me," Evelyn said. "I would have said the same about you."

The laughter rose one last time, and then the bunkhouse fell silent, except for the winds. Evelyn closed her eyes. She tried to remember the touch of Sarah's fingers on her skin and warmed with the memory. She was embarrassed, too, though. She must think I'm a rather brutish woman, she thought, with or without the male clothing. Her next thoughts were ones of puzzlement. *Why do I even care? This camp is changing me in more ways than I know.*

CHAPTER EIGHT

Sarah woke the next morning to a hush, and she knew the blizzard had passed. She stalled for a moment, huddling under her blanket, not quite ready to brave the cold. She thought about her visit with Evelyn. Everything about her enamored Sarah—her ability to feign being a man, her motherhood, her solemn strength, her persistence. She made Sarah feel weak and unsubstantial. Sarah was also drawn to Evelyn physically, though she doubted that she would ever have the opportunity to approach her in any way romantically. She didn't think Evelyn could fathom such a relationship, or would ever want one. She had her home, her children. She was settled, even with her husband gone.

The night before, after Evelyn left, Sarah had been disappointed, though she wasn't sure what she had expected. She had wanted... more. She craved closeness. She had tried to imagine Evelyn's hands sliding over her, touching her, exploring her curves, holding her. Sarah had slid a hand under her garments, then between her legs, and she rested her fingers on her clitoris. She was still moist and excited from her brief encounter with Evelyn. She began to rub her clitoris, gently, slowly, and as it hardened, she rubbed more vigorously. She could feel herself throbbing, and then her entire body quivered with a flood of relief. She thought of Abigail and began to weep quiet sobs until she fell asleep.

The early morning chill slipped through the shed's walls, and Sarah rose and quickly pulled her dress on over her underlayers. She stoked the fire in the woodstove and put on her coat, ready to head to the shanty. At the door, she heard Mack's and Annie's voices and loud scraping sounds, and she knew they were clearing a path from the shanty to her shed. Sarah attempted to pull the door open, but it barely budged. She pulled harder, using all her weight, and the door finally creaked open to brilliant sunlight.

"You made it through the night," Mack said matter-of-factly.

"I did," Sarah said. "It was a bit noisy, but the building's still standing."

She glanced about the camp. The snow was pristine and had drifted to nearly five feet in some places. The boughs of the evergreens bent beneath the weight, and she could hear light crashes throughout the forest, the accumulated snow sliding from limbs as the sun began to melt it.

"I've got to get some water and then I'll start breakfast," she said.

"It'll be a difficult trudge through the snow," Mack said. "Give me the buckets. I'll make a path to the river and get the water while you and Annie work on the grub."

Sarah handed him the buckets, and she and Annie headed into the shanty. As Sarah prepared pots of coffee and Annie set the tables, Sarah could hear the lumberjacks stirring outside. They were clearing the snow out of the common area, setting up the washtubs and a spot for haircuts and shaves. She could tell by some of the yelling and jeers that a good bit of roughhousing was going on, too. She quickly mixed up some shoepack pie and went to the fireplace to remove the pot of beans she had prepared the night before from the glowing coals. She thought about Evelyn the entire time. When the camp closed down in the spring, Evelyn would return to the farm and her children, and she would return home, where she would always be shadowed by memories of Abigail. She found the prospect daunting.

Mack returned with the water and rang the triangle, and just as Sarah and Annie finished pulling breakfast together, the jacks filed in. Sarah scanned the crowd of men until she saw Evelyn, and her heart flipped. Evelyn looked at her only briefly and then turned her attention to her plate. Sarah scurried about the shanty, refilling platters of food, pouring coffee, grabbing up plates as the jacks finished their meals. When the shanty finally cleared out, Annie went to get some more firewood, and Sarah began to wipe off the tables and sweep the floor, occasionally peering out the small window to see if the jacks were assembling outside yet. She was also keeping an eye out for Sam. His return was inevitable, and she didn't want to be caught off guard. She looked out the window one last time, and she finally saw Evelyn, taking her usual spot. Sarah went to the shed, gathered together the clothes that she wanted to wash, and a few items to mend. She put a needle and two spools of thread in her coat pocket and went outside.

Annie soon joined her, and they cleared away an area to build a fire and set up their wash tub. Then, as they had done many times before, they went to the river to get some water, following the trail that Mack had forged earlier. The snow in some places was so high and such a struggle to push through that they had to stop occasionally and catch their breath. When they finally returned, they started the fire, put the tub in place, and filled it with water. The whole time Sarah kept taking sideways glances at Evelyn, who was stooped over on the stump, focused on her stitching. Sarah kept waiting for a look her way, a meeting of the eyes, but Evelyn rarely lifted her head, and that was most often in response to some noise the other jacks were making.

With their tub filled with garments, Sarah and Annie sat on a log, one of them stirring the water now and then with the wooden paddle.

"Were you scared last night?" Annie asked.

"Not really," Sarah said. "A bit cold more than anything, but I kept the fire going all night."

"There were a few times I thought the shanty was going to blow down," Annie said. "I hope I never have to come up here again."

"Have you told your father?" Sarah asked.

"Now is not the time," Annie said. "He'd just worry. But when we return home... Do you think you'll be back next winter?"

Sarah chuckled.

"Most days I barely think I'm going to make it through this

winter," she said. "I have a small calendar and a pencil I use to keep track of the days—how many done, how many ahead. It seems like there's no end in sight."

"But we should only have about two months to go, right?" Annie asked, with a touch of desperation in her voice. "It is the end of February."

"I think we're at the mercy of nature," Sarah said.

She dug into her coat pocket and pulled out the two spools of thread and her darning needle. She was anxious to talk to Evelyn. She stirred the clothes in the tub and looked around. Most of the jacks were washing clothes or repairing equipment. Others gathered around the large stump that was used as a barber chair and waited for trims.

"I've got to return this thread that I borrowed from Bauer," she said.

"Sometimes I think you just like to have a reason to talk to him," Annie said. "I've never seen you talk to any of the other jacks."

"I've already told you that I'm perfectly happy with my life back home," Sarah said rather harshly, hoping to steer Annie away from any thoughts she might be harboring about her and Evelyn.

"Oh, I know," Annie said, blushing and falling silent.

❖

Sarah approached Evelyn, clearing her throat when she was beside her. Evelyn looked up, then quickly glanced around at the other jacks before settling her eyes on Sarah.

"You made it through the night," she said.

"I'm glad you made the trek back to the bunkhouse," Sarah said. "I was worried. The winds picked up quite a bit after you left."

"I held tight to that rope, that's for sure," Evelyn said.

Sarah sensed some uneasiness coming from Evelyn.

"Is everything okay?" she asked.

"Was questioned by a few of the jacks when I returned last night," Evelyn said. "Poker Pete thought I had snuck my way to your shed."

"Oh?" Sarah said.

"Of course I denied it," Evelyn said. "But it has me a bit worried that some of the jacks are even thinking that we, that you and I…"

"I brought your spool of thread back," Sarah said meekly.

She felt a distance between them that hadn't been there before, and she wondered, was it only because some of the jacks had questioned her, or was it… Maybe she had made her feel uncomfortable somehow. Did I touch her in a way I shouldn't have, she wondered. Evelyn took the spool from her.

"Just in time," she said. "I've got a pile of socks to mend."

Sarah rested a hand on Evelyn's shoulder, and Evelyn quickly shrugged it off.

"Not now," she said, sounding urgent. "We've got company."

Sarah removed her hand just as she heard a horse and wagon crunching over the freshly fallen snow. She turned around and saw Sam. She was instantly overcome with dread.

"Let's try to meet tonight after dinner," she said quietly before leaving Evelyn's side.

"If I can," Evelyn said curtly.

Sarah felt a bit hurt and slighted by Evelyn, but she didn't have time to dwell on it, as the jacks had already begun to help Sam unload the supplies from the wagon.

"We weren't sure you'd make it back," she heard one of the jacks say to Sam.

"I made it to town and was able to load up on supplies and get the horses to shelter just before the worst of the storm blew in," Sam said. He sounded quite chipper. "The wagon got stuck once on my way back, but a nearby farmer helped me get it out."

"You have any time to partake in some creature comforts, Mighty Man?" Poker Pete asked. "Maybe a bit of time with one of the gals from the saloon?"

Some of the jacks laughed.

"I knew that would be your main concern," Sam replied with good humor as he smacked Poker Pete on the back. "Now, let's get these goods to the shanty. Where are my flunkies?"

Sarah and Annie had already removed their clothes from the

washtub and hung them from a rope they had strung between two trees so they could soak up some fresh air before they took them inside. They emptied the tub, leaned it against a tree, and extinguished the fire. As they finished, Sam approached them, carrying a box. He settled his eyes on Sarah.

"You weathered the storm okay?" he asked.

"Everything's still standing," Sarah said.

She felt no joy at seeing him.

"Good enough," Sam said. "Let's get these supplies in the pantry. You know where everything goes."

He entered the shanty ahead of them and slid the box he was carrying under his bunk. Sarah wondered what he had in there—whiskey, perhaps. If nothing else he's in good spirits, she thought. We'll see how long that lasts.

She, Annie, Mack, and Sam spent the rest of the afternoon putting away the supplies. Sam remained in a pleasant mood, but Sarah couldn't help but notice that he missed no opportunity to stretch over her while placing something on a shelf, or brush against her when reaching for something. When everything was in its place, Sam looked about, seeming content. He picked up two water buckets and looked at Sarah.

"Let's go get some water while Mack and Annie start dinner," he said.

Sarah was startled. Sam had never fetched the water before, always sure to draw a clear line between which duties belonged to whom. He handed her one of the buckets and led the way outside. An uncomfortable silence ensued as they headed to the river, and when they finally reached it, Sarah stooped on the snowy bank and plunged her bucket into the water. Sam knelt beside her and, before she knew it, he wrapped a firm arm around her waist.

"Don't want you to slip in," he said.

He was so close to Sarah that his breath tickled her ear. She abruptly stood, breaking his grasp, but he rose with her, again lassoed her waist with his arm, this time from behind, and she could feel him, hard, butting up against her back. He turned Sarah toward him and moved to kiss her, shoving his tongue into her mouth and sucking her breath out of her. Sarah struggled against him to push away, but his grip was tight. When he finally removed his mouth from hers, Sarah gasped for air. She tried again to push him away.

"Sam, stop!" she said.

"Stop?" he said.

He pulled her in even closer.

"You're all I thought about when I was gone."

He forced a brutal kiss on her as he tried to wedge a hand between her legs. With his hand pushing against her, he stopped kissing her.

"Things up here could be so much better," he said. "For us both. Think about it."

"Stop," Sarah said again.

Tears began to fall down her cheeks.

"This is not what I want," she said adamantly.

Sam removed his hand and released her. He let out a deep laugh.

"You'll probably come looking for me tonight," he said. "Give it some thought."

He turned to Sarah with a smile and pointed to the path.

"You lead, I'll follow," he said.

He walked behind her the entire way, whistling some eerie tune. Sarah moved as gingerly as she could through the snow, tears slipping down her face.

❖

With Sam walking behind her, his eyes on her, Sarah felt mortified and sick. This man, all these men... She couldn't trust any of them, wanted nothing to do with them, dreamt only of running away from the dismal camp. In that moment, Sam had become the worst of all the jacks, and she had gone from simply disliking him to despising and fearing him. Abigail had been right about him all along. She had known her brother better than she thought. If Sarah would have heeded her warnings, she never would have even considered coming up to this land of isolation. She would have stayed home, in her and Abigail's house, and found some other means to support herself. *What was I thinking?*

Her body was wracked with regret. Now that Sam had made his intentions with her clear, she knew that he would be looming over her constantly, always chasing her down, filling her days with trepidation whenever he visited the home she had shared with Abigail. He would ruin all sense of home for her, and that was a future she didn't look forward to. Her heart sank at the thought of going back to Pine Creek. She didn't have much choice. She didn't know how else she would survive. That home, the sewing, was her livelihood. But now… Her chest heaved and she struggled to keep the tears at bay. The joy she had felt, clung to, when she thought about returning home had suddenly dissipated.

❖

When Evelyn was gathering the clothes she had mended and preparing to return to the bunkhouse, she saw Sam and Sarah heading back from the river with water buckets. Sarah's head was down.

As she and Sam neared the cook shanty, Poker Pete yelled out. "You got a minute to spare, Sam?"

"I reckon I do," Sam shouted back and placed his bucket of water in the snow.

Sarah lifted her head briefly and Evelyn eyed her closely. She looked distressed, as if she had been crying. Sarah lowered her head again and disappeared into the shanty. Evelyn swung her eyes in the other direction and saw Sam and Poker Pete talking, away from the others. Sam slung an arm around Poker Pete's shoulder and glared directly at Evelyn. His features were taut, and he was flushed. He fisted his hands, still staring at Evelyn, and rushed toward the cook shanty. Evelyn turned to look at Poker Pete, who had a smirk on his face. He pointed a finger at Evelyn, as if to say, you're in trouble now, and Evelyn knew exactly what he had told Sam. Poker Pete was always trying to stir the pot.

When she finally reached the cook shanty, Sarah felt a slight wave of relief. She entered without waiting for Sam and poured her bucket of water into the barrel. She looked up and saw Annie watching her. Sarah looked away. Annie put the pots of coffee on the stove and joined Sarah at the counter.

"Are you okay? You look… Have you been crying?"

Sarah couldn't even look at her. The shanty door creaked open and Sam stepped in and set his bucket of water on the floor. He turned his head toward Sarah and Annie, and a strange grin crawled over his face. He still maintained his seemingly cheerful disposition.

"Smells mighty fine in here," he said. "It's good to be back at camp. All the comforts of home. Isn't that right, Sarah?"

Sarah remained silent and he let out a loud guffaw. Annie looked from Sam to Sarah, waiting for Sam to go back outside before she spoke.

"Did he do something to you? Just now? When you went to fetch the water? Did he…?"

"We've got work to do," Sarah said stiffly.

She walked over to the other side of the shanty, to the hooks where their aprons hung, and she took down and put on her blue apron, her signal to Evelyn. She went to one of the counters, making eye contact with no one, and she grabbed a stack of tin plates and began to set the two long tables. Her only focus was on staying steady, trying to remain strong. Her biggest mistake would be to show any sign of weakness.

❖

When she entered the cook shanty that evening, Evelyn was not surprised to see Sarah wearing her blue apron. Earlier in the day, she had seemed so distraught that Evelyn had sensed that something had gone awry. Sarah moved around the tables pouring coffee, and Evelyn found a free seat next to Henry. They nodded to each other and held up their cups simultaneously. Sarah avoided their table, and Annie soon served them, the hot coffee steaming in the brisk shanty air. Evelyn looked about the shanty until she spotted Sam staring directly at her. She settled her eyes on him. She had a feeling he hadn't taken his eyes off her since she entered the room, and she felt a knot in her stomach and sensed that unavoidable trouble lay ahead.

Later that night, about an hour before lights out, Evelyn hesitated, then took out her pipe and tobacco and pulled on her coat and hat. When she reached the door, Poker Pete's voice rang out.

"Careful out there, Bauer," he said. "You never know what might be lurking in those woods."

Evelyn ignored him and continued out the door. As soon as she reached the trees, she heard the door to Sarah's shed creak open and then close. She heard footsteps crunching through the snow, and when she finished packing her pipe and looked up, her eyes met Sarah's.

"Are you all right?" she asked.

Sarah leaned against her. She was trembling.

"Sam tried to force himself on me," she said. "Down by the river."

Evelyn grabbed her hand.

"You need to talk to Johnny," she said. "He's the only one who will be able to do something."

"He won't do anything," Sarah said. "His hands are tied. Without Sam, the camp closes down."

"Well, I think Sam suspects there is something going on between us," Evelyn said. "I saw Poker Pete pull him aside and tell him something that seemed to put him in a rather foul mood. We need to distance ourselves or you won't be safe. Try to stick close to Mack and Annie."

Sarah began to cry, and she quickly wiped the tears from her face.

"I'm not going to make it up here," she said.

"We'll figure something out," Evelyn said. "You don't have that much time left here. Stay strong."

Sarah began to walk away, and Evelyn reached out and took her hand.

"I will," Sarah said. "I'll try."

Evelyn returned to a bunkhouse of thunderous snoring and incoherent groans. She lay down, but all she could think about was Sarah. She knew that the longer she had to be around Sam, the less safe she would be. Evelyn didn't know what she could do to help her, and she felt helpless and frustrated. She stared into the darkness that surrounded her. Only a slight flicker of light escaped from the woodstove, and she felt that same darkness settle in her—a heavy, oozing feeling. She was homesick—aching for both the children and her daily life on the farm. She was weary from her masquerade and the harshness of the male energy that pervaded the lumber camp. Evelyn reached into her pack and fingered the calendar. Those pages held her only hope. On one of those future days, she would be heading home, back to the world that was familiar to her. She wondered about Sarah, having to return home with Sam so nearby. *What will her future be now?* Even at the camp, with so many people around, Sarah's predicament, her proximity to Sam, worried Evelyn a bit more every day.

CHAPTER NINE

Evelyn had begun to feel a slight rush of excitement knowing the days remaining at the camp were numbered. Within a month, if all went well, she would be back on the farm, with the children. One morning, in the second week of March, she woke to what sounded like rain, a constant pitter-patter, and she smiled—the first thaw. That was the true indicator of winter drawing to an end. The sound of the triangle rang out, and as the men pulled on their outer layers, they were boisterous, light-hearted almost, sensing the end of the season.

When Evelyn stepped outside to head to the cook shanty, she looked about the camp. Icicles were dripping and chunks of snow were sliding off tree limbs. She entered the shanty with a sense of joy, but when her eyes settled on Sarah, the feeling quickly fled as she was reminded of Sarah's new predicament. She couldn't help but wonder what was going through her mind and how she now saw her future.

As soon as the men finished eating and began to gather their tools, Johnny Jones called them all together.

"The first thaw is setting in, which means that this season's chopping is done," he said. "Every jack's job now is to load the logs on the sleds, get them to the riverbank, and stamp them. They all need to be moved before the ice melts and the roads turn to slush. We don't know how much time we'll have, so every minute counts."

An excited murmuring traveled through the crowd of men, and they gathered up the chains and skidding tongs that they would need to move the logs. Whiskey Jack sidled up to Evelyn with a chain in hand and gave her a pair of tongs.

"There's a touch of spring in the air today, George," he said. "You feel it?"

"Felt it the moment I woke," Evelyn said. "Couldn't come soon enough, if you ask me."

"You ready to head back to that farm of yours?" Whiskey Jack asked.

"Been ready since the day I left," Evelyn replied.

She had been sensing a change in the weather, a slight quiver of warmth in the winds. The days were growing longer, with the sun climbing over the tree line earlier and sinking a bit later each night. All Evelyn could do was speculate as to when she might be able to leave the camp and head home.

❖

After the harsh days of February, the windblown days that ushered in March offered some relief, a slight touch of spring pushing in and winter edging out. Sarah had become more and more depressed, worrying about her daily interactions with Sam, being constantly on guard, and despairing over her future once her days at the camp came to an end. She felt lost. She felt completely unprepared for life, unanchored in regard to any kind of future. She knew that Evelyn would be returning to the farm and her children. They had spoken only sparingly since the altercation with Sam, and their talks were quick snippets of conversation, making Sarah feel even more alone. Evelyn would leave the camp without ever knowing that Sarah had grown to have feelings for her.

The atmosphere in the camp lightened with the shift in the weather. As much as Sarah despaired over her future, even she felt a wave of relief, until one night in late March. As Sarah prepared for bed that night, she could hear Sam outside her shed. She sat on the edge of her bed and listened as she brushed her hair to remove any lice. She thought she heard him mumbling to himself as he padded back and forth near her door.

At one point he stumbled against the building. He's drinking, she thought, and as she rose from her cot to wedge the chair under the doorknob, Sam crashed through the door, knocking her to the floor. Startled, Sarah quickly got up with the goal of escaping the shed. Sam lurched toward her, trying to grab her. He latched onto her dress, drew back an arm, and landed a solid slap on Sarah's cheek. She reeled back, stunned by the pain, and tried for the door again, pushing Sam off balance. In his drunkenness, he fell to the floor. She reached the door and Sam caught hold of her dress again. She heard the material tear and felt a moment of relief as Sam lost his grip.

She made it out of the shed and ran toward the cook shanty. As soon as she reached it, she grabbed the beater and struck the triangle, again and again, hoping someone would hear it—Mack or one of the teamsters. Sam was on her before she knew it, and he grabbed a handful of her hair and began to drag her toward the woods. Petrified at the thought of what would happen if he succeeded, Sarah started to scream and tried to fight him off. With his free hand, Sam slapped her hard again, still dragging her. He pinned her against a tree with one arm. She could smell the liquor on his breath. Sam began to undo his belt. Sarah tried to push him off her, and she screamed again, tears streaming down her face.

The days in the woods had grown longer and no less strenuous with the moving of the logs, and all the jacks, including Evelyn, edged sheer exhaustion. Evelyn's sleep became even more disturbed than usual, her thoughts constantly on the farm and all the tasks that would need to be accomplished when she returned to ensure a good crop that year. Her pulse quickened when she thought of seeing her children again. She wondered how much they had grown. Peter and Karl were probably a good bit taller than when she left, and Louise was probably talking up a storm.

With sleep evading her, she lay buried beneath her covers. She thought about stepping out for a smoke, thinking it might settle her down. She heard something outside, faintly rising over the sounds of the snoring jacks. She sat up and listened. The cook shanty triangle was ringing. Evelyn reached into her rucksack and pulled out her pocket watch, then lit a match—two o'clock, too early for breakfast. She heard the sound again, then some other noise—a voice, faint screaming. Someone's in trouble, she thought. She gently shook Whiskey Jack until he woke.

"What the hell, George?" he grumbled.

"Something's wrong," Evelyn said. "Someone's ringing the triangle, and it's too early for chow time."

Whiskey Jack climbed off the bunk, grabbing his coat and boots.

"I'll go with you," he said.

Evelyn led the way past the slumbering jacks and pushed open the bunkhouse door. She and Whiskey Jack let their eyes adjust to the darkness and turned toward the noise. The voice was Sarah's. Then another voice—Sam's. Evelyn immediately knew what was happening. She grabbed Whiskey Jack's coat sleeve.

"Sam's attacking the flunky," she said.

She broke into a run.

Sarah and Sam were about fifty feet from the cook shanty. As Evelyn neared them, she could see that Sarah's dress was torn. Sam had her pinned against a tree with one arm and was using his other hand to try to lower his pants.

Evelyn yelled, "Stop, Sam! Stop now!"

Whiskey Jack rushed Sam, trying to throw him off balance, but Sam reeled around and caught him with a swift right hook. Sarah broke free of Sam's grip and stepped back. Sam lunged toward her, trying to grab her again, and Evelyn quickly glanced about and picked up a good-sized branch off the ground. She approached Sam from behind and swung the branch with all her strength. The crack that followed when the branch connected with Sam's head resounded through the woods, and Sam toppled backward. A pool of blood spread out about him, soaking into the snow. For a moment, Whiskey Jack, Evelyn, and Sarah stared at him silently. Whiskey Jack reached down to check for a pulse, and Evelyn took off her coat and draped it over Sarah. Sarah's cheek was swollen and her left eye was nearly shut, the skin below already blooming into black and blue.

"Are you okay?" Evelyn asked. "Did he...?"

"No, but he would have," Sarah sobbed. "He cornered me in the shed. I barely made it out..."

She crumpled to the ground in defeat, and Evelyn bent over her, not knowing what to say.

"He's still alive," Whiskey Jack said.

The door to the teamsters' shed opened and Johnny Jones stepped out.

"What the hell's going on out here?" he asked as he pulled on his coat.

He then saw Sam on the ground, surrounded by blood. He looked at them.

"He attacked me," Sarah said. "I was barely able to escape out here and ring the triangle. They were only trying to help me."

"Who took him down?" Johnny asked.

"I did," Evelyn said without hesitation. "He wouldn't let her go."

"You're going to have to leave, George, get out of the camp," Johnny said. "Tonight."

"Leave?" Evelyn said. "You want me to leave tonight?"

Johnny nodded.

"When he finally comes to and recovers, you're a dead man. And who knows what the other jacks might do before then. Poker Pete's bound to rile some of them up."

"But what about..."

Evelyn gestured toward Sarah.

"You'll have to take her with you, make sure she gets home," Johnny said. "She can't stay here. She won't be safe."

"But how...?"

"Go get Jankowski," Johnny said. "You're going to have to take his horse if he'll let you. It's either that or walk."

"I can't leave without my wages," Evelyn said. "My farm will go under without that money."

Johnny hesitated for a moment. He looked down at Sam and then nodded.

"I'll draw up a check," he said. "You and Whiskey Jack need to move him into the shanty. Get him out of sight."

Shaking his head, he returned to the teamsters' shed. Whiskey Jack grabbed Sam beneath the armpits, and Evelyn hoisted up his legs. When they reached the shanty, Sarah, still sobbing, opened the door, and they dragged Sam inside. Evelyn looked at Sarah and took her gently by the shoulders to try to calm her.

"Pack your bag quickly and put on your warmest clothes," she said. "We'll meet you at the teamsters' shed."

Sarah nodded but glanced at Sam with apprehension.

"He's out cold," Whiskey Jack assured her. "I'll get Mack to tend to him once you're gone."

Sarah nodded again and turned to the shed to gather her belongings.

"Let's go get Henry," Whiskey Jack said to Evelyn.

"Meet us as soon as you can," Evelyn hollered to Sarah.

She and Whiskey Jack headed out of the shanty and toward the bunkhouse.

"I'll wake Henry while you grab your stuff," Whiskey Jack said.

They entered the bunkhouse quietly. Evelyn went to her cot to grab her belongings. She could feel her heart palpitating, and she felt a mix of emotions—anger, panic, elation. Things had not gone as planned, but she was heading home. Whiskey Jack woke Henry and told him he was needed outside. In a sleepy daze, Henry grabbed his coat, pulled on his boots, and followed Whiskey Jack and Evelyn out of the bunkhouse.

"I have to leave the camp tonight, and I'm going to need your horse to do it," Evelyn said. "I have to take the flunky with me. Sam attacked her tonight. There's been a bad fight."

"I'll ready the horse," Henry said. "I'll hitch a way back with one of the other jacks when we're done for the season, and I'll come get the horse after I return home."

"Thanks, Henry," Evelyn said.

"It's nothing, George," Henry said. "I owe you."

Evelyn and Whiskey Jack followed Henry to the teamsters' shed, where Sarah was already waiting, her satchel of belongings in hand. Evelyn and Whiskey Jack waited with her without speaking, and Henry finally emerged with his horse. Johnny Jones also joined them and handed Evelyn her check.

"You did good work, Bauer," he said. "Never caused any trouble. I know all about Sam and his ways, and I can't hold this against you."

"Thanks, Johnny," Evelyn said.

"You'll have to keep an eye out when you get home, though," Johnny said. "He'll come looking for you when he can."

"Sam has your wages," he said to Sarah. "There's nothing I can do."

Sarah, still crying, said nothing. Whiskey Jack extended a hand to George.

"This is it, George," he said.

Evelyn reached out and gave it a firm shake.

"It's been a pleasure, Whiskey," she said. "Help her up after I get on."

Evelyn fastened her pack and ax and Sarah's satchel to the back of the horse's saddle and climbed up on the horse, grabbing the reins. Whiskey Jack boosted Sarah up behind her, and Sarah wrapped her arms tightly around Evelyn's waist. Evelyn could feel her trembling, and she knew she was weeping again. The best thing she could do was get them to the farm.

"Safe travels, George," Whiskey Jack said.

Evelyn gently yanked on the reins and the horse slowly began to plod through the snow.

When Evelyn and Sarah were about an hour away from the camp, the moon dimly lighting the trail, Evelyn stopped the horse.

"Are you all right, Sarah?" she asked.

"I don't know what I'll do, where I'll go now," Sarah said. "I feel as if my life has been destroyed in one single moment. I must now call everything that I once knew into question."

Before heading to the camp, Sarah had assumed that she would return to Pine Creek, but Sam's brutal attack had undoubtedly changed her future. She wouldn't have any level of comfort or security at home, and she felt abandoned, strangely orphaned—again.

"I'm so sorry this has happened," Evelyn said. "I'm taking you with me to the farm. You can stay there until you decide what you want to do, where you want to go. I can always use an extra set of hands, especially now, with George gone. You might decide that you can stay in your home after all, but if not, my brother-in-law will take you there at some point so you can pick up some of your belongings."

As the horse plodded on, Sarah sat behind Evelyn, stunned—by Sam's brutal attack, by the blur that had become her life. Before the camp, before Abigail's death, her life had a clear direction. She questioned nothing. Now everything that had been securely in place had unraveled, vanished before her eyes. She felt physically ill, nauseated by her prospects, the bleak path ahead.

❖

As the sun began to descend, with the moon slowly climbing into the sky, they finally reached the farm. Evelyn pulled the horse to a halt as soon as it was in sight.

"There it is," she said to Sarah.

Sarah leaned over to look past Evelyn, her eyes settling on the farm. The house was small, but the lights faintly flickering in the windows looked welcoming. The barn seemed to be sagging to one side and was flanked by a silo. A few other small structures stood beyond them. Behind the farm was a wooded area, thick with trees. Evelyn nudged the horse again, and they headed to the house. When they arrived, Evelyn helped Sarah down from the horse, removed their gear, and tied the horse to one of the porch railings. The door to the house opened and a woman stuck out her head.

"Who is it?" she asked. "Can I help you?"

She took a close look at them and rushed outside. She took Evelyn in her arms. "Oh my God, you're back," she said. "You made it home."

"Did you have doubts?" Evelyn asked as Helen released her.

"I had some worries," Helen said. "I didn't expect you back this early."

"We had a bit of an altercation that cut the tour short," Evelyn said. "This is Sarah. She's a friend from the camp. I'll explain later. Sarah, this is my sister, Helen."

"It's a pleasure," Sarah said meekly, lowering her eyes.

Helen's eyes fell on Sarah. "That's quite a bruise you have there," she said. "Let's get you inside so we can fix you up."

Evelyn grabbed their belongings and gestured for Sarah to follow her. Sarah glanced about the small abode, the dwelling that would be her home, for a time. Compared to this house, her home with Abigail had been a rather luxurious one. The children, still eating their evening meal, first looked at Evelyn and Sarah with no sign of recognition. Then they screamed with joy, jumping up from the table and surrounding Evelyn with a tangle of arms. Evelyn's eyes moistened as she wrapped her arms around the children and pulled them close to her.

Sarah watched as Evelyn transformed from the robust and rigorous woman she had known as George into Evelyn, mother of three. She softened before Sarah's eyes, her shoulders relaxing, her eyes filling with tenderness. Evelyn tousled her children's hair and kissed them gently, and Sarah warmed at the sight, though she also felt a tinge of jealousy. That was the very affection she had craved since Abigail had passed away. When Evelyn finally let go of the children, she picked up the little girl and examined the boys.

"You boys have grown some over the winter," she said.

She fought back tears. The boys smiled proudly. Evelyn turned to Sarah.

"Children, this is a friend of mine from the logging camp," she said. "Her name is Sarah, and she'll be staying with us for a while. Sarah, this is Peter, Karl, and Louise."

"Hello, Sarah," the children all said politely.

"Hi," Sarah said timidly. "It's a pleasure to meet you. Your mother told me about you up at camp."

Sarah looked at each child. She could see some of Evelyn's traits in them. Peter had her strong cheekbones, and Louise had her build. Karl looked the least like her, and she thought he must resemble his father more. Peter looked at Sarah's swollen face and black eye.

"What happened?" he asked.

"A little trouble at camp," Evelyn said. "Now, you boys finish up your dinner, and when you're done, take the horse tied up outside to the barn and brush him down and feed him."

"Yes, ma'am," the boys said happily, returning to the table with Louise in tow.

"What's its name?" Peter asked.

"I don't know," Evelyn said. "For now, let's call her Henrietta."

"Okay," Peter said.

Helen smiled.

"I'll put on coffee," she said.

"Coffee would be good," Evelyn said. "But we need a change of clothes first. I know I must smell like a hundred stinking jacks. We'll take our things up to my room and be right down."

She led Sarah up the stairs and to her bedroom. Sarah took in the room. Like the rest of the house, it was simple and quaint. Evelyn lit a lantern on a table and looked at Sarah.

"It's no palace," she said.

"Compared to the camp it is," Sarah said, and for the first time since they had left the camp, she smiled.

Evelyn handed her a basin of water and a washcloth.

"You need to clean out that cut on your cheek," she said. "Why don't you sit and I'll find something for you to wear. After the children go to bed, we can heat up some water for bathing. Won't that be divine?"

Sarah nodded and tried to smile again, but she felt limp, as if she were wilting. Evelyn sat beside her and took her hand.

"Everything will work out, Sarah," she said quietly.

"Regardless, I thank you for having me here," Sarah said.

She didn't want Evelyn to think she was ungrateful.

"I wouldn't have had it any other way," Evelyn said. "I would never have left you to fend for yourself up there."

"I know," Sarah said.

"I need to find us some fresh clothes before we go back down," Evelyn said.

She went to the dresser and took out a shirt and a sweater, which she put on, and she looked at Sarah.

"I'm afraid my dresses would slide right off you," she said. "At least you can keep up a pair of my pants with a belt."

"Anything will be fine," Sarah said.

"We'll put all our clothes from the camp outside so we can burn them in the morning." Evelyn handed Sarah some pants, a soft flannel shirt, and a sweater. "I don't want any of the lice we might have brought back with us to settle into the house."

"I don't think I'd want to wear any of those clothes again, anyway," Sarah said.

"I agree," Evelyn said. "Now, the moment I've been waiting for."

She took off her mackinaw and long john shirt.

"Finally, I'll be able to breathe."

She reached down to unfasten one of the pins holding the wrap in place.

"Let me help," Sarah said.

She stood and unfastened the pins and then removed the wrap while Evelyn raised her arms above her head. With the wrap off, Evelyn released a long sigh.

"Never again," she said.

She put on a clean shirt and sweater, picked up the mackinaw and long john shirt that she had taken off, and pulled her other change of clothes out of her pack.

"Bring down all your clothes after you change," she told Sarah.

"All right," Sarah said.

Evelyn left, closing the door behind her, and Sarah sat on the bed. She ran a hand over her cheek and stood up to look at herself in the crude mirror sitting on the dresser.

"It looks as bad as it feels," she said.

She turned and surveyed the room. The wood on the floors and walls was a dark, knotted brown. Two photographs were on the dresser. One was a picture of three men standing side by side, cradling rifles in their arms, the man in the middle holding a large dead bird. The other was of two women, sitting on a porch, with children nestled in their laps. A few small trinkets were on the dresser, too—a small wooden box, a bird whittled out of wood, and a daintily decorated egg that had been hollowed out. In a corner of the room by the one window was a wooden rocking chair with a table beside it. There was another kerosene lamp on that table and a small stack of three books. Sarah picked one up—*Jane Eyre*. She smiled. All this to tend to and Evelyn still finds time to read, she thought. She admired her stamina.

She put down the book and glanced at the bed—big enough for two. She wondered if she'd be sleeping there tonight, with Evelyn. Her pulse quickened with the idea, the thought of some closeness. Then she felt a sense of doom as she wondered how long Evelyn would allow her to stay, and where she could go when she finally did leave. *What if the children don't like me? What if I can't keep up with the work? What if...? This is my life now—a bunch of ifs.*

When Evelyn returned downstairs, she put her camp clothes outside on the porch.

"I've got no more need for those," she said.

She closed the door and Louise ran to her. Evelyn hoisted her up and kissed her on the cheek. Louise snuggled into her neck.

"I missed you, Mommy," she said.

"I thought about you every day, darling," Evelyn said.

She moved to the kitchen table and sat on a bench, with Louise curling into her lap. Helen finished clearing off the table and set down cups of coffee for her and Evelyn.

"Would you like some soup?" she asked.

"Not now," Evelyn said. "Just sitting here is like heaven."

"How was it up there?" Helen asked.

"Dreadful," said Evelyn. "The conditions were deplorable, indescribable really. At first I thought I might lose my mind. It was the work that actually saved me. Inside the bunkhouse at night, with all those stinking jacks crammed in... Someone was always egging on someone, trying to start a fight."

"I can't even imagine," Helen said. "And Sarah?"

"She discovered I was a woman by accident a few months in," Evelyn said. "We became confidantes, friends. She had lived with a woman who passed away. That's why she was working in the cook shanty. The head cook was the other woman's brother."

"What happened to her?" Helen asked. "How did she get hurt?"

"The cook was also a drunkard," Evelyn said. "He was the one who attacked her last night. He was trying to rape her. Another jack and I intervened. I hammered him with a branch, hurt him pretty bad. That's why we had to leave."

"Where does she live?" Helen asked.

"That's the problem," Evelyn explained. "Until all this happened, she had planned to return to the house she had shared with the other woman in Pine Creek, but she probably won't be safe there now, not with him lurking around. The only thing I could think to do was to bring her here."

"Well, you can always use some extra help," Helen said.

"We'll just see how it goes," Evelyn said. "Right now I'm too tired to think."

❖

When Sarah joined them downstairs, carrying her clothes from the camp, Evelyn was sitting at the table with Helen. She had Louise in her lap and a cup of coffee in one hand.

"You can put those out on the porch," she said. "We'll tend to that in the morning."

When Sarah returned from the porch, Helen got her a cup of coffee and a bowl of soup.

"Please, sit and eat," she said to Sarah.

"Thank you so much," Sarah said.

She sat at the table across from Evelyn and Louise. She took a sip of coffee and ate some soup, finally beginning to relax.

"This soup is delicious," she said. "If I never have to eat another bean or piece of shoepack pie again, I'll be fine with that."

Evelyn took a gulp of coffee.

"I'll second that," she said.

The front door swung open and Peter and Karl entered, stomping their boots off on a mat.

"Horse is in the barn, Ma," Peter said.

"Thank you," Evelyn said. "You boys should get ready for bed now, and I'll bring Louise up in a bit. After you finish milking the cows in the morning, you can help me show Sarah the lay of the land."

The boys nodded and went over to Evelyn to give her a hug.

"I'm sure glad you're home, Ma," Peter said.

Evelyn smiled.

"Me, too," she said. "You have no idea."

"Good night," the boys said to Sarah, before turning around to give Helen hugs good night.

"Good night," Sarah said.

The boys hugged their aunt and raced for the stairs.

"They seem sweet," Sarah said to Evelyn.

"They're good boys," Evelyn said. "They have their moments, as all children do, but they have George's temperament. He was a steady man, not easily ruffled."

Sarah looked at Evelyn. She wondered if she still grieved for him, longed for him in his absence, as she did Abigail.

"How did things go here?" Evelyn asked Helen.

"The winter's been fairly mild, except for one storm," Helen said. "We only got about seven feet of snow, and that has now thawed down to about four or five in most places. We had some cold snaps, but beyond that, everything was business as usual. Peter and Karl made it to school most days after tending to the animals, thanks to Will. He was a great help. He made sure the woodpile was well stocked, made repairs when needed, kept the well from freezing over, and made sure the animals stayed healthy. A fox broke into the chicken coop one night and killed two hens, but he took care of that the next morning. Jess and I took turns taking care of Louise during the days so one of us could keep the school going."

Evelyn released a sigh of relief.

"It could've been worse," she said. "I was so worried, thinking about everything that could go wrong."

"Peter and Karl had some rough days, mainly just feeling the absence of you and George, I think. But they passed. They're growing up so quickly. They just wanted to know when you'd be coming back home."

"Well, I'm happy that it was sooner instead of later," Evelyn said.

Louise shifted in her lap. Evelyn looked down at her.

"Time to put this one to bed," she said.

Louise was cocooned against her, sound asleep. Evelyn rose from the table, cradling her in her arms, and took her up the stairs.

❖

Helen put her cup in the sink while Sarah sipped on her soup.

"Evelyn said you ran into a bit of trouble up at camp," Helen said. "I'm sorry to hear that."

Sarah nodded.

"I don't know what I would've done without your sister," she said. "I would have gone out of my mind if I hadn't been able to talk to her. I've never felt so isolated in my life. And Sam... I hate to think of what would have happened if Evelyn and the other jack wouldn't have intervened."

"She's a strong woman, a defender," Helen said. "What do you think you'll do now? Evelyn said that you had been living with a woman prior to going to the camp, but that she had passed away."

Sarah felt herself sinking. She had no idea how to answer that question. She had nowhere to go.

"Her name was Abigail," she said. "She died of pneumonia. She took me in from the orphanage when I was seventeen, taught me her trade. She was a seamstress and a tailor. I had planned on returning to the house when I left the camp, but that notion has since been ruined. Now, I…"

Her voice trailed off.

"You'll stay here until you figure things out, but I'm sorry for your loss," Helen said. "You and Evelyn are in somewhat the same situation. You are now both without the key people in your lives, your partners."

"I know," Sarah said. "The adjustment will take time."

"You might find you like life on the farm," Helen said.

"Where do you live?" Sarah asked.

Helen was so different from Evelyn that Sarah was intrigued that they were sisters. Helen was more petite than Evelyn, more refined, feminine, but Sarah wasn't drawn to her the way she was to Evelyn. She was enamored by Evelyn's melding of female and male characteristics, her ability to be so strong and resilient, and yet gentle and caring.

"I stay in town with another woman, Jess," Helen said. "We have a small house, and we run the town's school. That's how we support ourselves."

Sarah was relieved that she didn't have to hide her past relationship with Abigail. Evelyn would have no need to lie for her. Evelyn returned downstairs with an arm full of towels and a smile. She put the towels on the table and went to the sink and began to pump water into a large pot. She placed the pot on the woodstove and went to the pantry. She came out, pulling a large steel tub over the floor. She took it into the sitting room and placed it close to the fireplace. When she returned to the kitchen, she looked at Sarah.

"As soon as the water's hot, you can bathe."

"Never before would those words have caused such comfort," Sarah said. "I realize now how many things I have taken for granted."

"It's too late for me to head out tonight," Helen said. "I'm going to set up the cot in the sitting room when you're done with your baths."

Evelyn gave her a hug.

"I know you're ready to return home," she said. "I can't thank you and Jess enough for taking care of the children."

"They're my nephews and niece," Helen said. "And you know I'd do anything for you."

"I know," Evelyn said. "I've always known that."

When Sarah stepped into the tub of warm water and slowly sat, submerging her body, she felt such a release that tears streamed down her face. The water eventually relaxed her, and she realized that from the first day she had arrived at the sordid camp with Sam, she had been a bundle of anxious nerves, tense and taut, and ever hypervigilant. The days had taken more of a toll than she had realized, and though she wasn't home in her home, she was at least someplace safe, someplace warm. She could not imagine what the days ahead would be like, but she trusted Evelyn, and in that moment, that was enough.

❖

After Sarah finished bathing, Evelyn pulled the tub outside, emptied it, and returned inside to refill it.

"The moment I've been waiting for," she said to herself.

When she immersed herself in the warm, soothing water, her entire body loosened and unraveled. She felt as if her muscles were turning to jelly, and she rested her head on the back of the tub and closed her eyes. Only then did the exhaustion from the months of rigorous work overcome her. Even her bones felt weary. She felt as if she could sleep for a month and never stir, but she was excited to be home, back with her children, and she was invigorated by the thought of preparing for the spring planting. She knew that the work that lay ahead would be strenuous, but she was accustomed to that, and she also knew that the days would be without the tension and turmoil that were ever-present at the camp.

Evelyn finally forced herself out of the tub, dried herself off, and put her clothes back on. She emptied the tub outside and then returned it to the pantry. Helen and Sarah were quietly sitting at the table.

"That was a little piece of heaven," Evelyn said. "I never knew a bath could feel so wonderful."

Sarah smiled in acknowledgment.

"I can only imagine," Helen said.

She rose and gave Evelyn a quick peck on the cheek.

"Time for me to turn in, sister," she said. "I want to get to town in time to open up the school with Jess in the morning. Back to business as usual. I'll stop by Will's on my way in and let him know you're back."

"I'll see you in the morning," Evelyn said. "Breakfast will be ready before you go."

"Nice to meet you," Helen said to Sarah.

Sarah nodded and said, "Good night."

When Helen left the room, Evelyn looked at Sarah.

"I don't think I can stay awake another minute," she said.

"Me, either," said Sarah.

Evelyn led the way up the steps with Sarah trailing behind her.

"You can sleep with me in my bed tonight," she said. "Tomorrow we'll set up the cot in here."

"Okay," said Sarah.

When they reached the small bedroom, Evelyn went to the dresser and took out two nightgowns. She handed one to Sarah.

"You'll probably drown in this, but it will have to do for now, until you decide what to do. If you decide that you're going to stay here, at some point Will can take you home to gather some of your things," she said.

"I don't think I have any choice but to stay here, at least until I figure things out," Sarah said glumly, looking at Evelyn. "I believe my days in Pine Creek are over. I would never feel safe there with

Sam so close by and feeling as if the house is as much his as mine. I could never trust him again."

Each of her words was wrapped in defeat.

"Well, I'm happy to have you here," Evelyn said.

Sarah began to remove her clothes. Evelyn quickly turned her back to her and also began to undress. Sarah watched her from behind, and as Evelyn reached for her gown, Sarah caught a full glimpse of her. She was striking—a voluptuous woman with full curves. Sarah knew that when her hair grew back she would be even more attractive. As she reached for the nightgown Evelyn had given her, Evelyn drew back the covers on the bed and sat on the edge. When she looked up, Sarah was just pulling the gown over her head. Sarah let down her hair, and it fell to the middle of her back in gentle waves. Her breasts were full, firm, and she was slender and lithe.

Evelyn quickly shifted her eyes away and lay back on the bed, her body sinking into the softness beneath her. She was exactly where she wanted to be—home. She knew every inch of the house—which floorboards creaked, on which ceiling rafters the spiders liked to weave their webs. Home.

"Oh my," she said aloud. "Compared to that bunk…the bunkhouse…"

"I'm amazed you could actually sleep in that madness," Sarah said.

CHAPTER TEN

Evelyn's pent-up exhaustion could not compare to the exhilaration she felt from being home, and she woke the next morning before dawn, just as the day was being ushered in by crowing roosters. Her body ached from the previous months of labor, but she was so thrilled to be back on the farm that it seemed only a minor inconvenience. A slight breeze was rattling the windows, and she sat up in bed and stretched. She nearly gasped as her hand brushed against Sarah. She had almost forgotten that she was beside her. Evelyn gazed at her for a moment. She looked peaceful, despite all the turmoil that Evelyn knew she was feeling. She quietly got out of bed, dressed, and left the room, gently shutting the door behind her. The noise of the children getting up would wake Sarah soon enough.

She went downstairs and smiled. The embers in the fireplace softly lit the two rooms. She added some wood to the kitchen stove and the fire sparked. She reached for a cast iron pan and a baking sheet. She had waited for this moment for months—a breakfast of eggs, biscuits, and ham. She could already taste it. She glanced out the window. The sun was beginning to push above the tree line, spreading a silky sheen over the farmland. She pulled on her coat and went outside, trampling through snow to the chicken coop. She opened the creaking door and stepped in, rousing the birds as she searched for eggs. She gathered them into a basket as she found them—a total of thirteen. She put out some feed and headed back to the house. She was greeted by the nutty smell of coffee boiling on the stove.

"You're up," she said to Helen.

"I heard you coming down," Helen said.

"I'll get the breakfast started," Evelyn said.

"I can't wait to tell Will that you have returned," Helen said. "He'll be relieved."

Evelyn smiled.

"I'm sure he had his worries, just as you did. Ask him if he can come by sometime this week with the wagon to take Sarah home. We might need two wagons. I want her to be able to salvage as many of her belongings as she can before Sam returns. We can store some things in the barn if we need to."

"She has decided to stay?" Helen asked.

Evelyn nodded.

"For the time being," she said.

"I feel sorry for her," Helen said. "She's displaced now. The only home she knew is unsafe, and with no other family… You did the right thing bringing her here."

"I could never have left her there," Evelyn said. "She wouldn't have been safe, and our friendship has grown in the past few months."

Helen glanced at her.

"How do you think she'll fare here?"

Evelyn shrugged.

"All I can do is make her as welcome as possible. Maybe one day she can think of the farm as…home. Maybe she'll find another place to settle. I know she was used to a different kind of life before the camp, before this."

"Don't sell yourself short," Helen said. "The farm has its appeal, and so does this house. You know I love spending time here."

"I know that, but you, at least, have a reference point to farm living," Evelyn said. "That's how we grew up. This life takes adapting to."

Helen nodded. Evelyn cracked eggs into the hot skillet, and by the time the whites were spitting and setting, she could hear the children upstairs, scrambling to pull on clothes and boots. She knew they were as thrilled as she was to have everything back to normal.

❖

For the first time in months, Sarah woke to sunshine instead of darkness. She felt the cushiony bed beneath her and for a moment was disoriented. She scanned the room—Evelyn's. She was with Evelyn. She sat up on the side of the bed. *Look at me, from a logging camp to a farm. Who would have thought my life could have changed so drastically in so little time?* She wanted nothing more than to curl up in a cocoon, stay hidden away from the world, but she heard scrambling down the stairs and rose to get dressed. Ten minutes later, she joined everyone, and Evelyn glanced at her and laughed.

"I know you'll be happy when you can put on some of your own clothes," she said. "You're certainly drowning in mine."

Sarah smiled.

"I've got no complaints," she said.

They all gathered around the table before steaming plates of food.

"Do you hear that?" Evelyn asked Sarah.

Peter looked from Evelyn to Sarah.

"Hear what?" he asked.

"The quiet," Evelyn said. "Up at the camp, meal times were the loudest times, with more than fifty loggers crammed into a room not much larger than this."

"What else was it like up there, Ma?" Peter asked.

"Well, I felt like I never did get warm up there," Evelyn said. "And like here, the work was never done. We were up before the sun rose and down not long after it set."

"Were the lumberjacks nice?" Karl asked.

Evelyn's eyes met Sarah's for a moment.

"Some," Evelyn said. "My bunkmate was a man named Whiskey Jack. He was a decent fellow."

"Did he drink whiskey?" Peter asked.

"No drinking at camp," Evelyn said. "He must have gotten that name before he started working there."

"How many trees did you cut down?" Karl asked.

"More than I can count," Evelyn said. "That's the only thing we did all day, until we started to move the lumber to the riverbank."

"Did you cut down trees?" Peter asked Sarah.

"Oh, no," Sarah said. "Your mother had the stamina for that, but I worked in the cook shanty. I helped feed the jacks."

"Even that work was endless," Evelyn said. "Now, enough with the questions. We've got a full day ahead, and we need to show Sarah around the farm."

"How long is she staying?" Peter asked with a scowl on his face.

Silence filled the room for a moment, and Evelyn watched as a light blush crawled over Sarah's face.

"Sarah is welcome here for as long as she wants to stay," she said. "She might take a liking to the farm life."

"When does Daddy come?" Louise asked.

The room fell quiet as the boys' heads dropped. Evelyn pulled Louise onto her lap and wrapped her arms around her. She rested a hand on Louise's chest, over her heart.

"He's in a better place now, honey," she said. "But as long as you keep him here, in your heart, he'll always be with you. Isn't that right, boys?"

"Yes, ma'am," they said halfheartedly.

Evelyn studied them, then said, "But I'm here, and I'll never leave again. Do you hear me?"

"Yes, ma'am," the children said in unison.

"All right," Evelyn said. "Let's get started."

After Helen left and the kitchen had been tidied up, Evelyn sent the boys out to milk the cows. She took Louise upstairs to get her dressed and returned to find Sarah gazing out the window.

"What do you think?" she asked.

"The farm is bigger than I could have imagined," Sarah said. "I could barely make it out last night."

Evelyn joined her by the window.

"Ah," she sighed. "It's a beautiful day. That sun ought to do a good job of melting some more of the snow today. Spring's right around the corner. When the Chinook winds start to blow in from the southeast, they'll melt what remains. Are you ready for a tour?"

"Of course," Sarah said.

"Grab your coat and I'll give you a pair of galoshes to wear. We'll be traipsing through a good bit of mud."

When they stepped outside, Evelyn paused on the porch and took a deep breath. The sky was a clear, deep indigo, and the harsh call from a blue jay cut through the morning silence, accompanied by the distant drumming of woodpeckers hammering on dead trees and the chirping of sparrows on the roof of the house and in the nearby bushes.

"First things first," Evelyn said as she gestured toward the pile of her and Sarah's camp clothes. "I'll get a fire going in the pit over there so we can burn those."

She grabbed a few logs and some kindling from the pile that was stacked on the porch, and Sarah scooped up the pile of clothing. She followed Evelyn to the fire pit, with Louise humming happily between them, one hand clutching Evelyn's pant leg. Evelyn started the fire, and when it finally caught, they added the clothing, one piece at a time.

"Good riddance to these," Evelyn said happily.

"I couldn't agree more," Sarah said.

"Come on," Evelyn said. "Let me show you around."

She took Sarah's hand in one hand and Louise's in the other.

"I don't want you slipping," she said. "There are still some icy patches."

Sarah immediately warmed at the feeling of Evelyn's hand cupped over hers. Evelyn led her away from the house and stopped before they reached the barn.

"That, of course, is the barn," she said. "The cows, horses, and pigs stay in there during the winter. The horses we use for transportation and plowing. The cows provide us with milk, butter, and an occasional batch of ice cream until we take them to the butcher, and the pigs and chickens provide most of our meat."

She led Sarah and Louise to a fenced-in structure on the barn's right side.

"This is the chicken coop," she said. "We check it each morning to collect the eggs and spread the feed. They usually stay outside for a good part of the day, except for during the winter time."

She opened the door to the coop and ushered in Sarah and Louise. A cordon of hens and roosters were gathered near the door, their white heads jauntily cocked. Others were busy eating—clucking and peeping, their heads bobbing as they eagerly picked up kernels. Sarah felt as if she was in a foreign land.

"The main concern with the coop is keeping out the foxes," Evelyn said as they left the structure. "That's what the fence is for, but the foxes have learned how to burrow beneath it."

She gestured to a small building on the right side of the chicken coop.

"That's our smokehouse. We smoke most of our meats to preserve them. Come on. I'll show you the barn. The boys should be just about done milking."

"I don't think Peter is very pleased with my presence," Sarah said.

Evelyn squeezed her hand.

"Give him time," she said. "He's a bit more set in his ways than Karl and Louise and, being the oldest, his father's absence has weighed on him the heaviest."

"I can't imagine," Sarah said.

As they headed toward the barn, a loud, shrill, throaty jumble of sound arose. Sarah jumped slightly and looked at Evelyn, startled. Evelyn laughed.

"Those are the turkeys," she said. "They can usually be found behind the barn, roosting in the trees. They provide a windbreak for them from the drifting snow and winter wind."

"Do you feed them?" Sarah asked.

"We give them some grains when necessary," Evelyn said. "In the winter they eat nuts and whatever fruits they can find. In the spring and summer, they most often feast on buds, grasses, and grasshoppers from the fields."

Sarah looked over the vast plot of land. She had never even wondered what farm life was like before that moment, and she felt overwhelmed.

"What do you grow?" she asked. "How do you make your money?"

She felt naive, unlearned. Everything seemed so intricate and complicated.

"Our main money crop is potatoes," Evelyn said. "They grow well in the large field in the south, where the soil is sandier. We use the two smaller fields on the north side of the land to grow corn for animal feed and wheat for our own uses. There's also a good-sized plot on the other side of the house where we grow the garden. We'll be planting that soon enough. We get a good supply of provisions from that, pretty much everything we need for canning—tomatoes, green beans, corn, squash, lettuce, carrots, all the basic root vegetables."

"I'm good with gardens," Sarah said earnestly.

She didn't want Evelyn to think that she would be useless and more of a burden than a help, though she was unsure of how much help she could actually be, what she might have to contribute.

"Excellent," Evelyn said, nodding. "That will be under your charge, as I'll probably be spending most of my time in the fields with Peter. Tending to the crops was George's primary duty."

"Do you have any help besides the boys?" Sarah asked.

"Only during harvest season," Evelyn said. "Until then hiring hands just isn't cost effective. The plowing will be the most difficult part. I can always get some help from Will if I need it, but he has his own fields to tend to. I should be able to manage with Peter's help."

Sarah followed Evelyn across an expanse of snow to the barn, the thawing snow sinking beneath their feet. The sun was pressing higher into the sky and felt warm on her skin. Except for the occasional animal sound, the farm was quiet and peaceful, and Sarah realized how grateful she was to be away from the logging camp, Sam, and all the gregarious men and their nonstop noise. Evelyn pulled open one of the barn doors. They stepped in and were greeted by a menagerie of sounds—the horses' whinnies; the cows' low, melodic moos; and the pigs' lyric sopranos and tenors. Sarah's eyes took a moment to adjust, the lanterns only dimly lighting the monstrous structure, with slices of light breaking through some slats. The barnyard scents were strong, ripe, but they weren't nauseating—nothing like the stench of all the jacks huddled in the cook shanty. One set of stalls housed the cows, and a stall across from them was home to the horses. In the back of the barn, one large pen corralled the pigs. The sounds of the animals filled the vacuous space.

"As soon as spring arrives and the warm weather settles in, the horses and cows will be sent out to pasture for grazing. At the same time, the large pen on the west side of the barn will transform into the pigpen."

"It's so much to handle," Sarah said.

She wondered if she would be able to stack up to the abundance of work.

"It all comes together somehow," Evelyn said. "How are you boys doing?"

"Good, Ma," Peter said. "We've only got three more to go."

Both of the boys were sitting on stools, each near a cow's left rear side, with silver buckets placed beneath the cows' udders to catch the frothy milk. Peter moved from the cow he'd just finished milking to the next one in line.

"Have you ever seen a cow getting milked?" Evelyn asked Sarah.

"Can't say I have," Sarah said. "I've just always partaken in the outcome."

"Peter, why don't you show Sarah how it's done?" Evelyn said. "She'll probably be helping out some mornings."

"Okay," Peter said.

Sarah edged in cautiously. She had never even really seen a cow close up, and she thought the creature rather lovely in a docile sort of way. The eyes, more than anything, drew her in—the dark, glossy pools framed by thick curling eyelashes.

"You hold the teat like this," Peter said.

He spoke in an authoritative tone. He wrapped the thumb and forefinger of his left hand into a circle around the base of one of the cow's teats and gently squeezed it until a small squirt of milk was released.

"You pinch off the top of the teat with your finger and thumb," Evelyn explained. "That traps the milk in the lower part of the teat. You squeeze that out using your other fingers. The milk will squirt out through the hole on the teat's tip."

"It looks a bit complicated," Sarah said.

"It takes some getting used to, but you'll get the hang of it," Evelyn assured her.

"The first squirt gets rid of any dirt on the teat and lets you check the milk," Peter said. "If the milk is smooth and white, you milk the cow until her udder is empty. You have to milk every teat."

"Fascinating," Sarah said. "Most city folks have no idea of the labor that goes behind the supplies we eat daily. At least I never did."

"When the cows have been milked, we pour most of the milk into those tall metal canisters over there to keep it cool," Peter said.

"Some of the milk goes into the shallow dishes beside the canisters," Evelyn added. "We use that for churning butter. Once the cream rises to the top of the dishes, we skim it off and put it into the churn. It usually takes a good half day or so. Churning is a whole different deal. We'll show you how that's done this afternoon."

"Ma says I'm the best churner in the house," Karl said proudly.

"Perhaps you can teach me," Sarah said.

"Yes, ma'am," Karl said. "I'll show you how to do it right."

"You boys finish up here while I go feed the pigs," Evelyn said.

"Yes, ma'am," the boys replied.

Evelyn left Louise with the boys and led Sarah to the back of the barn. The pigs' snouts and ears were protruding above the pen's top rail as they crowded each other, waiting for food. Evelyn picked up a large scoop, plunged it into one of two wooden barrels beside the fence, and dumped the mess into a trough inside the pen.

"These beasts eat a variety of table scraps, vegetable peelings, whey from the milk, and a mix of ground barley and oats that thicken it up."

"They're a noisy lot," Sarah said.

Evelyn smiled.

"Only when they're hungry," she said. "After they eat they usually don't have much to say."

As Evelyn said, when the pigs were full, they became motionless, except for their flopping ears and wiggling tails.

"Next we tend to the horses," Evelyn said. She led the way back to the horses' stall. "The stallion with the dark maroon coat is Red, our primary plow horse. The gray mare is Smokey, and the brown and white mare is Patches. She's a decent backup for a plow horse, but Smokey's a bit older, and we use her only to pull the wagon. You already know Henry's horse, of course."

Sarah looked at the haggard beast. It would be a constant reminder of the world they had left, the world where they had met. It was also a reminder of Sam. Just as Henry would come back for the horse one day, Sam would come looking for George.

"They're beautiful," Sarah said.

"Hard not to like a horse," said Evelyn.

She lifted the lid of a box and scooped up a pan full of oats, which she dumped into the horses' feedbox at the end of the stall. She picked up a pitchfork and threw some fresh hay into the stall as well. She then went to a small box nailed to the wall, took out a brush and currycomb, and began to comb the horses one by one, working backward from behind the ears until their coats were shining. Sarah watched in awe—so much to do, and she knew there was more, much more. She was amazed by how Evelyn and her children fell into sync with each other immediately upon her return, as if she was never gone. Even with George's absence, Evelyn was clearly capable of holding the farm together.

"This is how the mornings start," Evelyn said. "After these chores are finished, we do whatever cleaning needs to be done in the barn—shoveling up the waste, laying down fresh hay, filling the troughs with water. Before, during the summer, with the boys home from school, they would usually do these chores while I tended to the garden, cleaned, did the laundry, cooked—whatever needed to be done. George would head out to the fields after breakfast and stay there most of the day. Now I'll be going to the fields with Peter while you and Karl do the milking and barn chores. He can help you with the garden, too."

Sarah remained silent for a moment. That seemed like so much to undertake. She had never thought about what farm life might be like, what it entailed. Never would she have envisioned this. No wonder Evelyn held up so well at camp.

Evelyn glanced over at Sarah and saw the same face she had seen a number of times at the logging camp—the panic of being in a realm not her own.

"Are you okay?" she asked.

"I'm just worried that I'll let you down," Sarah said. "That I won't be able to..."

Evelyn rested a hand on her shoulder.

"Everything will work out," she said. "We'll show you what you need to know. You just do what you can. Maybe this life will grow on you. If not, we can figure out something else, something that you might find more suitable."

Evelyn wondered if Sarah would be able to adapt to the farm, and she saddened a bit at the thought that she might not. She liked the idea of having another adult to help her on the farm and with the children, and she had to admit that she cared for Sarah, had grown fond of her, and wanted their friendship to continue.

By the time the morning chores were done, the sun had climbed to perch at its highest point in the sky—noon. Evelyn and Sarah and the children headed back to the house to warm up over a lunch of soup and bread. As Evelyn and Sarah cleared off the table, Evelyn glanced at Louise, who was quickly fading.

"Are you ready for your nap, little Louise?" she asked.

"Yes, Mommy," Louise said.

"I'll lay you down as soon as we're done here," Evelyn said. "I'll read you a story."

Louise grinned and clapped her hands.

"Karl, are you ready to churn the butter?" she asked. "The cream should have risen by now."

"Yes, ma'am," Karl said eagerly. "Can Sarah come?"

Evelyn looked at Sarah.

"I'd be happy to," Sarah said. "I might as well jump right in."

"Okay," Evelyn said. "I'll tend to the chores in here as soon as Louise goes to sleep, and then I'll start making dinner. Peter is going to chop some more wood this afternoon. The pile's running a little low."

Evelyn picked up Louise and headed up the stairs. Sarah and the boys got ready to go outside and headed out the door. Peter grabbed an ax and went to tackle some of the logs stored behind the house, and Sarah followed Karl to the barn. As they walked she looked down at him. He was good-natured and seemed less serious than his older brother.

"Do you like school?" she asked.

"Yes, ma'am," he said exuberantly. "I like math, and I like when we look at the maps."

"What about reading?" Sarah asked. "Do you like to read?"

"I like when other people read to me," Karl said.

Sarah laughed.

"When I go home to pick up my things, I'll bring some books back with me," she said.

"Do you want to leave your house?" Karl asked.

Sarah didn't immediately answer.

"I think I'll like it on the farm, with all of you," she finally said.

When they entered the barn, Karl led the way to the canisters of milk and the large bowls that he and Peter had filled in the morning.

"It's ready," he said as he examined the bowls.

The cream had separated from the milk and risen to the top. Karl got the tall wooden butter churn that sat beside the milk canisters. He skimmed the cream out of the bowls with a shallow saucer and put it in the churn. He put a lid with a hole in its center on the churn and inserted a round wooden stick with cross boards attached to the bottom through the hole. He then got the two stools that he and Peter had used for milking and set them near the churn.

"Now we're ready," he told Sarah. "I'll show you." He rested his hands on the wooden stick that protruded out of the churn. "This is the dasher."

He began to methodically move the dasher up and down as fast as he could, and after nearly half an hour, he looked at Sarah, who was watching intently.

"Do you want to try?" he asked. "My arms are getting tired."

"Of course," Sarah said, and she took hold of the dasher and started the same repetitive motions, up and down, up and down. "How will we know when it's ready?"

"The butter starts to get solid," Karl said. "It takes a long time. That's why it's easier if we take turns."

"I see," Sarah said as she worked the dasher.

"Wait until you taste it," Karl said enthusiastically.

Sarah grinned, and they continued with the churning, each taking turns, until the sunlight slowly began to seep out of the barn. After more than two hours, Karl peeked into the churn.

"It's ready," he proudly pronounced as he removed the lid. "Now we take it out."

He picked up a slender paddle and began to scoop out the butter, which he placed in a clean tin bucket. When all the butter was removed, he grabbed a wooden spoon and pushed down on the butter to separate the buttermilk, which he poured into a metal bowl.

"Ma will use this to make pancakes," he told Sarah.

"Ah, pancakes," Sarah said. "I think they're my favorites."

"Me too," Karl said.

When all the butter and buttermilk was gathered, Karl and Sarah cleaned out the churn and the bowls and then prepared to take their bounty to the house. Karl picked up the bucket of butter, and Sarah carefully balanced the bowl of buttermilk. When they stepped out of the barn, she was surprised to see the sun gradually beginning to sink, a swirling mix of violet-red taking over the sky. *Time does pass quickly on the farm. No time to waste.*

As she and Karl were heading back to the house, they saw Evelyn and Peter near the chicken coop, both with their backs to them. Evelyn raised an ax and swiftly lowered it, and a squawking screech penetrated the air. Evelyn dropped the ax to the ground, and when she and Peter turned around, Sarah saw that she was holding a headless chicken, its dripping blood staining the snow red. Her stomach lurched and she quickly set down the bowl that she was carrying. Before she could stop herself, she bent over and vomited, then dropped to her knees. Evelyn hurried to her side after handing the chicken to Peter. She placed a hand on Sarah's back.

"Sarah, are you okay?"

Sarah wiped her mouth on her coat sleeve.

"I'm fine," she said. "I've just never seen a dead…"

She bent over and vomited again, and Peter, who was now by Evelyn's side, snickered.

"That's enough of that, young man," Evelyn said sternly.

"Yes, ma'am," Peter said as he reddened. "Sorry, Ma."

"It's not me you should be apologizing to," Evelyn said.

Peter lowered his head. "I'm sorry, Sarah," he said.

Finally composing herself, Sarah turned to Peter.

"It's quite all right," she said. "The sight of that chicken sure did startle me, though."

She realized that it would take some time for the children to grow accustomed to her. I'm a stranger to them, she thought. I'll need to tread lightly. I'll need to earn their trust, their respect. The thought was a daunting one. She already felt as if Peter saw her as an intruder.

"Peter, you and Karl take the chicken to the house and start plucking it," Evelyn said.

The two boys walked toward the house, the chicken dangling from Peter's hand. Evelyn grabbed the bucket of butter, and Sarah picked up the bowl of buttermilk. Evelyn pointed ahead to the boys and the chicken.

"Tonight's dinner," she said. "I wanted to cook you something special."

Despite her embarrassment, Sarah smiled.

"I obviously never considered where chicken comes from until just then," she said.

They laughed and headed toward the house.

❖

They feasted well that night on roasted chicken, baked potatoes, pickled green beans, and rolls, and by the time the table was cleaned off and the dishes were done, the darkness of night had descended. Evelyn put the children to bed and went downstairs. Sarah was sitting by the fireplace, sleeping. Evelyn softly shook her by the shoulder. Sarah opened her eyes.

"It's been a long day," Evelyn said. "Let's take the cot upstairs and put some bedding on it so you can get some rest."

"All right," Sarah said. She yawned. "I had no idea I was so tired. The day went by so quickly."

"They always do," Evelyn said. "Come on."

Sarah followed her to the pantry and Evelyn pulled out the cot. They each took one end and carried it up to Evelyn's room.

"We can set it here," Evelyn said.

She pointed to the wall opposite of where the bed stood.

"Looks good to me," Sarah agreed.

They put the cot in place and made it up with sheets, a thick quilt, and a pillow.

"I have this, too," Evelyn said. She held up a coil of thick line and a blanket. "We can run the line across the room and drape this over it. I thought we could both use some privacy."

She stood on a chair and secured one end of the line with a hammer and nail, then moved to the opposite side of the room to secure the other end. As Sarah lifted the curtain to her, she had a sinking feeling. This is it, she thought. She is uncomfortable with me, here with her. The drape will be a separation. Once the curtain is drawn, silence will fall. She wondered if Evelyn thought that she needed the curtain as some symbol of protection from her.

"That should do," Evelyn said when she finished the task. "There's clean water in the basin. I've got a few more things to do downstairs and then I'll be up."

When she reached the door, she paused.

"You made it through your first day on the farm," she said. "What do you think?"

"It's a lot to take in," Sarah said. "Is it like this every day?"

"Pretty much," Evelyn said. "Life on the farm is rather routine, not much room for variation."

"Well, it is an admirable existence," Sarah said.

"I don't know about that, but it's the only life I know," Evelyn said. "Good night, Sarah."

"Good night," said Sarah.

Two days later, after breakfast, as the boys were about to go to the barn to do their chores, Evelyn heard clamoring outside and went to the window. Will pulled up in his wagon with Helen and Jess by his side. She went out onto the porch to greet them.

"Didn't think I'd see you again so soon," she said to Helen as they all got out of the wagon. "Morning, Jess."

"Hi, Evelyn," Jess said. "Welcome back home."

"We came to watch the kids while you and Will take Sarah to fetch her belongings," Helen said.

Evelyn warmed at the sight of Will, with his disheveled brown hair, crooked grin, and long arms hanging by his side. She thought of George. The brothers had been close, and she had always admired their kinship. In some ways she knew George's absence was probably more difficult for him than for her. George had been his only remaining family.

"How are you doing, Will?" she asked.

Will smiled.

"Happy to see you made it home safely," he said. "I hear you brought a guest back with you."

"Yes," Evelyn said. "Her name is Sarah. Come inside so I can introduce you."

"I didn't want to wait too long before coming," Will said as they all followed Evelyn into the house. "The thaw has already started, and soon the roads will be too flooded for travel until the river recedes."

As they entered the house, Sarah was putting away the last of the breakfast dishes and she turned toward them. The children ran to Will, and he gathered them around him with his lanky arms as they laughed and giggled.

"Sarah, this is Will, George's brother, and Helen's housemate, Jess," Evelyn said.

Sarah took in the tall, skinny man. She wondered if he looked like George. She sensed by the way the children took to him that he must be a mild-mannered, kind man. She then looked at the woman standing beside Helen. She was attractive, as petite as Helen was, with long, glossy black hair, so dark it had a purplish hue, and dark brown eyes.

"Pleased to meet you both," Sarah said.

Will grinned and hoisted Louise into the air. "Likewise," he said.

Jess nodded at her and smiled.

"I can't thank you enough for keeping the farm in one piece while I was gone, Will," Evelyn said as she handed him a cup of coffee.

He passed Louise into Helen's arms and took the cup, sipped, and smacked his lips. "My coffee never is as good as yours," he said. "You've got those two boys of yours to thank for keeping the farm going. They did a mighty fine job, stepped right up. Their father would've been pleased."

The boys beamed with pride.

"As am I," Evelyn said.

She gave Peter and Karl each a hug. Sarah warmed at the sight of the scene before her—family. She wondered if she would ever belong.

"Boys, I need you to go get the wagon ready," Evelyn said. "We should get on the road if we're going to make it back in time for dinner. Your aunt and Jess will stay with you while we're gone."

"Yes, ma'am," the boys replied.

"Where are you heading?" Peter asked.

"Pine Creek," Evelyn said. "A small town to the west, probably very similar to Maple Grove."

"Can you bring us back a treat?" Karl asked.

"You do deserve one," Evelyn said. "Sarah, does your Pine Creek have a mercantile store?"

"I recommend the Wileys'," Sarah said. "They have a fine selection of sweets."

"You hear that, boys?" Evelyn said as she pulled on her coat and wrapped a scarf around her neck. "Sounds like you're in luck. Now, go get the wagon ready."

"Okay, Ma," the boys said excitedly and rushed out the door.

The ride to Pine Creek was a quiet and solemn one. Will led the way with his wagon, and Evelyn and Sarah trailed behind. Evelyn occasionally took a side glance at Sarah, wondering what she was feeling about returning home to a place where she could not stay, and what memories the journey must be stirring up of Abigail.

Sarah became more morose as the wagon jolted and rumbled over potholes in the dirt road and focused on the scenery surrounding her. The road from the farm to Pine Creek was a winding one. First, nothing was in sight, and finally a few farm buildings became visible, surrounded by fields waiting to be cultivated, the road flanked with barbed wire fences. Large crows flying overhead, flapping their long black wings, made shadows as they passed by, their hoarse caw-caws breaking the silence. Red-winged blackbirds perched beside potholes that were filled with water from melting snow.

"How do you feel?" Evelyn asked.

"I'm not sure," Sarah said. "I had never thought about not

returning to Pine Creek, even with Abigail gone. It's the only place I've known, the only life I've known, besides the orphanage."

"I know your life there was much different from life on the farm," Evelyn said. "The farm is quite secluded, less social. Do you think you'll be…lonely?"

"Not lonely," Sarah said. "I just… I haven't really had time to adapt to the idea of life without Abigail. After her death, I was in shock, numb. Then I was rushing to prepare for the camp. Everything has been so…surreal. A part of me feels as if I have walked into a dream, and no matter how much I try, I just can't wake."

Evelyn took the reins in one hand and gently placed an arm over Sarah's shoulder.

"Everything takes time," she said. "When I saw Will pull up this morning, all I could think of was George. We must both now partake in different kinds of lives, lives we never expected."

Tears began to trace down Sarah's face and Evelyn's heart sank. She began to doubt that life with her and the children on the farm could ever fulfill Sarah or represent a life that she would want to lead.

When they arrived in town, Sarah straightened in her seat. She felt her chest tighten. Familiar buildings came into view—the small schoolhouse, the blacksmith shop, the mercantile store that she and Abigail had always shopped in, the feed store. Will pulled his wagon over on the side of the road and halted, waiting until Evelyn pulled her wagon up beside his.

"You'll have to lead the way to the house," he told Evelyn.

Evelyn looked at Sarah.

"Will do," she said.

"The house is on the other side of town," Sarah told Evelyn. "Stay on the main road and I'll tell you where to turn."

"Okay," Evelyn said. "Let's go, Smokey."

She took hold of the reins and set the horse into motion. The horse plodded on, and twenty minutes later, with most of the town behind them, Sarah finally spoke.

"Turn down the next road," she said. She released a jagged breath. "It's the fourth house on the right."

"Got it," Evelyn said, and her stomach flipped.

She was anxious about seeing where Sarah once lived with Abigail. She knew that her life on the farm would greatly pale in comparison. Sarah pointed out the house when it came into view, and Evelyn felt that her worries had been substantiated. It was like one of the many houses she had admired whenever she and George traveled to Maple Grove, much like the home Helen shared with Jess. The house was like a quaint cottage, with two front doors, windows flanked by shutters, and a spindled porch that wrapped around the front. She pulled the wagon up to the house and Will followed. They climbed out of the wagons and stood before the house for a moment.

"You two head in and I'll tie up the horses and put down some tarps in the wagons," Will said.

"Are you ready?" Evelyn asked Sarah.

"Yes," she said. Her voice slightly shook. "I think so."

Evelyn followed Sarah into the house and scanned the hallway that led to the parlor. Such a different life, she thought. The floors were finished, polished to a glow, and the walls were covered with decorated paper. The parlor held two stuffed chairs, a rocking chair, a brass standing lamp, a writing desk, and a small woodstove. The dining room nearly took Evelyn's breath away—a cherry-wood cabinet that held pieces of china and glasses, a beautiful round table with four wooden chairs, and a light that hung from the ceiling. The kitchen was twice as big as the one on the farm, and everything in it was shiny and in place, the cupboards and drawers fashioned from unscarred wood. The sink was porcelain, bone white, with no stains or scratches. Beyond the kitchen was the bedroom. Sarah led the way in—lace curtains over the windows, a decorative rug centered on the floor, and a bed that looked like one could melt into it. Everything represented a peace and femininity that was not prevalent on the farm.

Evelyn noticed two photographs hanging over the dresser and

went over to look at them. Sarah, she recognized. The other woman must be Abigail, she thought, as she studied the picture closely. The woman was as beautiful as Sarah was. Evelyn felt, again, like a clumsy oaf in comparison.

"Well, this is it," Sarah said. "This is…was…home."

She sat on the bed, ran a hand over the flowered quilt, and bent over, cradling her head in her hands. Evelyn sat beside her.

"Are you all right?" she asked. "I thought that once you returned you might change your mind about leaving, despite your reservations."

Sarah sat up straight and looked at her.

"I could stay in this house only if I could move it," she said, Her voice quivered. "Trust me, I can't believe that I have to leave this, that I'm losing this because of Sam."

Her eyes began to swell with tears, and Evelyn placed an arm around her.

"I'm sorry," she said. "I'm so sorry. If there was anything else I could do…"

Sarah held back her tears.

"You've already done more than enough," she said. "My life here would have never been the same again anyway without Abigail. Maybe it's time for a change. I can't forever lament over what I no longer have."

"Things take time," Evelyn said. "This is a rather monumental change. You've got reason for lamenting."

Having seen the living that Sarah was accustomed to, Evelyn began to doubt her decision to take her to the farm, but she had no idea what else she could have done.

"Let's get some things together," Sarah finally said. Resilience crept into her voice. "I know Will doesn't have all day to tarry around here. First things first—clothing."

She went to a trunk on the other side of the room and opened it.

"Much of what I need is in here," she said. "The rest is in the closet. I'll try to find my most practical pieces."

"Bring what you are used to wearing," Evelyn said. "There's no need for you to change every aspect of your life. What about furniture, or trinkets? I'm sure you must treasure many of the things here."

"I hadn't planned on… The farmhouse doesn't have much free space."

"What we can't find a place for in the house we can store in the barn," Evelyn said. "I want you to bring as much of your life with you as you can. I want my home to feel like your home, too, for as long as you're there."

"I'll go through the clothing," Sarah said. "You could see what we might need from the kitchen. Baking is my forte, so we should take my baking pans and utensils, and there might be a few pots or pans that we can use. Also, I know you like to read, so you should go through the bookcase and pick out some books."

"All right," Evelyn said.

She left the room and went to the kitchen. She heard the front door swing open.

"I'm in the back, Will," she called out.

He entered the room, balancing empty wooden crates in his arms.

"There are more crates on the porch if you need them," he said. He set them down and shifted from foot to foot, looking about. "I think I'll ride into town while you two sort through things here. I reckon it'll be hard on her, leaving this place. I'll be back in a few hours to help load up the heavy stuff."

"Thanks, Will," Evelyn said.

She knew he wanted to avoid any emotional outbursts that might ensue. Evelyn continued to go through cupboards and drawers. She felt strange, rummaging through Sarah's and Abigail's belongings, and a wave of empathy overtook her. Compared to this house, the standard that Sarah was accustomed to, everything on the farm was so rustic, raw and unfinished. That is my norm, Evelyn thought, as she placed items that Sarah might need for baking on the table, along with a few other assorted pieces of cookware. When she finished she returned to the bedroom, where she found Sarah folding a few last pieces of clothing and placing them in a trunk.

"Can I help with anything?" Evelyn asked.

"Those blankets and quilts can go in a crate," Sarah said. "I've no doubt we can use them on the farm. All the clothes I need are in the trunk."

"What else do you want to take?" Evelyn asked. "What about furniture?"

"I don't really want much," Sarah said. "We could take the chairs from the parlor, and I'd like to take the rocker. It's my favorite reading chair. I already put a few keepsakes in the trunk. Just some…memories. I packed my old checkerboard, too, so I can teach the children how to play. It was the one game I took with me when I was sent to the orphanage."

"You've had to leave so much behind," Evelyn said.

Silence descended over the room like a shadow, Sarah slowly, sorrowfully, accepting that she had, again, been delivered to a life of transience.

When Will returned, they had already moved the filled crates onto the porch, as well as the chairs and rocker from the parlor. Will helped them move the dining room table and accompanying chairs, which they had finally decided would make a fine addition to the farmhouse. They tied everything down and climbed into the wagons, and as they started to make their way down the street, out of town, Sarah took one last glance back, and then turned to find Evelyn looking at her pensively.

"Everything will be fine," Sarah told her. "I'm ready to begin again. We need to make one last stop in town so I can withdraw the money Abigail and I have in the bank. Otherwise, it'll end up in Sam's hands."

"All right," Evelyn said. "In the meantime, I'll pick up some treats for the children."

By the time they made it back to the farm and unloaded the crates and the furniture, the purplish bruising of dusk filled the sky. Will left with Helen and Jess to return them to town and then head back to his farm. Inside, Evelyn, Sarah, and the children gathered around the table for the dinner that Helen and Jess had prepared, and Evelyn opened a bottle of dandelion wine that she had made the summer before. She poured her and Sarah a glass, and then raised her glass in the air.

"A toast," she said to the children and Sarah. "Now that it's official, let's welcome Sarah home."

The children, even Peter, raised their cups of milk, and they sang out in unison, "Welcome home, Sarah."

Sarah didn't yet feel the home as hers, but she felt embraced in the moment.

That night when Evelyn went upstairs, Sarah was still awake, reading. Evelyn drew the curtain across the room and got ready for bed. She dimmed the kerosene lamp until darkness filtered into the room.

"You must think me so weak," Sarah said.

She put down her book.

"Why would you say that?" Evelyn asked.

"You don't think me dependent, unable to forge my own way?" Sarah said. "First, Abigail took me in, and now you. I've never really been on my own."

"Neither have I," Evelyn said. "George and I married only a few months after my father passed away. We all find our own way to manage our lives, to survive. Sometimes it seems as if a path is already laid out before us. I don't fault anyone for the path that he or she takes, except maybe a few of those stinky jacks!"

Sarah laughed.

"Good night, Evelyn," she said.

"Good night," said Evelyn.

Her last thought was that everything was as it should be.

CHAPTER ELEVEN

The last weeks of March slowly eked by, and the weather shifted from winter to spring in bursts. Evelyn and Sarah found their rhythm running the farm together and caring for the children. Sarah took over the bulk of the cooking and baking, and Evelyn oversaw the livestock and the constant maintenance of the barn and the house. Something always needed to be done—a fence to repair, a loose board to nail down, supplies to replenish. In the mornings, the focus was on the animals, and the remaining chores consumed the afternoons. Evenings were the time when they all settled in together. When dinner was over they often huddled in the sitting room, where Evelyn and Sarah mended clothes or read to the children. Some nights, with the children finally in bed, Evelyn and Sarah would sit on the porch and watch as the stars dotted the sky with sprinkles of blinking light.

The days were long ones for the children, as they anxiously waited for the full-fledged days of spring and summer to arrive with more time to play outside, go fishing, romp through the surrounding woods, or swim in the river and pond. Evelyn and Sarah sat outside one night after a day of intermittent rain.

The boys had argued with each other over every little thing all day. At one point, Peter had attempted to fix a fishing pole with its line tangled in the reel. Karl had been playing with the various flies and dropped one through a crack in the wooden floor. Peter had exploded.

"See what you did, Karl? It's gone now. That was one of Pa's favorites."

He had stomped out of the room as Karl began to cry. Remembering the scene, Evelyn glanced at Sarah.

"I'm sorry about the boys' behavior today," she said.

"It's to be expected," Sarah said. "They've been cooped up inside all winter."

"Do they overwhelm you?"

"The children?" Sarah said. "Goodness, no. They're good children. They bring life to the house."

"I just wondered," Evelyn said. "You're not used to having children around."

"No," Sarah said. "I do enjoy them, though. When I was with Abigail, I visited the orphanage that I grew up in every weekend to take the children clothing or go with them on outings."

"You did?" Evelyn said. "That was kind."

"They say one should never forget where he or she comes from," Sarah said. "Those children need all the love they can get, and the staff is always short on help."

"My children seem to be settling in with you," Evelyn said.

"Well, I've still got my work cut out for me in regard to Peter," Sarah said.

"He'll come around," Evelyn told her. "He's already letting down his guard."

"I know," Sarah said. "I'm in no rush."

She knew the children needed time to adapt. But she felt differently when it came to Evelyn. No part of Sarah could envision a life without intimacy, passion, and she wondered if Evelyn would ever realize that, or feel the same way.

"What was your life like with George?" she asked.

"Pretty much like it is now, except I'll be working the fields this season," Evelyn said. "Other than that, the routine is the same. As you know by now, farming doesn't leave much room for variation."

"What was George like?"

Evelyn sat quietly for a moment, thinking.

"He was a kind, gentle man," she said. "The farm meant

everything to him, and he loved the children. He never laid a hand on me or them."

"I'm glad you weren't with a brute," Sarah said.

"I never would have wanted children if I had been with a bad man," Evelyn said. "I got the luck of the draw."

"Was he handsome?" Sarah asked.

She had never seen even a picture of George. Evelyn sat quietly, pondering the question.

"He had his attractive qualities," she finally said. "Not that it really mattered. Our physical interactions were more about the means to an end than any attraction to each other. We both wanted children."

"I see," Sarah said.

She looked at Evelyn. I guess you can't miss what you never had, she thought. Her relationship with Abigail had been so different, their intimacy fueled by desire.

The next morning, just as their breakfast was coming to an end, Evelyn heard some noise outside and went to the window.

"We have company," she said.

She watched as a wagon with two men pulled up near the house.

"Keep the children inside while I see who it is," she told Sarah.

As she stepped outside and approached the wagon, she recognized one of the passengers—Henry Jankowski. Forgetting that he had known her only as George, she addressed him.

"Henry," she said.

"Yes," Henry said.

A puzzled look crossed over his face as he crawled down from the wagon. He looked at Evelyn with no sign of recognition.

"I reckon you've come for your horse," Evelyn said.

Henry scratched his head and peered at her. Evelyn stepped closer to him.

"I'm Evelyn," she said. "At the camp I was George…George Bauer."

"You were George?" Henry said. "What do you mean?"

"When I was at the camp I was disguised as my husband, George," Evelyn said. "He had passed away last autumn, and that was the only way they would let me work at the camp."

Henry looked at her closely. Her hair had grown, and she had the physical attributes of a woman.

"Well, I'll be," he said. He sounded unconvinced. "I never would've guessed."

The front door creaked opened and Sarah stepped out.

"You remember Sarah, one of the flunkies, don't you?" Evelyn asked.

"Her I recognize," Henry said. "Sam was mad as a bull when he finally came to after the fight, said he'd spend the rest of his days tracking down both of you. He was like a rabid dog. He almost took off Johnny's head for letting you go. The other jacks, except for Poker Pete and his pals, sided with Johnny, though, so Sam backed down."

Evelyn and Sarah looked at each other.

"We've been expecting both you and Sam, though I'm awfully glad you showed up first," Evelyn said. "I was wondering when the camp would close for the season."

"We finished up about a week and a half ago," Henry said. "This is the first chance I had to come for the horse."

"Peter, come out here," Evelyn called out.

Peter stepped out of the house, with Karl and Louise following behind him.

"This is one of the jacks from the lumber camp," Evelyn said. "His name is Henry. Henry, these are my children."

The children looked at him in awe.

"Go get Henrietta out of the barn, Peter," Evelyn said. "Henry's ready to take her home."

"Henrietta?" Henry said with a smile.

"Never did know the horse's name," Evelyn said.

"Lady," Henry said. "Her name is Lady."

"Peter will fetch her for you," Evelyn said. "Would you and your friend like a cup of coffee?"

"Almost forgot he was with me," Henry said sheepishly. "This is my brother Joseph. Want a cup of coffee, Joe?"

"I'm good," his brother said. "But thanks for offering, ma'am."

"We can't stay," Henry said, unable to keep his eyes off Evelyn. "We dropped our mother off in Maple Grove so she could buy some supplies. I still can't believe you were George."

"I'm glad the disguise was a success," Evelyn said.

Henry smiled.

"Sam will be confused as hell when he comes looking for George," he said.

Evelyn looked at Sarah.

"I guess we'll deal with that day when it arrives," she said.

Peter returned from the barn with Henry's horse, and Henry ran his hands over the animal.

"I'm surprised she's still standing," he said.

"She got us home safely," Evelyn said. "I can't thank you enough for that."

"It's only fair," Henry said. "You treated me better than anyone else up at that camp."

Henry tied the horse to the rear of the wagon and then walked over to Evelyn.

"I guess this is good-bye," he said. "I don't imagine our paths will cross again."

"Not at that camp, they won't," Evelyn said. "Take care of yourself, Henry."

"It's nice to have met you...Evelyn," Henry said.

He held out his hand and Evelyn firmly shook it. She and Sarah watched in silence as he climbed back into the wagon and he and his brother headed down the road, a cloud of dust trailing behind them.

"I guess we should be expecting a visit from Sam sometime soon," Evelyn said.

Sarah recoiled at the thought of seeing him again.

"What should we do?" she asked.

"Keep the guns loaded," Evelyn said matter-of-factly.

"Oh," Sarah said in surprise.

"Just in case," Evelyn said.

"Of course," said Sarah.

She knew that Evelyn would do anything to protect her children and the farm, even her.

"Come on, children," Evelyn said.

The children ran to her and they all went back into the house.

❖

During the last week of March, the days began to warm a bit, and by the second week of April, one could hear the sap from the maple trees dripping into the buckets that were in place beneath the spigots tapped into the trees. The snow was nearly gone, and only a few drifts that had blown in on the shaded sides of some buildings and trees remained. Geese flew over in large formations, returning from their winter getaways, their honking echoing across the sky. The spring was arriving gently and casually, with the frost leaving the ground and the first shoots of green grass beginning to appear through the brown growth of the preceding year. The children were out of school, ready to help on the farm for the spring and summer, and Evelyn had already made the trip to town to buy the seeds she planned on sowing that season.

"The ground has finally thawed," she announced one morning at breakfast. "Peter and I will start to plow the fields today."

"Does that mean I can break ground in the garden?" Sarah asked.

"Sure does," Evelyn said. "You'll find everything you need in the small tool shed near the barn. Louise, do you want to help Sarah with the garden?"

"Yes," Louise said.

She clapped her hands.

"You don't mind the company?" Evelyn asked Sarah.

"Not at all," Sarah said.

She took one of Louise's hands.

"What do you want me to do?" Karl asked.

"You can start to collect the maple syrup," Evelyn said. "Do you remember where you and Peter tapped the trees with your uncle?"

"Yes, ma'am," Karl said earnestly.

"Make sure you come back home when Sarah rings the lunch bell. No dawdling."

"I will," he said.

Evelyn looked at Sarah.

"Peter and I will take some lunch with us and return in the early evening for dinner," she said.

Sarah nodded and took a deep breath. *This day will be a test. Can I pull my own weight?*

When breakfast was over and everything was cleaned up and put in its place, everyone headed in different directions. Karl gathered the buckets he would need out of the root cellar and took off for the woods. Evelyn and Peter went to the barn to prepare Red for a day of plowing. Sarah helped Louise put on a light jacket and gave her a wicker basket filled with packets of seeds to carry. They went to the tool shed, and Sarah took out a hoe, a spade, a trowel, and a pair of work gloves.

In the barn, Evelyn put a collar on Red and attached some straps to the harness, adjusting them so they would fit the collar. She fastened the traces to them and put the surcingle around the horse, attaching a fastening to the traces to keep them from sagging. After that, she took the bit and made a bridle of the halter by fastening it with a couple of snaps and attached the reins.

"Does it look right?" she asked Peter.

He inspected the rig.

"Yes, ma'am," he said.

"We're ready, then," Evelyn said. "I'm going to go tell Sarah the layout for the garden, and then we can get started."

"Okay," Peter said.

Evelyn left him in the barn and went to join Sarah and Louise at the garden plot. Sarah was sorting through the packets of seeds, and she looked up as Evelyn approached.

"I forgot to tell you the layout for the garden," Evelyn said.

"The layout?"

"You have to put the plants where they'll flourish the most," Evelyn explained. "The tomatoes need to go in the western corner, where they'll get the most sunlight. The string beans will grow up along that trellis on the east side, and the greens do well in this patch here."

"You don't think I know what I'm doing?" Sarah asked.

Evelyn looked at her, startled. *Am I being too bossy? Am I treating her like a child?*

"I just know how it needs to be done," she said. "We depend on the garden for most of our food."

"I know, but where do the flowers go?" Sarah asked.

Evelyn almost laughed, thinking Sarah was kidding, but she stopped herself. Sarah was serious.

"The flowers?"

"A home needs food and flowers, Evelyn," Sarah said.

"Of course," said Evelyn.

That never would have crossed my mind, she thought, scanning the garden for a place to plant the flowers.

"The flowers would do well here," she told Sarah.

Sarah became flushed.

"You don't think it's silly, do you?" she asked.

"No," Evelyn said. "Not at all."

Sarah released a quiet sigh of relief.

"I'm ready, then," she said.

"I'll see you at the end of the day," Evelyn said as she turned to go join Peter.

❖

"Let's get this plow on now," Evelyn told Peter when she returned to the barn.

Peter helped her maneuver the plow into place, and with the ends of the reins tied together, Evelyn passed them over her right shoulder, crossing her back and under her left arm, so that her hands were free to guide the handles of the plow. She was truly stepping into George's shoes. They exited the barn and headed to the field where they would plant the potatoes. Evelyn set the plow upright, lifted the handles to allow the point of the share to enter the ground, and then gave Red the command to move forward. Peter followed closely behind her, using a harrow to work the soil that the last of the snow had left moistened. They moved down the plot until they reached the end, and then Evelyn stopped Red and bore down on the plow's handles to pull it out of the sod so she could turn Red around and begin a furrow in the opposite direction. By the time a quarter of the field was plowed, it was lunchtime. Evelyn and Peter fetched their lunch bucket and sat beneath a tree.

"After lunch you can take the plow," Evelyn said as she handed Peter a sandwich and an apple.

"Yes, ma'am," he said.

As they ate a soft breeze blew. The only noise was the sound of the insects whirring and buzzing by.

"How do you feel these days about Sarah being with us?" Evelyn asked.

He finished chewing and gulped.

"I didn't like it at first, but I guess it's all right," he said begrudgingly. "She's a good baker."

"She does know how to bake," Evelyn agreed. "I'm happy she's here. I can't run the farm and take care of you and your brother and sister on my own."

"I know," Peter said. "I just wish... I miss Pa."

Evelyn hugged him close to her.

"I know that," she said. "We all do. Sarah isn't here to replace him, you know. No one can replace your father. Just give her a chance. This is all new to her, too."

"Yes, ma'am," Peter said.

Evelyn ran a hand through his hair.

"You look more like your father every day," she said. "You ready to take up that plow?"

"Sure am," Peter said.

They set aside the lunch bucket and rose to return to Red, who was grazing in the grass.

❖

Sarah finished turning the soil in the large garden plot, with Louise trailing behind her, and stood back to admire her work. The dirt looked dark and fertile. She glanced up at the sky, the sun climbing to its noonday high.

"We should probably take a break and get some lunch together," she said to Louise. "Are you hungry?"

"Yes," Louise said.

Sarah set her tools aside, and as she took Louise's hand, she heard screaming coming from the woods.

"Karl!" Louise said.

"I hear him," Sarah answered.

She hoisted up Louise and ran toward Karl's voice, grateful that Evelyn had given her a thorough tour of the land beyond the house and barn.

"He's back by the pond," she said, mainly to herself. Panic crawled into her voice. "I hope he didn't try to cross it."

When she pushed through the woods into a small clearing, the pond came into view and she spotted Karl, frantically flailing in the murky waters, thin sheets of ice engulfing him.

"Damn it!" she said.

She put Louise down and looked around for something, anything that she could use to reach Karl. She found a long tree branch that would suffice and bent down until she was at eye level with Louise.

"Louise, I have to help Karl," she said. "I need you to stay right here and hug this little tree until Karl and I get back. Don't let go. Just hold on to the tree. Okay?"

She took Louise's little arms and placed them around the trunk of a slender birch tree.

"Do you understand?" she asked. "Hold on tight."

"I will," Louise said as she began to cry. "Karl! Karl!"

"Just hold on!" Sarah said. "I'll get Karl!"

She grabbed the branch off the ground and ran toward the pond and Karl. She plunged in and immediately lost her breath. The water was bone chilling, and her wet dress and undergarments felt like an anchor, weighing her down. Still, she pushed forward steadily. Karl was fighting even more frantically as she moved toward him, then he sank below the surface and popped back up, choking and wheezing, trying to catch his breath.

"Karl!" Sarah shouted. "Grab the branch, Karl!"

She extended the branch until it was less than an arm's length away from Karl, while trying to maintain her balance and planting her feet on the muddy bottom of the pond.

"Karl!" she shouted again. "The branch!"

Karl finally locked his eyes onto hers, stretched his arms out, and latched onto the branch. Sarah slowly and steadily pulled him toward her. She didn't want him to lose his grip.

"Hold on," she called out. "Hold on."

When Karl was close enough for her to reach him, Sarah released the branch, grabbed him under his armpits, and pulled him to her. She lifted him up, his body shivering uncontrollably, and painstakingly trudged out of the pond as the remaining sheets of ice broke around her. When she stepped out of the pond, they both fell to the ground, trying to catch their breath. Sarah eventually stood and gathered Karl into her arms. He was crying, choking in jagged breaths of air. Louise ran to them and flung herself against Sarah.

"Grab on to my dress, Louise," she said. "Hold on tight. We need to get to the house as fast as we can."

She felt Louise against her and started to walk as quickly as she could, pushing past bushes and trees and making sure that Louise was still by her side. The weight of Karl slowed Sarah down, and when the house finally came into view, she sighed with relief.

"We're almost there, Karl, just a little ways to go," she said.

When they reached the house and went inside, she sat him down on the bench in the sitting area, put Louise beside him, and ran upstairs to grab the blankets off her and Evelyn's beds. She stood Karl up, removed his wet clothing, and wrapped a blanket around him. She started a fire in the fireplace, wrapped the other blanket around herself, and sat beside Karl, pulling him close to her, hoping that the warmth of the fire and her own body heat would eventually suck the cold out of him.

After nearly an hour had passed and Karl had calmed down, his small body pulling in the heat from the fire, Sarah stood up.

"You two stay put," she said. "I'm going to put on some dry clothes, and then I'll warm up some soup for all of us."

Karl and Louise huddled next to each other, and Sarah went upstairs and quickly changed. When she returned downstairs, she went down to the root cellar and found the jar with the leftover soup from the night before. She put the soup in a pot and set it on the stove. By the time she had served herself and the children their late lunch and cleaned up the kitchen, the sun was lowering in the sky.

Sarah sat with Karl and Louise near the fireplace. She felt anxious as she waited for Evelyn and Peter to return from the fields, as she feared that Evelyn might blame her for the incident and find her inadequate. Of course this would happen on my watch, she thought.

"It's warm as a hothouse in here," Evelyn called out when she and Peter finally entered the house. "What's going on in here?"

"We're in the living room," Sarah answered. "We had an accident."

"An accident?" Evelyn said as she stepped into the room with Peter behind her.

When she saw Karl, she rushed over to him and looked at Sarah.

"He tried to cross the pond," she said. "Louise and I heard him screaming for help."

Evelyn sat beside Karl and wrapped her arms around him as he began to sob against her. Peter sat on the floor with Louise by his side.

"I am so glad you're okay," Evelyn said to Karl.

"I'm so sorry," Sarah said.

"You saved him," Evelyn said. "If you hadn't been here, he would've had to fend for himself. Who knows what might have happened."

Sarah dropped her head.

"It's true," Peter said.

Sarah glanced at him. She could tell from the look on his face that, though he wasn't particularly happy about it, it was indeed the truth.

"It's just fortunate that you were still in the garden," Evelyn said. "If you had been in the house, you never would have heard his screams."

With that, Karl started to sob again.

Evelyn took one of Sarah's hands in her own and squeezed it.

"Thank you," she said.

"I'm just relieved that I made it to him in time," Sarah said.

When they all gathered for dinner that evening, the mood was joyous. Everyone was happy that Karl was safe. Bowls were passed around the table and the kerosene lamp flickered over the room.

"I imagine it was pretty scary when you fell into that pond," Evelyn said to Karl.

"It sure was, Ma," he said. "I got stuck, and there was so much ice."

"You know you shouldn't have crossed, Karl," Peter said.

"I know, but it looked solid," Karl said defensively.

"The lakes and ponds are deceptive this time of year," Evelyn gently said.

Karl lowered his eyes.

"Yes, ma'am," he said.

"It's a good thing Sarah knew how to save you," Peter said earnestly.

Sarah looked up from her plate. For the first time, she felt as if she might have a chance with Peter, that he might eventually accept her presence on the farm. She had finally done something to prove herself worthwhile.

After the children went to bed that evening, Evelyn and Sarah sat on the porch with cups of coffee. They sat silently, the sonorous hooting of an owl in a tree on the edge of the woods filling the air.

"I feel terrible about what happened today," Sarah said.

"Why?" Evelyn asked.

"I should have kept an eye on Karl, checked on him at some point," Sarah said.

"Can't be in two places at one time," Evelyn told her. "The important thing is that he's all right. The day could have taken a dreadful turn."

Their eyes locked, and Sarah yearned to lean over and softly place her lips on Evelyn's, but she was frozen in place. Eventually, she told Evelyn good night and retreated to the house.

Damn it. At some point I must be able to cross this bridge, tell her how I feel.

❖

Two weeks later, after the fields had finally been plowed, torrential rains began to fall. The children busied themselves in the barn and in the house, and Evelyn and Sarah focused on various tasks—sorting through the root cellar and pantry, doing some minor household repairs, and cleaning away the dust and grime that had gathered over the winter. On the third day of rain, Evelyn traveled into town for supplies, and Sarah stayed with the children, trying her best to keep them occupied. They were growing more restless with each passing day. She put Louise down for her nap and returned downstairs to find Peter and Karl playing a game of cards on the kitchen table.

"Come on, boys," she said as she took bowls and baking sheets out of the cupboard. "You can help me bake while we wait for the rain to stop."

Peter reared up. "Baking is for girls," he said.

Sarah chuckled.

"That's nonsense, especially in this house," she said. "You know how it goes here. Everyone pitches in."

"That's right," Karl said. "And after this chore, we at least get a reward."

Sarah looked at Peter. Karl had bonded with her since the

incident at the pond, but Peter continued to resist, though less adamantly than before.

"What do you say?"

He shrugged.

"I guess, but only until the rain stops. I've got fishing to do," he said.

He glanced out the window, the rain still streaming down.

"What are we going to make?" Karl asked.

"We're going to roll out some sweetened dough and make fruit pastries," Sarah said. "I'll show you."

She sprinkled flour on a wooden board and spread it about. She then took a ball of dough and began to flatten it with a rolling pin.

"Peter, can you get the pot that's simmering on the stove?" she asked.

"Okay," Peter said.

When he returned with the pot, Sarah took it from him and stirred it.

"What's that?" Karl asked.

"This is our filling," Sarah said. "It's just some stewed apples with a bit of sugar and cinnamon."

"It smells good," Peter said.

"Tastes even better," said Sarah. "Now the fun part begins."

She cut the flattened dough into small squares and gave each boy a spoon.

"Put a generous dab of stewed apples in the center of a square, cover it with another square, and pinch the four corners together like this," she said. "Then brush each one with butter and sprinkle it with sugar. Once we have a sheet full, they'll go in the stove until they're golden brown."

She showed them how to do the first one, and they followed suit, filling the baking sheet in no time. Sarah placed the sheet in the stove's potbelly and poured glasses of lemonade for the boys.

"They'll take about twenty minutes or so," she said.

They sat at the table and watched the rain fall. The water traced down the windows, and the sound resounded off the roof.

"It's coming down pretty steady," Peter said. "Bad for fishing, but good for the crops."

"And the garden," Sarah added.

"Did you have a garden at your house?" Karl asked.

"Yes, but it wasn't nearly as big as this one, and I grew mostly flowers," Sarah said.

"Why can't you go back?" Karl asked.

"My friend who I lived with passed away, like your father," Sarah said. "The house was hers."

"Why don't you go back to your ma and pa?" Karl asked.

"I don't have parents anymore," Sarah said. "They've both been dead since I was little. I grew up in an orphanage."

"You did?" asked Peter, sinking in his seat. "Didn't you have anywhere else to go? Didn't anyone else want you?"

"I didn't have any other family," Sarah said. "I don't have any aunts or uncles. Not like your Aunt Helen and Uncle Will."

"Then you need a home," Karl said emphatically.

"I do," said Sarah.

Peter nodded in agreement. Sarah checked on the pastries, then removed them from the stove and placed them on a platter.

"You boys can fill up the baking sheet again, and I'll go check on Louise before I go down to the root cellar and gather some things for dinner," she said.

"Okay," Peter and Karl said.

As Sarah headed up the stairs, she paused on the steps for a moment and glanced at the boys, focused on their pastries. They were good children, and they were definitely growing on her. They were, after all, Evelyn's.

When Evelyn returned from town, the rain had just begun to lighten up, and the boys ran out to greet her and help her unload the provisions from the back of the wagon. They entered the house with crates of goods and wiped their feet on the mat near the door. Evelyn took a deep breath.

"Smells mighty good in here," she said.

"We helped Sarah bake," Karl said. "We made pastries."

"Is that so?" Evelyn said. She glanced at Peter.

"That's right," Peter said, almost proudly. "Sarah taught us."

Evelyn had noted a slight shift in his disposition since the day Sarah rescued Karl. She looked at Sarah, who smiled and turned away. Evelyn had watched Sarah's relationship with her children evolve since the day she had arrived on the farm with her. Peter had been rather territorial when it came to the farm, not sure about having a stranger around, and he was less than pleased with Sarah's presence, though he had recently begun to warm up to her a bit. Louise had taken a liking to her nearly right away, which hadn't surprised her. Sarah was warm and affectionate, when she thought it was welcome, and Louise was a little girl who loved to cuddle and snuggle. Karl was becoming attached to her, too, their friendship sealed when she pulled him out of the pond. He loved when Sarah read to them, and when she joined him in churning the butter. That was his time. It makes him feel special, Evelyn thought. They were slowly becoming a cohesive unit, and together Evelyn knew that she, Sarah, and the children could keep the farm going. That gave her hope, but the same doubt constantly nagged her. *Is Sarah truly happy on the farm? Would she want to stay?*

Two days later, the clouds finally parted and the glaring sun pulsed through. Business on the farm went back to usual. Evelyn and Peter continued with the plowing, while Sarah, Karl, and Louise worked in the garden and tended to the chores in the barn and the house. Evelyn and Peter returned from the fields early one afternoon so Evelyn could fix a loose horseshoe on Red. Evelyn led the horse to the barn, and Peter went into the house to join Karl and Louise, who were peeling potatoes for the evening meal. Sarah had already taken the washtub outside and filled it with water and was doing the laundry, vigorously rubbing each piece of clothing over the washboard.

As she was hanging the clothes up to dry, she heard the faraway whinnying of a horse and looked to see someone heading down the road, toward the farm—a big man with short-cropped hair. He wasn't anyone Sarah knew, and thinking it was someone coming to see Evelyn, perhaps someone to help her with the horse, she turned her attention back to the laundry. When she reached down to take the last piece of clothing out of the basket, she glanced down the road again. This time the person on the horse was close enough to identify, and Sarah's heart nearly stopped—Sam. He had cut his long hair and looked like a different man. Her chest tightened. Before she could move or call out for help, Sam reined in his horse, stopping about twenty feet from her. He removed his rifle from the carrier on the side of the saddle.

"So this is where you ran off to," he said gruffly, cradling the rifle in his arms. "To lay your head next to that farmer's."

Sarah stiffened.

"Things aren't as they appear, Sam," she said.

"They seem mighty clear to me," Sam said.

❖

In the barn, Evelyn picked up Red's hoof with the loose horseshoe and rested it on her thigh. She picked up a pair of nippers and began to clip the clinches where they were bent on the outside of the hoof wall. Then, realizing that she might need Peter's help to pull off the shoe, she put down the nippers. As she was about to head out of the barn, she heard voices, Sarah speaking to someone, and she looked out the partially opened door. She saw it was Sam. *I knew he'd show up. I guess today's the day.* She quickly stepped back into the barn and took down a rifle from the rack hanging on the wall. She took a deep breath and stepped out of the barn, into the sunlight.

"Where can I find that farmer of yours?" Sam asked Sarah. "I've got a bone to pick with him, if you recall. Bauer's a fool if he thought I would forget what he did. Took me a week to recover from that blow to the head."

"He's not here," Sarah said. "He's never been here. You don't understand…"

Sam got off his horse and stood before her, the rifle still in his arms. Evelyn hurried toward him and Sarah, and when she was close enough to see Sam clearly, she slowed her pace and raised her rifle.

"Oh, I think I understand," Sam said.

He edged in toward Sarah.

"I'd stop right there if I was you," Evelyn said, her voice slightly quivering.

Sam looked at her and stopped moving.

"I've got a right to be here," he said. "I'm looking for a man named Bauer—George Bauer. When I find him, I'll leave."

"There's no George here anymore," Evelyn said. "It's just me, her, and my kids. George passed away last fall, near the end of the harvest season."

Sam trained his eyes on Evelyn. She took a deep breath, wondering when he would finally notice her, but he showed no sign of recognition. He obviously could not stretch his imagination far enough to envision her as the man he had known as George Bauer. She had her hair down and was wearing a blouse with her trousers.

"That right," Sam said, his words carrying his disbelief. "We had a man named Bauer came to work at the logging camp this last winter. He said he had a farm in these parts, and I've got some business to settle with him. Is there another George Bauer nearby?"

Sam's eyes darted back and forth, from Evelyn to Sarah. Evelyn could tell by the look on his face that he was becoming irritated.

"You don't understand," she said. "There was no George at the camp, no real George. I was George."

"What are you talking about?" Sam asked.

He took another step toward Sarah, and Evelyn focused her rifle on him.

"George was my husband," she said. "He died late last September. The farm hadn't been doing well, and I needed the money. I went to the camp disguised as George. That was the only way I could get the work I needed. I was George."

Sam stared at Evelyn, his eyebrows knitting together.

"I don't know what you're talking about," he said.

His eyes settled on her chest.

"I cut my hair and bound my breasts so I could pass as a man," Evelyn said. "My name is Evelyn—Evelyn Bauer. George is buried in the back, behind the house."

Sam looked at Sarah.

"She's telling you the truth," Sarah said. "I didn't discover that she was really a woman until we had been at the camp for a couple of months. I found out by accident."

For a moment, they stood in silence, and then Sam glared at Evelyn.

"So you're the one who…?"

He rubbed his hand over his head and shifted his feet.

"You didn't leave me much choice," Evelyn said.

"You could have stuck to your own business," Sam snarled.

"That never entered my mind," Evelyn said.

She stepped closer to Sam and raised her rifle a bit higher. She feared he wouldn't back down. She then saw him move his gaze to something, and she quickly glanced back. Peter wasn't far behind her, his rifle trained on Sam, also. Sam was outgunned.

"You'll always be outnumbered here," Evelyn said. "If it's not me and one of my boys, it'll be me and my brother-in-law. My sister's a damn good shot, too."

There was silence again, and then Sam focused on Sarah as he lowered his rifle a bit.

"Abigail always did say that liquor got the best of me," he said. "She said it could turn any man into a devil. It was never my intention to…"

Sarah didn't look away from Sam. She stared at him without fear, unwavering.

"You tried to rape me," she said.

Sam dropped his head, loosened his grip on his rifle, and finally lowered it to his side.

"I don't even remember that night," he said. "I didn't…I reckon I was a bit out of my mind."

He stopped talking. His face looked blank, and he shifted his feet again.

"I haven't done anything to the house," he said to Sarah. "I wasn't really sure where you had gone. If you want to return there, you'll have no problems from me."

Evelyn looked at Sarah. *Does she want to go? Maybe it would be best.*

"I would be a fool to trust you," Sarah said, her voice strong with resolve. "This is home to me now. That house would only taunt me with Abigail's absence, and Evelyn needs my help here."

"I see," Sam said.

He glanced around the farm.

"If you ever change your mind," he said.

"I don't foresee that happening, Sam," Sarah said.

"Well, I should probably head back, then," Sam said. "That boy doesn't seem to be taking too kindly to my being here."

"He's just protecting his home," she told Sam. "Like I said, you'll always be outnumbered here."

He nodded and slowly moved to his horse. When he reached it, he mounted it and put his rifle back in its carrier.

"Guess that's it, then," he said.

He grabbed the reins and prodded his horse into motion. Evelyn and Sarah watched silently until the horse and Sam disappeared around the curve in the road. They both took deep breaths, and Evelyn finally lowered her rifle. They walked back to the house, though Evelyn couldn't keep from glancing over her shoulder. When they reached Peter, Evelyn rested a hand on the stock of the rifle he was holding and lowered it.

"Who is that, Ma?" he asked.

"His name is Sam," Evelyn said. "He was the cook at the logging camp."

"Did he come looking for Sarah?"

"He mainly came looking for your father, or the person who he thought was your father," Evelyn said.

"You?"

"Yes," Evelyn said. "That would be me. He's the reason I had to bring Sarah to the farm. He's the man who attacked her."

"He looked mighty mean," Peter said.

"He does have a mean streak, but you do know I would never want you to actually shoot someone, don't you?"

"I know, Ma," Peter said. "Pa said the important thing is to let them know you're willing."

"I see," she said. "That's good to know. Where are your brother and sister?"

"I told Karl to take Louise down to the cellar."

"You can go fetch them now," Evelyn said.

She watched as he walked toward the cellar. He's growing up more every day, she thought, but his father did teach him well. She knew he would do anything to defend the family. She turned her attention to Sarah, who was nervously pacing, occasionally pausing to look out a window.

"Do you think Sam will come back again?" Sarah asked.

"I don't think so," Evelyn said. "I really don't think he means you any harm. Not anymore."

"I would hate to put you and the children in danger," Sarah said.

"I think that chapter is closed now," Evelyn said.

"I hope so," Sarah said. "Those were some of my darkest days. Those days changed my life. I had always thought that Sam was harmless, that as Abigail's brother he posed no threat."

"You never know with people," Evelyn said. "That camp could bring out the worst in anybody. Add alcohol to the situation and… I'm just grateful that we both escaped safely and we never have to return."

"After that, being here is like being in heaven," Sarah said.

Evelyn wondered if Sarah truly felt that way or if she had simply settled into the circumstance. *It's not as if she had any choice but to come here. If Sam hadn't attacked her, she inevitably would have returned to Pine Creek. If. If. If…* Sarah did turn down Sam's offer to return to the house she lived in with Abigail, but Evelyn believed that decision was due more to her continuing distrust of Sam than her desire to stay on the farm.

That night, Sarah lay awake, thinking about Sam, Abigail… Even though she was surrounded daily by Evelyn and the children, she felt loneliness growing within her, gnawing at her. Some nights, after Evelyn dimmed and turned off the kerosene lamp, Sarah would listen to Evelyn's breathing and wonder what she was thinking about. *The farm? The children? Does she ever think about me?* Some nights she ached so badly for warmth, touch, tenderness, that she wanted to get up, pass through the blanket that served as a wall, and crawl into bed beside Evelyn, but she couldn't make herself move.

Any time that Evelyn touched her, whether she was taking her hand or placing an arm around her, Sarah became confused. She wondered if Evelyn was ever touching her as a woman or if she was always just caring for her as she did her children. She was never sure, and she was so frustrated sometimes that she wanted to scream, confront Evelyn, say something, anything, but uncertainty left her tongue-tied. She couldn't help but wonder if Evelyn sometimes, maybe, harbored the same feelings toward her, but she had no idea how she would ever broach the subject.

CHAPTER TWELVE

The days were settling into summer, mid-June, and work on the farm was in full force. Sarah woke early one morning after listening to Evelyn cough on and off all night. She got dressed and drew back the blanket that separated them. Evelyn opened her eyes and squinted in the sunlight that slanted through the window.

"Are you okay?" Sarah asked. "You were coughing all night. How do you feel?"

"My throat's a bit scratchy," Evelyn said. "I might have a little cold coming on. I did have the chills throughout the night."

"You need a day of rest," Sarah said.

"There's too much to do," Evelyn said as she rolled over and groaned, sitting on the edge of the bed. "The crops are just reaching their peak. Before we know it harvest and canning season will be upon us. We begin to harvest the spring wheat in mid-August, and I haven't even arranged for farmhands yet."

She started to stand, and Sarah crossed the room, lightly rested a hand on her forehead, and gently pushed her back onto the bed.

"You're warm," she said. "You have a slight fever. I know you are the cog that holds this machinery together, Evelyn, but the children and I can manage a day or two without you, whether you believe it or not. If you don't get some rest, you'll be too sick to help anyone. Nip the cold in the bud before it gets worse."

"Are you bossing me?" Evelyn asked.

"If I have to," Sarah said. "You've been working nonstop since the day we returned from the logging camp. At some point, you need to take a break."

Evelyn smiled slightly. "So have you," she said.

"I'd say the work you do requires a bit more stamina than the work I do," Sarah said.

"A strong cup of coffee and I'll be ready for the day," Evelyn told her.

"I'll send one of the children up with some hot water and honey while I fix breakfast," Sarah said. "That'll be more soothing than coffee."

"If you insist," Evelyn said as she snuggled back under her covers, her eyes fluttering shut.

"I insist," Sarah said as she left the room.

Peter was the first to emerge from upstairs that morning, muttering an unenergetic hello. He was always a bit irritable when he first woke. Sarah stirred the coals in the woodstove, put a pot of water on top of it, and took down the frying pan. She glanced at Peter.

"Peter, you need to go gather the eggs so I can start making breakfast."

Peter wiped a hand over his eyes.

"I don't take orders from you," he said. "You're not my ma."

Sarah looked at him sternly.

"I know I'm not your mother, but I am an adult and I deserve your respect, just as you deserve mine," she said. Her voice shook slightly. She didn't know how Evelyn would feel about her reprimanding one of her children. Up until that moment, she'd had no need to. "You're mother isn't feeling well, and the only way she'll get some rest will be if we work together for the next few days. I'm going to need your help more than anyone else's. Do you understand?"

"Yes," Peter said, straightening up and reddening. "Sorry, Sarah. I'll go fetch those eggs now."

Sarah handed him a basket.

"Thank you," she said.

She watched as he went out the door, and then she went to the counter to cut some bread. Karl came down the stairs with Louise behind him. Louise ran over to give her a hug before joining Karl at the table.

"Good morning, sweetheart," Sarah said.

"Morning," Louise said.

"Good morning, Karl," Sarah said. "Did you sleep well?"

"Sure did," Karl said. "Where's Ma?"

"She's upstairs," Sarah said. "She's coming down with a bit of a cold, so she's going to get some rest. We'll all have to pitch in a little extra for the next few days."

"Okay," Karl said good-naturedly.

Peter entered the house with the basket of eggs and set it on the counter near the woodstove.

"Good day for the hens?" Sarah asked.

"Nine eggs," said Peter.

"Good enough for breakfast," said Sarah.

She put the skillet on the woodstove, added some butter, and began to crack the eggs on the side of the pan. She poured some hot water from the pot on the stove into a mug, added a dollop of honey, and handed it to Peter.

"Take this up to your mother and tell her I'll bring her some breakfast shortly," Sarah said.

"Okay," Peter said.

He took the mug from her.

"Thank you, Peter," Sarah said. "Karl, can you set the table?"

"Yes, ma'am," Karl said.

❖

There was a knock on Evelyn's door and she sat up in the bed.

"Come in," she said.

Peter pushed the door open and handed her the mug as she sat up in the bed.

"I'm sorry you don't feel good, Ma," he said. "This is hot water with honey. Sarah said she'll bring breakfast up soon."

"Thank you," Evelyn said. "I'm sure I'll feel better in no time."

Peter turned to leave and Evelyn patted the space beside her on the bed.

"Sit down for a minute before you go," she said.

"Yes, ma'am," Peter said.

He sat.

"I heard you talk back to Sarah earlier, when she asked you to go get the eggs," Evelyn said.

Peter turned red and lowered his head.

"Peter, she's a part of this home now, if she wants to be. You know I need her help with the farm, the chores, everything. We wouldn't be able to manage this alone. You know that."

"I know," Peter said.

"I want you to show her the same respect that you show me," Evelyn said.

"Okay," Peter said. "Sorry, Ma."

Evelyn rested a hand on his back.

"It's all right," she said. "I know it takes getting used to, for all of us, but things will get easier as time goes on."

"Yes, ma'am," Peter said.

"Do you know what you need to do in the fields today?" Evelyn asked.

"Sure do," Peter said. "I need to check the crops for any signs of bugs and get to the weeding."

"That's right," Evelyn said. "Can you handle that by yourself?"

"Yes, ma'am," Peter said proudly.

"All right," Evelyn said. "I'll want a report from you at the end of the day."

"Okay," Peter said.

He leaned over to give Evelyn a hug.

"Thank you, Peter," Evelyn said.

He turned, smiled, and then left the room.

❖

"I want to make a pot of soup today," Sarah said as they were sitting down to breakfast. "It'll help your mother to feel better."

"What kind?" Peter asked.

"Chicken vegetable," said Sarah.

"You'll need a chicken for that," Peter said.

"That's my one problem," Sarah told him. "I have no idea how to…"

"I do," Peter said with authority. "I'll help you before I go to the fields."

"That would be great," Sarah said. "Thank you."

They all finished eating, and Sarah left Karl and Louise to clean up the kitchen as she went outside with Peter. He led the way to the chicken coop and pointed out a plump bird.

"That one there looks good," he said.

"Perfect," said Sarah.

Peter picked up the squawking bird and put it into a feed bag with a hole cut in one corner so the chicken's head could poke out. He led the way outside to the tree stump that was used for butchering. He set the bird on the stump and looked at Sarah.

"You hold it still and I'll chop off its head," he said.

"All right," Sarah said hesitantly, as she studied the bird in the bag, unsure of where to place her hands.

"Grab it in the middle," Peter told her. "Hold down the wings."

"Okay," Sarah said.

She took a deep breath and tightly grabbed hold of the bird.

"You ready?" Peter asked.

"As ready as I'll ever be," she said.

"Hold it as still as you can," Peter said.

Sarah held on to the struggling bird, and Peter picked up the ax and raised it over his head.

"On the count of three," he said. "One, two, three."

He swung the ax in one swift movement, severing the chicken's neck. Its screeching came to an abrupt stop and blood spurted out in a red stream. Sarah removed her hands from the bag and, as much as she tried not to, she felt herself getting sick. She leaned over with her hands on her knees and vomited.

Evelyn finished the breakfast that Sarah sent up and sat by the window to sip her hot water. She saw Peter and Sarah with a chicken in a burlap bag near the butchering stump and had a moment of panic.

"Oh no," she said as she watched Peter place the bird on the stump.

She watched with dread as Sarah held it down. As much as she wanted to turn away from the scene, she continued to watch, long enough to see Sarah double over and throw up after the chicken's beheading. She left the window and returned to her bed, shaking her head the whole time. She felt a strange queasiness.

I never meant for her to have to do that, she thought, though I guess it had to happen at some point. She must think this place is as dreadful as the camp at times. I owe it to her to offer her another option. The next time I'm in town I'll ask Mary Boyd if she needs some extra help in her shop. That would be more suitable for Sarah. Even as she thought that, though, sadness set in. She seemed to be in a constant battle between knowing how much she had grown to depend on Sarah and feeling the need to help her escape the drudgery and daily toiling of farm life. She returned to her bed and lay down. Grogginess overtook her, and she drifted off to sleep.

Sarah eventually regrouped from the chicken's crude beheading and stood up. She looked at Peter.

"Sorry," she said.

He shrugged.

"It was your first time."

"Now what?"

"We need to wash it off in that barrel of water. Then we need to put it in a pot of boiling water so that it's easier to pluck."

"Okay," Sarah said.

She followed him to the barrel. Peter doused the dead bird in the water, washed it off, and then pulled it out.

"Now we need the boiling water," he told Sarah.

"That I can do," Sarah said.

They went to the house and Sarah put a large pot of water on the stove.

"That's a mighty big bird," Karl said.

"Sure is," Sarah said. "We'll get an extra-big pot of soup out of this one."

When the water finally reached a boil, Peter handed the chicken to Karl.

"You take the bird," he said. "I'll carry the pot outside."

Before he went to the stove, he stopped at the bottom of the stairs and hollered up.

"We just killed a chicken, Ma. Me and Sarah."

"You did?" Evelyn called down.

"Sure did," Peter said. "Sarah threw up."

He took the pot off the stove and headed outside, with Karl and Louise in tow. Sarah stood in the quiet kitchen alone, embarrassed. She wished she hadn't vomited in front of Peter again.

"Sarah?" Evelyn called down from upstairs. "Are you okay?"

"I'm fine, Evelyn," Sarah replied. "I'm going to make a pot of soup."

"Soup will be good," Evelyn said, and the house fell quiet once again.

❖

Sarah went outside to join the children just as Peter was lifting the chicken out of the pot of water. He set it on a tarp, and he and Karl started to pluck the feathers.

"What happens after the plucking?" Sarah asked.

"I'll finish dressing it," Peter said. "Karl will bring it to you when we're done. I'll have to go to the fields as soon as we finish."

"Sounds good," Sarah said, pleased. "Thank you so much."

"You're welcome," Peter said. "I can't wait for the soup."

"Me, too," Louise piped in.

"Since you have everything under control here, Louise and I will go tend to the garden," Sarah said, taking her hand. "Karl, after you take the chicken in, we'll do the chores in the barn."

"Yes, ma'am," Karl said as he and his brother continued to pluck.

Sarah checked in on Evelyn throughout the day, between chores. Evelyn's fever persisted and her skin had a pallor hue. Sarah gently roused her a few times, urging her to sip on some tea or to drink some water.

"You need fluids for the fever," she told Evelyn.

The last time she checked in on her, before she started to prepare the soup, Evelyn was asleep, and Sarah left her undisturbed. Back in the kitchen, she put Karl to work chopping potatoes, carrots, and onions. She filled a large pot with water, placed it on the stove, and added the pieces of chicken and a bundle of herbs tied together with twine. After the chicken had boiled for some time, she added the vegetables and stirred everything together, leaving the soup to simmer.

"This will take a few hours," she said. "We'll have a little lunch and then go finish our chores."

"Okay," Karl said.

Sarah got out some fixings for sandwiches and started to prepare lunch. Only noon and it seems as if we've done a week's worth of work, she thought. She was pleased to find herself slowly settling in to the ways of the farm, the land, a household of children. More and more, she felt as if she had found her place—home. For the first time since Abigail had passed away, she had a sense of place, of belonging. She felt as if she had something to offer.

After Peter returned from the fields, Sarah and the children gathered around the table to eat the soup that had cooked throughout the afternoon.

"How did it go in the fields today, Peter?" Sarah asked.

"Good," Peter said. "I did a lot of weeding. I think we've got some bugs infesting the potato plants, though. Ma needs to check it out. She'll know what to do."

"What makes you think there are bugs?" Sarah asked.

"Something is nibbling on the leaves, and some of the plants have brown spots," Peter said. "Probably potato bugs or aphids."

"When will Ma be better?" Karl asked.

"Hopefully, soon," Sarah said. "The good thing is that we managed on our own so she could get some rest. Everything's still standing."

"Did you think it would all fall down?" Peter asked with a grin on his face.

"Well, not exactly," Sarah said.

"Can we read stories tonight?" Louise asked.

"There's been so much happening since I arrived here that I nearly forgot that I had brought my checkerboard with me. I thought I'd teach you and your brothers how to play after we finish cleaning up," Sarah said.

The boys looked at Sarah and eagerly nodded in approval, and Louise clapped. The children fell silent then, concentrating on their bowls of soup and sopping up the rich broth with chunks of bread.

Sarah took a bowl of soup up to Evelyn while the children cleaned up in the kitchen, and she opened the door to find Evelyn sitting up in bed, reading.

"You've got some color back in your cheeks," Sarah said.

"I feel better," Evelyn said.

Sarah set the bowl of soup and a spoon on the small table beside Evelyn's bed. She perched on the bed and pressed a hand against Evelyn's forehead.

"Your fever finally broke."

"The soup smells wonderful," Evelyn said. "I am sorry that you had to deal with the chicken, though."

"It was a rather gruesome sight," Sarah said. "But I seem to have survived."

She smiled. A wisp of hair fell over her face, and Evelyn instinctively reached over to push it back in place. Her fingers rested for a moment on Sarah's cheek. She felt a wave of tenderness wake through her, and in that moment, she… Evelyn at times became so confused about how she felt toward Sarah. She cared about her, was attracted to her in some strange way, but she didn't know what that even meant. She took a sip of the soup and sighed.

"The soup is delicious," she said.

"Thanks," Sarah said. "I'll come up later to get the bowl and see if you need anything else."

She went to her trunk and took out the checkerboard and a bag of disks that she had packed.

"I'm going to teach the children how to play checkers tonight," she said.

"I wish I could join you," Evelyn said. "Tell the children to come see me before they go to bed."

"Of course," Sarah said as she left the room.

Downstairs, Sarah took the checkerboard and bag of disks to the sitting room, and she and the children sat on the floor. She laid the wooden board, with its red and black squares, on the floor. She then opened the bag and dumped out the red and black disks. The children looked at her excitedly.

"How do you play?" Peter asked.

"Only two people can play at a time," Sarah said. "I'll teach you and Karl how to play the first game."

"Okay," Peter said.

He earnestly rubbed his hands together.

"You boys sit across from each other," Sarah told Peter and Karl.

She moved the board so that each boy had a red square on the right side closest to him. She divided the disks between the boys, giving Peter the black ones and Karl the red ones.

"Put your disks on the black squares closest to you."

The boys listened closely to her instructions as Sarah told

them how to move their disks and capture each other's pieces. Before long, they were immersed in the game, with Louise closely following each move.

Sarah moved to a chair and opened the sewing basket that she kept in the sitting room. She took out some gingham cloth with grass green and white squares that she had asked Evelyn to pick up on one of her trips into town, and she began to stitch. She was making curtains for the house, starting with the kitchen. By the time the boys and then Karl and Louise had played a game of checkers, bedtime was upon them.

"Put away the disks and the board so you can get ready for bed," Sarah said.

The children picked up, and Peter and Karl headed up the stairs. Sarah took Louise's hand and they followed. The children went to their room to change their clothes, and Sarah peeked in on Evelyn.

"The children are getting ready for bed," she said.

Evelyn put down the book she was reading. She looked at the cloth in Sarah's hand.

"What do you have there?" she asked.

"I'm making curtains. These are for the kitchen windows."

"Curtains?"

"I know they're not particularly practical, but they bring a sense of warmth to a room," Sarah said. "I thought they might make things more…homey."

"I'm embarrassed to say the thought never entered my mind," Evelyn said.

"I'm sure you had your hands full," Sarah said. "I can see why curtains never came to mind, but they'll make a difference. You'll see."

The children burst into the room and gathered around Evelyn's bed.

"I'll be up in a bit," Sarah said as she left them with their mother.

"Good night, Sarah," they all said cheerfully, before they began to explain checkers to Evelyn.

When Sarah went upstairs that night, Evelyn had already turned off the lamp and pulled the blanket across the room. Sarah started to change out of her clothes and Evelyn spoke.

"The children love the checkers," she said.

"I'm so glad," Sarah said. "It was my favorite game as a child."

"And I appreciate the curtains," Evelyn said.

Sarah smiled and crawled under her covers.

❖

A Saturday late in June, Helen and Jess joined Evelyn, Sarah, and the children for an evening picnic in the yard. As Sarah and Jess prepared the table outside and started a fire, Helen helped Evelyn get the food ready.

"Jess and I want the children to stay with us for the Fourth of July festivities in town," Helen said. "We can pick them up late Friday afternoon. Is that okay with you?"

"Is it that time already?" Evelyn said.

"One week away," Helen said. "What do you think?"

"I think that's a great idea," said Evelyn. "Sarah and I can manage fine here for a day or two, and the children will be thrilled. They deserve a break."

"Oh, and I ran into Mary Boyd," Helen said. "She said to tell you yes."

"She did?" Evelyn said. "I can't wait to tell Sarah."

"About what?" Helen asked.

"The last time I was in town I asked Mary if she might want to hire some extra help in her tailor shop. Sarah could work for her, and she has a spare room in her boarding house."

Helen looked at Evelyn.

"Are you two having problems? Has Sarah told you that she wants to leave the farm?" she asked.

"Well, no," Evelyn said. "But I thought…Her life in town would be more like what she is accustomed to, like the life she had before. I worry that she's unhappy here."

"Have you asked her? She's been here nearly three months

now. It appears things are working out fine, and she seems perfectly content to me."

"I just…" Evelyn stammered.

"Is that what you want? Do you want her to go?"

"No, I don't want her to go, but…"

"What do you want, Evelyn?" Helen asked.

"I want her to stay, but…"

"But what?"

"I want her to be happy. I never want her to feel like this is her only option," Evelyn said. "Ever since the altercation with Sam…I would never want her to feel beholden to me. I want her to be here by choice."

"And you don't think she is?"

"I don't know," Evelyn said. "I really don't know. She didn't have much choice when I brought her here."

Helen settled her eyes on Evelyn and shook her head.

"What?" Evelyn asked.

"I don't think Sarah will be happy with your news," Helen said.

"Why not?"

"I'm quite sure this is where she wants to be," Helen said. "She cares about the children, and I've seen how she looks at you when you're not aware," Helen said.

"What are you talking about?" Evelyn asked.

Helen laughed lightly.

"She looks at you the same way you look at her when you think no one is looking."

"What do you mean?"

Evelyn felt herself blushing. She knew what her sister meant.

"You two act like shy teenagers," Helen said. "You're clearly attracted to each other."

"I don't think—"

Evelyn started to deny the truth, but stopped.

"I do have feelings for Sarah, and I've grown to care for her, but I can't imagine…"

"What?" Helen asked.

"That she would feel the same way."

"You sell yourself short, sister," Helen said. "You are one of the kindest and strongest people I've ever known."

"But being with a woman..." Evelyn said. She felt both shy and confused. "I don't...I can't...I hardly knew how to be with George."

She didn't even know how to explain what she was feeling. Helen rested a hand on one of hers.

"You know, Evelyn, you should just let things happen. Everything is not black and white. If you hadn't cared about Sarah, you never would have brought her here, to your home."

"I wouldn't have left her there," Evelyn said.

"I know that," Helen said. "You would've helped her leave the camp, but you wouldn't have brought her home, to be with you and your children."

"Well, I never thought about it that way," Evelyn said. "There's so much I never thought about, so much that I've accepted without questioning. I do have feelings for her, but I've always just assumed that I am who I am—Evelyn, who was married to George, with three children."

"You are," Helen said. "You were, but that doesn't mean your future can't hold something different for you."

"But I don't—"

"Things will happen naturally if you let them," Helen said. "But at some point you need to tell Sarah how you feel."

"I don't know what I feel," Evelyn said.

"You know what you feel," Helen said. "It just scares you because it's new to you."

Evelyn looked away. She knew Helen was right.

"Anyways, I really don't think she'll be happy with your surprise," Helen said.

"We'll see," Evelyn said. "I need to at least give her an opportunity for a life other than this."

Peter and Karl ran into the house then, and their conversation ended.

"Jess said you can bring the food out now," Peter said. "The table's ready and the grill is hot."

"You can get the watermelon out of the pantry," Evelyn told him. "Karl, get a platter out of the cupboard."

"Okay," Karl said.

"I'll take out the potato salad and biscuits," Helen said.

"I've got the sausages," Evelyn told her.

Peter came out of the pantry cradling the watermelon in his arms, and Evelyn looked around the kitchen.

"I guess that's it," she said. "I'll come back in to get the lemonade."

❖

Throughout the meal that evening, Evelyn kept mulling over what Helen had said. Her stomach was so unsettled that she could barely eat. She nibbled on a bit of sausage and some potato salad. The children chattered excitedly about the coming Fourth of July celebration—games, fireworks, races, contests. Evelyn suddenly dreaded the prospect of them being absent from the farm, leaving her alone with Sarah. She would be without a buffer.

When dinner was over, they cleared off the table and gathered on the porch while the children played. Evelyn poured them all cups of wine, and the sky darkened, with sporadic flashes of fireflies scattering throughout the fields. Evelyn occasionally glanced at Helen and Jess, who sat close together, pressing into one another. She thought about what it might be like with Sarah absent from the farm. She knew she could hold the farm together, succeed in making it function as it needed to, but she liked the idea of a companion, someone besides the children. The children couldn't fill every void. Even though she and George had not had a passionate relationship, he had been a steady companion, someone she could rely on, talk to. Though he had been a man of few words, she had always known that he was listening.

Louise left the company of the boys and climbed onto Evelyn's lap. Sarah watched as Evelyn combed through Louise's hair with her fingers and kissed her on the forehead. She was excited about the idea of having some time with Evelyn while the children were gone. Ever since they arrived on the farm, every moment seemed filled, and the children were always close at hand. At times, when Sarah and Evelyn were near each other, washing the dishes or preparing a meal, Sarah would find herself breathing in their proximity, edging in closer to Evelyn, and just when she thought the moment might be right for a fleeting kiss or a knowing touch, the moment would be shattered—the children barging in from outside, or Evelyn suddenly moving on to some other task she had forgotten.

The only time Sarah could engage with Evelyn alone was when they retired for the evening, but by then they were both exhausted and their talk was mainly about the farm and the children, and tasks that had to be done. Sarah needed a chance to talk to Evelyn frankly, tell her how she felt. Some days she thought she would burst. She wanted to grab hold of Evelyn, draw her near, taste her lips, feel her warmth. She hoped that time would soon arrive. At least then Sarah would know where she stood. She would know what kind of future she and Evelyn could have together. She often wondered if Evelyn ever contemplated or envisioned an intimate relationship with her, but there was a part of her that was too afraid to ask, fearing what the answer might be.

The afternoon that Helen and Jess were to return the children from the holiday festivities, Evelyn and Sarah stood beside each other at the kitchen counter, cutting apples into wedges and slicing bread and cheese for a light lunch. They'd had so little spare time since the children had been gone, with Evelyn leaving extra early to head to the fields and Sarah taking over the chores in the barn and the garden.

"I have a surprise for you," Evelyn said as she arranged apple slices on a plate.

"What?" Sarah asked.

"I found you a position in town if you want it, working with the seamstress, Mary Boyd," Evelyn told her. "She even has a spare room."

She turned to see Sarah's expression. Sarah put down her knife, cupped her hands over her mouth, and ran up the stairs, closing the door behind her. Evelyn stood in the kitchen, dumbfounded. That was not the reaction she expected. *Maybe Helen was right.* She set down her knife, removed her apron, and headed upstairs. When she reached the door to the bedroom, she lightly knocked and then entered. Sarah trembled as tears began to slide down her cheeks.

"Sarah, what is it?" Evelyn asked. "I don't understand. I thought you would be happy."

Sarah didn't look at her.

"Why are you doing this now, when I'm just starting to feel like I belong here, like I might be a part of your…Don't you care for me at all?"

"Of course I do," Evelyn said.

"Then why this?"

"I wasn't sure if you liked being here, with me and the children," Evelyn said. "I know it's a big change from your usual life. Ever since we arrived here, I have worried that you might be unhappy. I want you to have a chance to have a life like the one you had before."

"But you never even asked me," Sarah said. "I've just now gotten close to the children. How could you assume…"

Evelyn crossed the room and sat beside Sarah on the bed. Sarah stood up and began to pace.

"This is my fault," she said. "I don't know what I was thinking. I should have been honest with you about my feelings all along."

She kept pacing, wringing her hands.

"What do you mean?" Evelyn asked.

"You don't understand," Sarah said. "At the camp, before I knew you were you, Evelyn, I was already attracted to you, just the person who you were, even as George. You stood out so among the other jacks that I was drawn to you, which confused me greatly. Trust me. Then, when I discovered you were a woman, everything made sense to me. But I knew all along that you had your children and the farm, and I had planned to return to Pine Creek, even with Abigail gone, until Sam...Then all that changed, and I thought that perhaps it was a sign, that we were meant to be...There were times at the camp, and here, that I thought you might also...What was I thinking? I should have known that you could never...We were never meant to be. Perhaps you're right...The job in town...I need some air."

Sarah left the room, went downstairs, and hurried out of the house. Evelyn wanted to stop her, call after her, but she simply sat for a few moments, stunned. *She wants to be with me. She's attracted to me somehow. Why am I pushing her away?* She went after Sarah. When she stepped outside, she caught a glimpse of Sarah as she headed into the woods, on the trail that led to the pond. A breeze whirled around Evelyn, and she glanced up at the sky to see a mass of clouds gathering in the north. She stepped off the porch and hurried to the woods, in the same direction that Sarah had gone. When she reached the pond, she saw Sarah, sitting on the bench that George had built there years ago. Evelyn slowed her pace as she approached her.

"Sarah," she said quietly as the winds picked up around them.

Sarah looked at her. Her face was wet with tears.

"I'm so sorry," Evelyn said. "I'm just...I thought..."

Sarah looked as if she was wilting before her. Evelyn dropped her head. She felt herself sinking. She never meant to cause sadness. She never meant to hurt Sarah. The winds churned around them, and the trees swayed, the sky quickly darkening. A slash of lightning flashed across the sky, followed by a loud boom of thunder. Another jagged slice of lightning cut through the sky, and the thunder that followed was so ear splitting that it echoed over the land. Sarah jumped in her seat.

"We have to go in," Evelyn said. "It's not safe in the woods with the lightning."

Before she could say anything else, Sarah sprinted through the woods. The winds grew even stronger, and rain began to sprinkle down. Evelyn headed toward the house, reaching it just as the skies opened and the light sprinkle of rain became a deafening downpour.

She entered the house to find an empty kitchen. She peeked into the sitting room, which was also empty, and then heard noise upstairs. She climbed the steps and stopped in the doorway of her and Sarah's room. Sarah was frantically going through her things, stuffing some items into the trunk she had brought with her to the farm and other things into a large satchel.

"What are you doing?" Evelyn asked.

Sarah did not look at her.

"I'm packing," she said. "I might as well leave as soon as possible. I can't see any reason to draw things out. If you want me to go, I'll go. Maybe Helen and Jess can take me to town with them when they return with the children."

This is all wrong. This is not how I meant things to turn out. She thinks I want her to leave, that I don't want her here. But I was only thinking about her, about...

"You don't have to..."

"What, Evelyn? I don't have to what? I need to pack my things. The furniture you can keep. It's got no meaning for me anymore."

"But wait," Evelyn said.

"Wait for what, Evelyn?" Sarah asked.

"I didn't mean..."

Evelyn didn't know how to explain herself. She had no words. Sarah continued to pack, keeping her back turned to Evelyn. Evelyn glanced out the window. The rain had dwindled into a light sprinkle.

"I need to go tend to the animals," she said, unsure of what else to do. "We can talk more when I return."

"I don't think we have anything more to say," Sarah said curtly.

She was so hurt that she cloaked herself in anger. Evelyn walked over to the doorway. Sarah refused to look her way, and Evelyn finally left the room and went downstairs.

❖

As Evelyn was returning to the house from the barn, Helen and Jess pulled up in their wagon and the children happily climbed out and ran to her, all of them talking at once, reliving the events in town. Hoping to soothe the situation between her and Sarah, Evelyn invited Helen and Jess in for coffee before they headed back home, and as they all entered the house, Sarah was coming down the stairs, carrying the large satchel. Louise ran over to her to give her a hug, and she set down the bag.

"Where's Sarah going?" Peter asked Evelyn.

Helen and Jess both looked at Evelyn, and she felt herself blushing. No one spoke.

"I was hoping your aunt would let me ride with her into town," Sarah finally said.

Peter grimaced.

"Why?" he said.

"Your mother has found me a position there," Sarah said flatly. "A job in a shop, evidently."

She had a blank look on her face.

"I knew you wouldn't stay," Peter said angrily and then ran up the stairs.

"I don't want you to go," Karl squealed and then started to cry. "Why does she have to go?"

He looked at Evelyn and then, following his brother's lead, escaped up the stairs. Helen and Jess were still standing in the doorway as if they had frozen in place, and Sarah stooped down to pick up the satchel. Louise ran to Evelyn and wrapped her arms around one of her legs.

"Can't she stay, Mommy?"

Evelyn tried to stutter out a word, anything, and then Sarah spoke, her words sounding frantic.

"Helen, can you drop me in town? I assume you know where the shop is. I hope she's expecting me."

Helen looked at Sarah and then at Evelyn.

"Of course," she said. "If this is how it's going to be."

Sarah looked at Evelyn one last time, and Evelyn stood before her, tongue-tied, caught in the whirlwind that she had somehow created. With her satchel in hand, Sarah walked out the door. Jess followed her out, and Helen lagged behind for a moment.

"What happened?" she asked Evelyn.

"I don't know," Evelyn said, her voice edging hysteria. "I thought…She took it the wrong way."

"Oh, sister," Helen said.

"Go," Evelyn said as she sat in a chair and pulled Louise onto her lap. "Just go."

Helen quietly departed and Evelyn sat at the table and silently cried.

CHAPTER THIRTEEN

The morning after Sarah left, Evelyn woke earlier than usual, before the sunrise. She hadn't been able to sleep, had tossed and turned throughout the night. The children had been somber and silent during suppertime. Karl sat glumly, slumped at the table, while Louise tightly clung to her. Peter, the one to resist Sarah the most, was angry and refused eye contact with Evelyn. She realized that the main reason for his resistance had been the fear of losing someone else.

Sarah's departure had, once again, magnified the absence of the children's father. Evelyn felt regret. The children had gone through so many changes in so little time—George's death, her own time away at the logging camp, and now Sarah's departure.

Evelyn got out of bed and dressed. She looked at the empty cot, and the silence of the room suddenly grated on her. She and Sarah had always chatted in the mornings as they got ready for the day—about the weather, their list of things to do, what to cook. When Evelyn went downstairs to start making breakfast, she stood for a moment and gazed out the window. The sun was beginning to bloom above the horizon—a light, golden glow. She fingered the curtains that Sarah had sewn. Sarah was right. They added a sense of warmth.

Peter was the first to come down that morning, and he mumbled an unhappy hello.

"There's a pot of oatmeal on the stove," Evelyn told him.

"I'm not hungry," he said.

"You'll need your energy for the day," Evelyn said.

Peter shrugged, and when Karl and Louise came down the stairs, Evelyn filled their bowls without asking. As they ate, Evelyn drank some coffee, and the children said little, to her or to each other.

"I'm going to have to work the fields alone now," Evelyn told Peter. "I'll need you here to tend to the animals and help Karl with the work in the garden. You'll have to keep an eye on him and Louise."

"If Sarah was here—" Peter started.

"I know," Evelyn said softly. "But she's not."

"Why did you make her go?" he asked in an accusatory tone.

"I didn't make her go," Evelyn tried to explain. "I thought she might want an opportunity to try something different."

"What's wrong with being on the farm?" Peter asked.

"Nothing," Evelyn said. "You know that. But farm life isn't for everyone."

"Sarah seemed to like it," Peter said.

Evelyn looked at Peter. She tried to rest a reassuring hand on one of his, but he pulled it away.

"She can come back if she decides she wants to," she said.

Peter turned away from her and looked at Karl.

"Hurry up and finish so we can get started," he snapped.

"Be kind to your brother and sister, and make sure you all eat some lunch," Evelyn said.

Peter looked at her and glowered.

Sarah woke to uncomfortable silence her first morning in town—no crowing roosters, no children's voices, no clanging of pots and pans in the kitchen. Mary Boyd had been kind enough when she arrived. She'd been startled by Sarah's sudden appearance more than anything. She let Sarah settle into her spare room and then heated up a late dinner for her. As the morning sun shined in, Sarah

sat up in bed and surveyed the room that was now her new home—
another new home. It was sparsely furnished—a bed, dresser, chair,
and table—but it had a feminine touch, with a soft, rose-colored rug
in the center of the floor and lacy white curtains on the windows.
When Sarah was at the logging camp, she had yearned for such
comforts, but on that morning, she missed nothing more than the
rustic trappings of the farmhouse, even with its flaws. With a heavy
heart, she forced herself out of bed and began to get dressed.

When she went downstairs, Mary Boyd was sitting at the
kitchen table with a cup of coffee. Sarah knew little about her. She
was an older woman, a widow, with long gray hair that she kept
coiled on the top of her head and, from what Sarah could ascertain,
she had a timid but kind personality.

"Help yourself to coffee," she told Sarah, gesturing toward the
stove.

Sarah poured herself a cup and then sat.

"Evelyn told me that she met you at the logging camp," Mary
said.

"Yes," Sarah said. "I was working there as a flunky."

"I can't imagine," Mary said. "I found it most admirable,
though, that Evelyn had endured the camp and the labor for the sake
of her children."

"She's a good mother," Sarah said, and she felt her chest heave.

"You didn't care much for the farm life?" Mary asked.

Sarah hesitated before she spoke.

"Actually, the farm was beginning to grow on me, and the
children. They're so well behaved, and the way they pitch in on the
farm should be applauded. I will truly miss them."

"Why are you here, then, if you don't mind my asking?"

Sarah remained quiet for a moment.

"Well, Evelyn had made these arrangements with you without
my knowledge," she eventually said. "I think she feared that life
on the farm wasn't suitable for me, that the life I'd had before
going to the logging camp was more to my liking. I had worked as
a seamstress before, until the woman whom I worked for passed
away."

"I see," said Mary. "I could definitely use some help, but if you ever decide that you want to return to the farm, I won't hold you back. I would understand. The Bauers are wonderful folks."

"They truly are," Sarah said.

You have no idea how much I want to return to that farm, she thought.

"Finish your coffee and I'll show you the room that I use as my shop," Mary said. "We'll be doing most of our work in there. When we aren't working, you're free to do whatever you please."

"Thank you," Sarah said.

Her days in Mary Boyd's shop went slowly compared to her days on the farm, everything seeming so mundane and unimportant—trousers to hem, holes to patch, a dress that needed fitting. She found herself gazing out the window, trying to assess the time using the sun's position in the sky, wondering what was happening on the farm in that moment.

In the evenings, after a quiet meal with Mary, she would often take a stroll on the town's quiet streets or retire to her room to read. She felt without purpose. She had only been gone from the farm for a little more than a week, and she missed Evelyn and the children so much that she ached. She wished she had challenged Evelyn when she told her about the arrangements in town, instead of reacting out of emotion, thinking that Evelyn no longer wanted her on the farm. She had felt wounded at the time, though, and she acted too hastily. Now all she could feel was emptiness and the dullness of each day.

❖

Evelyn's first day working the fields alone was a long one, and she had stayed out later than usual, until dusk, trying to accomplish what she and Peter would have in one day's time. When she returned to the house, she found the children impatiently waiting for her. They were hungry.

"What did you have for lunch?" she asked, as she rummaged through the pantry for items she could use to make a quick meal.

"Peter made sandwiches," Karl said.

Evelyn put some leftover baked beans and sausage in a pot and set it on the woodstove, opened the door to the stove, and stirred the coals.

"I'm sorry I'm so late," she said as the children gathered around the table. "Time got away from me. Did you finish your chores?"

She looked at Peter.

"Most of them," he said.

"Not all of them?"

"We forgot to churn the butter," Karl said.

Evelyn frowned, and Peter glared at Karl.

"You're the one who forgot," he said.

"Peter, settle down," Evelyn said. "It's no one's fault. We just need to adjust."

"Seems like we're always adjusting these days," Peter said.

Evelyn didn't reply right away. She knew he was angry and frustrated. She was asking him to assume much responsibility.

"Things will get a little better every day," she said.

She put the pot and some bowls and spoons on the table, and they all ate in silence. When they finished, Louise climbed into Evelyn's lap and began to quietly cry.

"I miss Sarah," she said.

Peter and Karl looked at Evelyn.

"It's been a long day," she said. "Go up and get ready for bed. I'll come after I clean up the kitchen."

Peter stood and stomped up the stairs. Karl took Louise's hand and they followed him. Evelyn cleared the table, filled the basin with water, and began to wash the dishes, tears trailing down her cheeks.

What have I done? What was I thinking?

❖

Every day that Sarah was gone grew more difficult instead of easier, with Evelyn trying to manage the farm and house on her own. She could barely keep up with the work, even with help from the children. The household was becoming unruly and strained, the children were arguing with each other more than usual, and Peter became more morose each day.

On the tenth day, Evelyn returned from the fields early; the sweltering heat had taken a toll on her. She was soaked with sweat, and she knew the children would need a break, some time to swim in the pond. When she reached the house, she was greeted by the sight of Peter and Karl, wrestling on the ground. Louise was sitting on the porch steps, howling.

"Damn it," Evelyn said. "Boys!"

She broke into a run and rushed over to them, pulling Peter off Karl.

"Stop this now," she said sternly. "What is going on?"

"Karl pushed Louise," Peter said. "She fell and hurt her knee."

Evelyn glanced at Louise.

"I'll be there in a minute, honey."

She returned her attention to Peter and Karl.

"That's enough of that," she said. "You both know better."

Peter and Karl looked at her sheepishly as they brushed the dirt off their clothes. Evelyn went to Louise and bent down to examine her knee, and Louise wrapped her arms around her neck.

"I don't like them fighting," she cried.

"I know," Evelyn told her. "It's okay. Let's go inside and I'll clean this up for you."

She took Louise's hand and helped her up.

"Come on, boys," Evelyn said. "We're going to go swimming. We all need a break."

As Evelyn and the children were heading out of the house in with towels draped over their arms, they could see Helen coming down the road in her wagon. When she reached the house and reined in the horse, the children ran to her. She got out of the wagon and they surrounded her—a tiny swarm. Evelyn embraced her as well.

"You're off for a swim?" Helen asked.

"We all need some relief," Evelyn said.

"Sounds delightful," Helen said. "This heat is oppressive. Why don't we rustle up a few things and make it a picnic?"

"Can we, Ma?" Karl asked.

"I don't see why not," Evelyn said. "You can wait out here and your aunt and I will put a basket together."

For the first time since Sarah left, the children showed some signs of joy. Evelyn and Helen went into the house, and Evelyn went to the pantry. Helen looked about her.

"Goodness, sister, the place is in a bit of a shambles," she said.

"Don't think I haven't noticed," Evelyn said, slightly irritated. "I can't keep up."

"How long has Sarah been gone now?" Helen asked.

"A little over a week," Evelyn said. "Ten days. And they've been long ones."

"Well, maybe after a little more time passes…"

"I don't think time will make a difference," Evelyn said. "The children are miserable. I didn't realize how attached they had become. I don't know what I was thinking."

She shook her head as she and Helen put some fruit, bread, and cheese in the picnic basket.

"And you?" Helen asked. "How are you doing?"

The silence that followed the question seemed to linger forever.

"I miss her more than I thought was possible," Evelyn said. "I feel so downhearted. I can't…"

Helen put an arm around her.

"That's one of the reasons I came out today," she said. "I stopped by the shop the other day. Mary Boyd left town for a few days to go visit her sister. If you'd like, I could stay with the children tomorrow so you can go to town. Maybe you can talk to Sarah."

Evelyn looked at Helen and sighed.

"I think that would be good," she said. "Helen, I…I think I… love her. I need her here."

"I know," Helen said. "I know. Let's go take that swim."

They went outside and the children circled around them and then ran ahead, leading the way to the pond. The children wasted no time splashing into the cool water. Evelyn took a quick dip and then joined Helen on a blanket they had laid out.

"This is the most relaxed I've been since Sarah left."

Her words hung in the air.

"At least you know now how you feel," Helen said.

"That doesn't necessarily mean anything will change between Sarah and me," Evelyn said. "After what I did, she might not…"

"Just give it a chance, Evelyn," Helen said. "See what happens. Even though you were wrong, you were acting in her best interest."

The children eventually got out of the pond and joined them on the blanket, and Evelyn and Helen set out the food.

"Did that feel good?" Evelyn asked.

"Yes," the children said in unison.

Evelyn was relieved—a moment of happiness.

"How have you children been these days?" Helen asked. "I've not seen you since the holiday."

"We miss Sarah," Peter responded quickly.

"Sure do," said Karl.

Louise nodded fervently.

"I think Ma does, too," Peter said. "She doesn't sing or hum anymore. She was happier before."

Evelyn looked at him.

"You're right, son," she said.

He leaned over and, for the first time in more than a week, he hugged her.

❖

Mary Boyd had departed for a five-day trip and had left Sarah a few pieces of clothing to work on in her absence. Sarah was happy to be alone, to have some time to gather her thoughts, but the empty house seemed to echo around her. She went to the window. A half moon was propped up in the sky, surrounded by sparkling stars. They looked almost effervescent. She envisioned Evelyn, sitting on the porch, taking in some fresh air before heading inside to go upstairs. They would be seeing the same moon. She wondered if Evelyn had any idea how much she missed her. *Does she miss me?*

Do the children care that I am gone? She turned from the window and looked at her room. *This cannot be the rest of my life. I need to take control.* She needed to carve out some kind of plan for her future. A part of her thought about asking Evelyn to let her return to the farm, but she didn't want to go back if she wasn't wanted, and she truly had no idea how Evelyn felt, if she felt anything.

❖

Evelyn hesitated outside Mary Boyd's house. She had been haunted by the words that Sarah had spoken on the day she left the farm. She had said that she had been drawn to Evelyn even at the logging camp, that she believed they might have been able to forge some kind of relationship. Evelyn hoped that Sarah still felt the same way, that what she had done hadn't squashed those feelings, and she knew there was only one way to find out. She knocked on the door and fidgeted in place as she waited for Sarah to answer. After a few minutes, she knocked again, and the curtain that hung over the door window was pushed aside. Sarah peeked out.

"Evelyn, what brings you here?" she asked.

Evelyn looked at Sarah. She displayed no sign of happiness at seeing her, but Evelyn couldn't move her eyes from her. She had her hair down, cascading over her shoulders, and the dress she was wearing was a striking shade of green, almost emerald.

"I came in town for some provisions," Evelyn said. "I wanted to see you."

Sarah hesitated for a moment.

"Do you need something?"

Evelyn was taken aback by Sarah's cold curtness.

"I thought we should talk," Evelyn said.

Sarah hesitated and then she gestured for Evelyn to enter. She led her into the kitchen and they sat.

"How are you faring here?" Evelyn asked.

"What do you want, Evelyn?" Sarah asked.

Her voice was flat, rigid. Evelyn took a deep breath.

"I wanted to talk about us," she said.

"About us?" Sarah said. "There is no us, Evelyn. There will be no us. You made that quite clear, and I cannot handle any more changes. This life is too disruptive."

Evelyn knew that she had hurt Sarah's feelings, and all she wanted to do was find a way to mend them now.

"Sarah, please give me a chance to explain," she said. "I was afraid."

"Afraid?"

"All this time, these feelings that I have for you have grown, taken root, but they are new to me, and after what happened with Sam, I was worried. I didn't want you to feel as if you owed me anything, and life on the farm is so different from the life you had before, with Abigail—"

"Abigail is gone! That life is gone!" Sarah's voice rose and cracked. "George is gone!"

"I know that," Evelyn said. "I know they're both gone."

"Then what do you want?" Sarah asked. "Why are you here?"

Evelyn began to pace around the kitchen. She looked out the window at an overcast sky.

"The children and I...I can't manage the farm alone," she said. "The children miss you. I miss you."

"So you want me to come back as what?" Sarah asked. "A farmhand? A hired worker?"

"No," Evelyn said. "You know better than that."

"No, I don't," Sarah said. "I don't understand what you want, Evelyn. I can't be coming and going based on your whims and moods, and I certainly don't want to spend the rest of my life sleeping on some spare cot. I need to decide what I want to do with my life. I can't second-guess what is happening, what you are feeling."

Evelyn opened her mouth, only silence escaping, and the next thing she knew she felt tears, warm on her cheeks. Sarah stood and went to her. She wrapped her arms around Evelyn, and they looked at each other steadily.

"I love you," Evelyn said. "I want you and me...The children... We could be a family."

Sarah leaned in and her lips brushed against Evelyn's. The kiss was long and gentle. Sarah raised a hand and wiped the tears from Evelyn's cheeks. Rain began to pound down on the roof, and the room grew dark. Sarah and Evelyn looked at each other silently, and Sarah took one of Evelyn's hands in her own and led her to her room, where she gently kissed Evelyn again and helped her to undress. Sarah removed her own clothing then, took Evelyn's hand, and pulled back the covers to her bed.

❖

After making love for the first time, sometimes fumbling awkwardly, sometimes giggling, they dozed off. Sarah woke before Evelyn, and she quietly lay beside her, watching her. Evelyn eventually woke up from the nap, and her lips slightly parted, but she said nothing. Sarah had a moment of panic, thinking that everything was too much for Evelyn, that she would change her mind.

"Are you all right?" she asked Evelyn. "You look almost... frightened."

"Frightened?" Evelyn said. "I'm not frightened."

"What then?"

"Startled maybe. I never...felt so much before. I've never been physically drawn to someone like this before."

"Ever? Not even George?" Sarah asked.

"There's only been George," Evelyn said. "I loved the man, but with him things were more...I never felt the way I feel right now."

Sarah kissed her softly. She cupped a hand over one of Evelyn's cheeks and traced a finger down, past her lips and along her neck, finally resting it on one of Evelyn's breasts. She gently pulled on the nipple and kissed Evelyn again. She stopped and gazed down at Evelyn.

"Are you thinking about Abigail?" Evelyn asked.

"No," Sarah said. "I'm thinking about us. Are you sure?"

"Am I sure?"

"About us?" Sarah said. "About me returning to the farm? I cannot handle any more drastic changes to my life, Evelyn. I need some stability. I need some place to belong—not for three months, not for three years. I need…As much as I wanted this, it seems so sudden now."

"I know what I feel, Sarah," Evelyn said. "At the camp I was so confused. I knew I was drawn to you. I thought you were attractive, as the other jacks did, but I thought all that was because I was pretending to be a man, that it was affecting me somehow. When we got back to the farm, the feelings didn't subside. They grew instead. I didn't know what to do, what to say. No part of me believed you would reciprocate."

Evelyn looked steadily at Sarah and took one of her hands in her own.

"I love you," she said. "We can be a family—me, you, and the children. Please trust me."

"What will we tell the children?" Sarah asked.

"Tell the children?" Evelyn said.

"About us."

"Nothing," Evelyn said matter-of-factly.

Sarah withdrew.

"Nothing," she said. "Are you ashamed?"

"Of course not," Evelyn said. She reached out and pulled Sarah back toward her. "But they wouldn't understand if we did tell them. They've never once asked about Helen and Jess. When they ask questions, we'll tell them. That's when they'll be ready to know. Okay?"

"Okay," Sarah said.

She relaxed and nestled back into Evelyn. Curling into one another, they dozed off once again.

The next time they woke, Evelyn looked at Sarah and smiled broadly.

"What is that for?" Sarah asked.

"I haven't slept like that in ages," Evelyn said.

Sarah laughed.

"That's the lovemaking," she said. "It's like a sedative."

"A lovely sedative," Evelyn said.

She looked out the window and then at Sarah.

"I need to get back to the farm before dark so Helen can head home," she said.

She kissed Sarah and got out of bed to dress. Sarah watched her, taking in every slope and curve. Evelyn was a majestic woman.

"I'll try to find some time to prepare the house for your return," Evelyn said as she put on her clothes.

"What do you mean?" Sarah asked.

"It's a bit of a mess these days," Evelyn said. "I'd like to spruce it up a bit and put the cot back in the pantry. We won't need it anymore."

Sarah smiled.

"I'll come as soon as Mary returns and I settle my business with her," she said. "I'll make arrangements with Helen."

Evelyn bent down until her lips met with Sarah's. They kissed and she straightened.

"I'll finish the rest of the curtains before I come back," Sarah said.

"I'll be waiting. We'll all be waiting," Evelyn said as she turned to leave the room and Sarah, still in the warm, soft bed.

When Evelyn entered the house, she was humming to herself, and the children and Helen, who were sitting at the kitchen table playing checkers, looked at her. She stopped humming and smiled.

"I saw Sarah when I was in town," she said. "She's going to come back to the farm."

"She is?" Peter asked.

Evelyn nodded.

"She misses us as much as we miss her," she said.

The children cheered and a feeling of relief spread over the room. Helen went to her.

"You cleared the air?" she asked.

"Yes," Evelyn said. "Thank you."

Helen hugged her.

"You deserve happiness," Helen said. "So do they."

"Come on," Evelyn said. "I'll walk you out."

Helen nodded.

"Good-bye, children," she said.

The children all said good-bye, and she and Evelyn went out on the porch.

"Sarah said she'll contact you when she's free to return," Evelyn said. "She doesn't want to leave Mary in the lurch."

"When she's ready, I'll be ready," Helen said.

She untied her horse, climbed into her wagon, and waved good-bye. Evelyn watched as the wagon receded down the road. She gazed at the tissue-paper blue sky and took a deep breath. She felt warm, peaceful, and free.

❖

That night after dinner, a warm breeze blew, scented by the rain earlier in the day, and Evelyn and the children sat on the porch, picking out constellations.

"There's the Big Dipper," Peter said.

Karl pointed at the sky.

"Little Dipper," he said.

"Let's see if we can find Leo," Evelyn said.

They all surveyed the sky. Louise huddled against Evelyn.

"When is Sarah coming?" Peter asked.

"The woman who owns the tailor shop left town for a few days," Evelyn said. "When she returns and Sarah finishes her work with her, she'll come. Meanwhile, we can do a few things to prepare in our spare time."

"Like what?" Peter asked.

"I want to make some room for a few more of her things that are in the barn, maybe one of her chairs and her sewing table. She'll feel more at home."

"Where will we put them?"

"I'll take down the cot in the bedroom," Evelyn said. "She can use that space."

"Where will she sleep?"

"I'll share my bed with her," Evelyn said. "It will all work out."

"Okay," Peter said. "I'm glad she's coming back."

"Me, too," Evelyn said. "Has anyone found Leo yet?"

"No," Karl and Louise said.

"Well, maybe we'll have better luck tomorrow night," Evelyn said. "Time to get ready for bed."

They went inside and the children went upstairs. Evelyn followed soon after and put them to bed. She went to her room, and when she lay down, she smiled, knowing she would sleep well that night and that soon Sarah would be beside her.

While Evelyn and the children awaited Sarah's arrival, Evelyn kept a small list of tasks she wanted to complete—sweep and wash down the floors, launder all the bedding, wipe the windows clean in preparation for the curtains.

"We never cleaned the windows before," Peter said.

"We never had curtains before," Evelyn said.

"What should we use?"

"I think vinegar might work," Evelyn said. She handed him a bottle. "Why don't you try?"

"Okay," Peter said.

Later that day, Evelyn took Louise and Karl with her to the garden to pick some flowers.

"What are we going to do with them?" Karl asked as he laid them in a basket.

"We'll put some on the porch and some in the house," Evelyn said.

"They'll be pretty," Louise said.

"I think so," Evelyn agreed.

"I guess," Karl said.

When they went back to the house, Evelyn filled an old

watering can with some water and arranged some long-stemmed black-eyed Susans in it. She set the watering can on the porch steps. She snipped off the heads of some mums and floated them in a bowl of water that she centered on the kitchen table. She was looking at her home in a way she never did before. She was seeing it through Sarah's eyes.

❖

When Sarah returned to the farm, it was midmorning, near the end of July, and Evelyn was near the barn, talking to the three farmhands she had hired to help with the harvest of the spring wheat. The children stopped doing their chores and ran toward the wagon. Helen and Sarah got out of the wagon and the children surrounded them.

"We're glad you're back, Sarah," Peter said earnestly as he took her satchel from her.

"So am I," she said.

Louise clutched her dress, and Karl wrapped his arms around her waist. Evelyn excused herself from the workers and began to walk toward the others, and then she broke into a run.

"You're here," she said when she reached them, and she took Sarah in her arms. "Thank you, Helen."

"It was no problem," Helen said. "At least everyone seems happier now."

She lightly rested a hand on Evelyn's back.

"Can you stay for coffee?" Evelyn asked.

"I'm heading right back," Helen said. "Martha Tarry's been under the weather these days, and Jess and I want to pay her a visit."

"Sorry to hear that," Evelyn said. "Send her my regards. Children, say good-bye to your aunt."

The children said good-bye, and when Helen started up the road, Evelyn looked at Sarah and the children.

"Children, you can finish up your chores now," she said. "Sarah and I will call you when lunch is ready."

Karl and Louise headed to the garden, and Peter went behind

the house to chop some wood. Sarah picked up the satchel, and she and Evelyn hooked arms and headed to the house.

"The flowers are a nice touch," Sarah said when they reached the house.

"I think so," Evelyn said, pleased.

She led Sarah up the stairs and to their room.

"I thought you might want a few more of your belongings in the house," she said.

Sarah looked over to where the cot once stood. Her favorite chair was there, with a standing lamp beside it, and on the other side of the lamp stood her sewing table. She walked over to it and ran a hand over its smooth finish.

"Thank you," she said.

A warm feeling oozed through her. She opened her satchel and took out some cloth and rods.

"I made the rest of the curtains," she said.

Evelyn leaned over and lightly kissed her.

"You go start lunch and I'll hang these," Sarah said.

Evelyn started to leave and then stopped.

"We begin again," she said.

"We do," said Sarah.

❖

When the children entered the house for lunch, Evelyn told them to wash their hands and to go see the curtains that Sarah had made for their room.

"Moons and stars," Karl called down. "I like them! Thank you, Sarah."

"You're welcome," Sarah hollered up.

Down below, she and Evelyn listened to the children's comments as they inspected the new additions to their room.

"If we pull them together at night, the sun won't be so bright in our room in the morning," Peter said.

"You still have to get up, though," Evelyn said, loud enough for them to hear. "Come down for lunch now."

The children laughed and headed down the stairs, where they all gathered around the table for sandwiches and slices of apples. They discussed the remaining chores for the day, and they picked up where they had left off. Evelyn would head to the fields with the hired hands, Peter and Karl would churn the butter, and Sarah would clean up the kitchen, work the garden with Louise, and get dinner started. The hot July day hummed around them, with crickets gathering in the grass and bumblebees circling the flowers and plants.

That evening after dinner, Evelyn got the large tub out of the pantry and took it outside. With the heat of the day lingering after sunset, the water from the pump was cool enough to be soothing. The children all bathed. Evelyn helped them prepare for bed and then refilled the tub for Sarah. When Sarah finished bathing, she went inside, up to their room, and Evelyn filled the tub for herself. The cool water caressed her, and she leaned her head back against the tub, settled her eyes on the night sky, and sighed. She was both content and excited. She, Sarah, and the children were together—a different kind of family.

After Evelyn finished bathing, she turned the tub upside down in the grass and went inside. When she went upstairs and entered the bedroom, Sarah was in bed, only the sheet draped over her. The flame of the kerosene lamp was low, spilling a faint glow over the room. Evelyn removed her robe, hung it on a hook, and Sarah pulled back the sheet. Evelyn lay down beside her.

"Welcome home," she whispered before she kissed Sarah.

A gentle breeze blew in through the open windows and pushed them toward each other, together.

About the Author

Jane Hoppen (http://www.janehoppen.com/) grew up in Wisconsin and has been settled in the New York City area for more than two decades. While working as a technical writer for the government and the software industry for more than twenty years, Jane has always done fiction and essay writing on the side and has been published in various magazines, including *Room of One's Own*, *Off Our Backs*, and *Story Quarterly*. She now focuses primarily on her fiction. Her first novel, *In Between*, was a finalist for a Lambda Literary Award and won the Golden Crown Literary Society "Goldie" Award for Debut Author. She has also published a novella, *The Man Who Was Not*.

Books Available From Bold Strokes Books

A Country Girl's Heart by Dena Blake. When Kat Jackson gets a second chance at love, following her heart will prove the hardest decision of all. (978-1-63555-134-1)

Dangerous Waters by Radclyffe. Life, death, and war on the home front. Two women join forces against a powerful opponent, nature itself. (978-1-63555-233-1)

Fury's Death by Brey Willows. When all we hold sacred fails, who will be there to save us? (978-1-63555-063-4)

It's Not a Date by Heather Blackmore. Kade's desire to keep things with Jen on a professional level is in Jen's best interest. Yet what's in Kade's best interest...is Jen. (978-1-63555-149-5)

Killer Winter by Kay Bigelow. Just when she thought things could get no worse, homicide Lieutenant Leah Samuels learns the woman she loves has betrayed her in devastating ways. (978-1-63555-177-8)

Score by MJ Williamz. Will an addiction to pain pills destroy Ronda's chance with the woman she loves, or will she come out on top and score a happily ever after? (978-1-62639-807-8)

Spring's Wake by Aurora Rey. When wanderer Willa Lange falls for Provincetown B&B owner Nora Calhoun, will past hurts and a fifteen-year age gap keep them from finding love? (978-1-63555-035-1)

The Northwoods by Jane Hoppen. When Evelyn Bauer, disguised as her dead husband, George, travels to a Northwoods logging camp to work, she and the camp cook Sarah Bell forge a friendship fraught with both tenderness and turmoil. (978-1-63555-143-3)

Truth or Dare by C. Spencer. For a group of six lesbian friends, life changes course after one long snow-filled weekend. (978-1-63555-148-8)

A Heart to Call Home by Jeannie Levig. When Jessie Weldon returns to her hometown after thirty years, can she and her childhood crush Dakota Scott heal the tragic past that links them? (978-1-63555-059-7)

Children of the Healer by Barbara Ann Wright. Life becomes desperate for ex-soldier Cordelia Ross when the indigenous aliens of her planet are drawn into a civil war and old enemies linger in the shadows. Book Three of the Godfall Series. (978-1-63555-031-3)

Hearts Like Hers by Melissa Brayden. Coffee shop owner Autumn Primm is ready to cut loose and live a little, but is the baggage that comes with out-of-towner Kate Carpenter too heavy for anything long term? (978-1-63555-014-6)

Love at Cooper's Creek by Missouri Vaun. Shaw Daily flees corporate life to find solace in the rural Blue Ridge Mountains, but escapism eludes her when her attentions are captured by small town beauty Kate Elkins. (978-1-62639-960-0)

Twice in a Lifetime by PJ Trebelhorn. Detective Callie Burke can't deny the growing attraction to her late friend's widow, Taylor Fletcher, who also happens to own the bar where Callie's sister works. (978-1-63555-033-7)

Undiscovered Affinity by Jane Hardee. Will a no-strings-attached affair be enough to break Olivia's control and convince Cardic that love does exist? (978-1-63555-061-0)

Between Sand and Stardust by Tina Michele. Are the lifelong bonds of love strong enough to conquer time, distance, and heartache when Haven Thorne and Willa Bennette are given another chance at forever? (978-1-62639-940-2)

Charming the Vicar by Jenny Frame. When magician and atheist Finn Kane seeks refuge in an English village after a spiritual crisis, can local vicar Bridget Claremont restore her faith in life and love? (978-1-63555-029-0)

Data Capture by Jesse J. Thoma. Lola Walker is undercover on the hunt for cybercriminals while trying not to notice the woman who might be perfectly wrong for her for all the right reasons. (978-1-62639-985-3)

Epicurean Delights by Renee Roman. Ariana Marks had no idea a leisure swim would lead to being rescued, in more ways than one, by the charismatic Hudson Frost. (978-1-63555-100-6)

Heart of the Devil by Ali Vali. We know most of Cain and Emma Casey's story, but Heart of the Devil will take you back to where it began one fateful night with a tray loaded with beer. (978-1-63555-045-0)

Known Threat by Kara A. McLeod. When Special Agent Ryan O'Connor reluctantly questions who protects the Secret Service, she learns courage truly is found in unlikely places. Agent O'Connor Series #3 (978-1-63555-132-7)

Seer and the Shield by D. Jackson Leigh. Time is running out for the Dragon Horse Army while two unlikely heroines struggle to put aside their attraction and find a way to stop a deadly cult. Dragon Horse War, Book 3 (978-1-63555-170-9)

The Universe Between Us by Jane C. Esther. Ana Mitchell must make the hardest choice of her life: the promise of new love Jolie Dann on Earth, or a humanity-saving mission to colonize Mars. (978-1-63555-106-8)

Touch by Kris Bryant. Can one touch heal a heart? (978-1-63555-084-9)

A More Perfect Union by Carsen Taite. Major Zoey Granger and DC fixer Rook Daniels risk their reputations for a chance at true love while dealing with a scandal that threatens to rock the military. (978-1-62639-754-5)

Arrival by Gun Brooke. The spaceship *Pathfinder* reaches its passengers' new homeworld where danger lurks in the shadows while Pamas Seclan disembarks and finds unexpected love in young science genius Darmiya Do Voy. (978-1-62639-859-7)

Captain's Choice by VK Powell. Architect Kerstin Anthony's life is going to plan until Bennett Carlyle, the first girl she ever kissed, is assigned to her latest and most important project, a police district substation. (978-1-62639-997-6)

Falling Into Her by Erin Zak. Pam Phillips, widow at the age of forty, meets Kathryn Hawthorne, local Chicago celebrity, and it changes her life forever—in ways she hadn't even considered possible. (978-1-63555-092-4)

Hookin' Up by MJ Williamz. Will Leah get what she needs from casual hookups or will she see the love she desires right in front of her? (978-1-63555-051-1)

King of Thieves by Shea Godfrey. When art thief Casey Marinos meets bounty hunter Finnegan Starkweather, the crimes of the past just might set the stage for a payoff worth more than she ever dreamed possible. (978-1-63555-007-8)

Lucy's Chance by Jackie D. As a serial killer haunts the streets, Lucy tries to stitch up old wounds with her first love in the wake of a small town's rapid descent into chaos. (978-1-63555-027-6)

Right Here, Right Now by Georgia Beers. When Alicia Wright moves into the office next door to Lacey Chamberlain's accounting firm, Lacey is about to find out that sometimes the last person you want is exactly the person you need. (978-1-63555-154-9)

Strictly Need to Know by MB Austin. Covert operator Maji Rios will do whatever she must to complete her mission, but saving a gorgeous stranger from Russian mobsters was not in her plans. (978-1-63555-114-3)

Tailor-Made by Yolanda Wallace. Tailor Grace Henderson doesn't date clients, but when she meets gender-bending model Dakota Lane, she's tempted to throw all the rules out the window. (978-1-63555-081-8)

Time Will Tell by M. Ullrich. With the ability to time travel, Eva Caldwell will have to decide between having it all and erasing it all. (978-1-63555-088-7)

Change in Time by Robyn Nyx. Working in the past is hell on your future. The Extractor series: Book Two. (978-1-62639-880-1)

Love After Hours by Radclyffe. When Gina Antonelli agrees to renovate Carrie Longmire's new house, she doesn't welcome Carrie's overtures at friendship or her own unexpected attraction. A Rivers Community Novel. (978-1-63555-090-0)

Nantucket Rose by CF Frizzell. Maggie Jordan can't wait to convert a historic Nantucket home into a B&B, but doesn't expect to fall for mariner Ellis Chilton, who has more claim to the house than Maggie realizes. (978-1-63555-056-6)

Picture Perfect by Lisa Moreau. Falling in love wasn't supposed to be part of the stakes for Olive and Gabby, rival photographers in the competition of a lifetime. (978-1-62639-975-4)

Set the Stage by Karis Walsh. Actress Emilie Danvers takes the stage again in Ashland, Oregon, little realizing that landscaper Arden Philips is about to offer her a very personal romantic lead role. (978-1-63555-087-0)

Strike a Match by Fiona Riley. When their attempts at matchmaking fizzle out, firefighter Sasha and reluctant millionairess Abby find themselves turning to each other to strike a perfect match. (978-1-62639-999-0)

The Price of Cash by Ashley Bartlett. Cash Braddock is doing her best to keep her business afloat, stay out of jail, and avoid Detective Kallen. It's not working. (978-1-62639-708-8)

Captured Soul by Laydin Michaels. Can Kadence Munroe save the woman she loves from a twisted killer, or will she lose her to a collector of souls? (978-1-62639-915-0)

Under Her Wing by Ronica Black. At Angel's Wings Rescue, dogs are usually the ones saved, but when quiet Kassandra Haden meets outspoken owner Jayden Beaumont, the two stubborn women just might end up saving each other. (978-1-63555-077-1)

www.ingramcontent.com/pod-product-compliance
Lightning Source LLC
Chambersburg PA
CBHW030514020726
47494CB00004B/1089